THESE OUR

NOBLE SONS

AN AMERICAN STORY

THOMAS WADE OLIVER

ISBN: 0692464778
ISBN 13: 9780692464779
Substance Press
Los Angeles, CA

THE AIRMAN'S CREED

I am an American Airman.
I am a Warrior.
I have answered my Nation's call.

I am an American Airman.
My mission is to Fly, Fight, and Win.
I am faithful to a Proud Heritage,
A Tradition of Honor,
And a Legacy of Valor.

I am an American Airman.
Guardian of Freedom and Justice,
My Nation's Sword and Shield,
Its Sentry and Avenger.
I defend my Country with my Life.

I am an American Airman.
Wingman, Leader, Warrior.
I will never leave an Airman behind,
I will never falter,
And I will not fail.

ACKNOWLEDGMENTS

As someone who shared many of the same experiences with my fictional characters as we grew up in Fort Leavenworth and the civilian community of Leavenworth, Kansas, I felt I knew them well in their youth as they came to life in these pages. Portraying young service members with some semblance of reality was another matter altogether. To capture that realism, I decided to walk the path of a young American joining the Air Force and becoming an airman medic. In August 2014, armed with a research approval letter from the Department of the Air Force Public Affairs and National Media Outreach in New York City, I spent a week in San Antonio, Texas, learning how to become what is now called an Airman Warrior.

Today's military is one of technology and extremely expensive weaponry. Unlike the days in our past when an enlistment might be an alternative to a prison sentence, our armed forces today more than ever require ranks of motivated problem solvers and intelligent thinkers. Nowhere is that more evident than the Basic Military Training campus at Lackland Air Force Base and the Basic Medical Technician Corpsman Program facility nearby at Joint Base San Antonio-Fort Sam Houston.

I would like to offer my profound thanks to the following individuals, who welcomed me to their training program without reservation and provided me with a firsthand view of how our young people become the noble defenders of our great nation.

Lackland Air Force Base
Basic Military Training Program

USAF CMSgt. (Ret.) Robert "Chief" Rubio, Public Affairs Officer (Tour Coordinator and Guide)
USAF SMSgt. Christopher Bell, 737 TRSS, Military Training Instructor
USAF MSgt. Danny Spaide, 737 TRSS, Military Training Instructor
USAF SSgt. Thomas Little, 737 TRSS, Military Training Instructor

Fort Sam Houston
Medical Education and Training Campus

USN LCDR (Ret.) Lisa Braun, Public Affairs Officer METC (Tour Coordinator and Guide)
USN CDR Stephen Guidry, BMTCP Program Director
USAF TSgt. Candice Lesane, Instructor, BMTCP
USAF TSgt. Kimberly Hoh, Instructor, BMTCP
USAF TSgt. Joel Alvior, Instructor, BMTCP
USAF SSgt. William Walker, Instructor, BMTCP

I would also like to thank US Army LTC (Ret.) Eric Hollister and 1SG (Ret.) Wayne Cogdill for their outstanding presentations during my tour of the Leavenworth High School JROTC program. Thousands of young people have learned the value of honor and patriotism under your tutelage and example. To you and all the brave military members who assisted me with this project, thank you so much for your service and God bless you and your families.

This is a work of fiction. Unfortunately, young Americans being killed overseas on our behalf is very real.

"True greatness is not in nor of the single self; it is of that larger personality, that shared and sharing life with others, in which, each giving of his best for their betterment, we are greater than ourselves; and self-surrender for the sake of that greater belonging, is the true nobility."

Joshua Lawrence Chamberlain

THESE OUR

NOBLE SONS

BOOKS BY
THOMAS WADE OLIVER

Of Guardians and Angels

Valor's Measure

Best Story

To Watch the River

-In memory of Sean McHenry Oliver #22

CHAPTER 1

I hadn't anticipated spending the night in Bangor, Maine. I wasn't even supposed to be there in the first place. And the truth is, if I'd actually thought there was an inkling of a chance that I would end up in Bangor in the middle of a blizzard, I would have stayed home.

Where I was supposed to be was 235 miles south in Boston. I was supposed to have just interviewed Kelly Leduc, a Boston Bruin who had earlier in the day been officially suspended indefinitely by the NHL for clocking a Toronto Maple Leaf across the back of his head with a hockey stick during a game two nights earlier. Now it was looking more and more like that interview wasn't going to take place, and that was a major problem for me because this was a huge story and I'd begged to be the guy to write it. The NHL Network was even calling my desk at the *Boston Globe* to schedule an on-air interview with me about the article I had yet to write.

In my haste I'd flown to Toronto to catch up with the Bruins the morning after the game, only to find they'd already moved on to their next stop in Montreal by the time I got there. I managed to sneak

1

onto a last-minute flight to Montreal, but by the time I arrived at the Bruins' hotel, Leduc had already learned of his suspension and was on his way back to Boston without me. If I thought I was screwed then, imagine how I felt when my red-eye to Boston was diverted to Bangor. Who knew Bangor had an airport big enough for commercial airliners? My Delta pilot sure did, and he decided spending the night at the Comfort Inn across the street from the runway was a much better idea than flying blindly through a snowstorm.

It had been snowing and sleeting all week—God only knows how I managed to get out of Boston in the first place—and there was no indication from the weather experts that there was going to be a break for another couple of days. I sure as hell wasn't going to sit around in Bangor waiting for a flight that might or might not happen in the next twenty-four hours, so I cashed in a favor with a colleague who has a travel account at the *Globe* and had him book a rental car for me that I could pick up in the Bangor terminal when the rental car offices reopened in the morning. The only thing I could do at that point was find a quiet corner in the already nearly vacant terminal to stretch out and try to get some sleep.

Delta had sent just about everyone else on my stranded flight to nearby hotels. I had no idea how many of those people were going to bail on the airline and try to rent a car in the morning like me. I decided it was best to make sure I was first in line when the Budget counter opened at seven. I'd slept in airports many times before—it was no big deal. Doing it completely sober this time would have been more irritating if I hadn't been so exhausted.

Bangor International was completely shut down; the only signs of life were a janitorial crew and a security guard who walked by when he needed to stretch his legs. I found a row of seats facing the tarmac where I could watch the snow flurries outside whipping wildly with each bone-chilling gust. I wadded my coat into a ball for a pillow and propped my feet up on my carry-on bag. I made a final check of my e-mails and text messages, set the alarm on my phone for six thirty, and tucked my cell phone into one of the side compartments on my bag. I was surprisingly comfortable and didn't have any problem dozing off. Funny how watching the havoc of a winter squall can be quite soothing from a safe, warm place inside, particularly when it's accompanied by the tranquilizing effect of generic office music emitting from an overhead PA system. The only thing to arouse me from my sleep was the occasional rattling of the larger windowpanes when a particularly strong blast of frozen air slammed into them. I believe I drifted off shortly after eleven.

I was already beginning to dream when real voices woke me. I lifted my head and turned toward the open terminal to see three old ladies walking down the middle of the hallway with paper grocery bags in their hands. All three were wearing blue jeans and oxford shirts with a pattern of the American flag splashed across the front.

I was just beginning to assemble an idea of who they were when another group, this one about fifteen deep, appeared at the end of the hallway and headed toward me. This group was clearly with the first; they were all senior citizens, the women wearing the same American flag shirts and jeans, but this group also had a few men in it and they all wore dark blue or black veterans' caps. Based on their age and attire, and because they were carrying items more associated with a potluck than airline travel, I assumed they were a group of local volunteers who were there to set up a USO display or something similar.

We'd been at war in Iraq and Afghanistan for several years already, and I'd seen media coverage of small groups across the country, mostly consisting of senior citizens, going out to airports and providing military people with something to eat and drink while they waited for their next flight. I leaned back to return to my sleep.

Much to my dismay, the group stopped in my nice quiet terminal and began assembling folding tables and setting up a buffet line. I was at first irritated by the racket, but if what they were doing was what I thought it was, who was I to be pissed about such a minor inconvenience? Instead of grumbling about it, I simply gathered my belongings and relocated to the adjacent terminal where I could get on with the business of getting some sleep.

Suddenly, loud applause and celebratory whistling broke the peace of my slumber. I sat up and turned around to see what was happening and saw the group of senior citizens had nearly doubled in size, and they were standing in two parallel lines adjacent to the steel door leading to the tarmac. Through the door a steady stream of military personnel all dressed in camouflage fatigues stepped into the terminal, each grinning ear to ear. Some were clearly moved by the welcome and others appeared to be more jovial, probably just relieved to be back on the ground. I rose up and watched proudly. Part of me wanted to go over and join the applause, yet the part that always tells me not to get involved kept me in my place. So there I stood like a true journalist, watching from the sidelines as life happened to someone else in front of me.

I never saw the plane they exited, but it must have been a big one. Well over a hundred people, mostly very young, filled the terminal and began milling around. One of the men in the welcoming group called for their attention when it was clear the plane was empty and formally welcomed the servicemen and servicewomen home to the United States. After a few words of praise for their sacrifices, he told the group to help themselves to the buffet that had been provided for them. There was plenty of coffee, hot chocolate, and cold drinks. His last words were a reminder that their thirty-minute layover would go quickly, so they shouldn't stray too far from the terminal.

When I heard that I knew there was no point in trying to go back to sleep. I sat up and looked at my watch and checked my phone again. It was one fifteen and it felt like the whole world was in bed except for those of us in that Bangor airport. I didn't have anything to read, I'm not one to play games on my phone, and without my interview I didn't have a story to write, so I sat and watched the old people interacting with the young military personnel.

I couldn't tell what branch of the armed forces they were from because they all wore the same basic uniform. I couldn't tell anyone's rank, either. I picked out a few I thought were in charge because they were older and managed to isolate themselves from the younger ones. I thought about a Pink Floyd song I used to listen to when I was a teenager: "Forward he cried from the rear and the front rank died. And the generals sat, as the lines on the map moved from side to side."

I wondered if any of those officers had been responsible for sending younger service members to their deaths and how much, if at all, it bothered them. Then I wondered if possibly it wasn't the officers who had separated themselves from the younger service members, but it was the younger enlisted ones who had distanced themselves from their superiors. I thought about what it must be like to be a nineteen-year-old kid from some small town getting stuck fighting a war in a desert in the Middle East because he couldn't find a job back home. This was 2013, long after the Twin Towers attack. No one was joining the military anymore out of their patriotic duty to go to war with the terrorists who already tried or would inevitably try to kill us first. As a country we were desperately trying to get out of the two wars we'd been so eager to fight only a few years before.

I'd never been in the military or around military people. I always appreciated their service, but there was something inside me that said it was madness to let someone put a gun in your hand and then surrender them the power to force you into enemy fire. I remembered watching the first thirty minutes of *Saving Private Ryan* and the film's depiction of the storming of Normandy Beach during the allied invasion of France in 1943, and I remember thinking at the time that you couldn't find fifty thousand Americans from my generation to do that. We just wouldn't.

I began to study the younger service members' faces and became very emotional about their sacrifice. I felt self-conscious about being an outsider in a crowded terminal full of people who were placing themselves in harm's way so I could live a nice, tidy life where the most important thing in my day was the outcome of a football or hockey game. Somewhere on that train of thought I realized I had a choice; I could sit and feel emasculated, or I could get up and go over and thank every one of those young patriots for what they were doing for me and my country. That was my intention when I stood up, scanned the room, and tried to decide where to begin.

I first spotted the lone serviceman while I was securing my bag. He was sitting by himself, much like I was, avoiding the bustle of the crowd in a quiet corner facing the snowstorm outside. He was one of the few to exit his flight with a duffel bag, which he had placed in the seat next to him. I noticed that he hadn't taken advantage of the buffet and was only sipping occasionally from a water bottle as he stared out the window. I'd awoken enough to think a cup of coffee and one of the cupcakes at the end of the buffet line would make a nice snack, so I walked over to one of the old ladies stationed at the table and asked her if I could take a couple drinks and cupcakes over to a soldier who was sitting alone. She said, "Absolutely," and poured me two cups of coffee while I selected two cupcakes from the stack. She handed me the Styrofoam cups after I filled my pocket with creamers and sugar packets. I managed to balance the coffee and cupcakes together in one trip, although I did arrive at the serviceman's side with very hot coffee spilling onto my left hand. "Could you grab one of these for me?" I asked the young man as I backed into the seat next to him.

"Sure," he said.

"That's for you, by the way," I told him as I sat down.

"Thank you, sir," he answered, his voice deep and sure.

"I brought you one of these, too." I offered him one of the cupcakes adorned with red, white, and blue sprinkles.

"Thank you, but I'm okay," the serviceman replied. He was holding the cup strangely as if he didn't know what to do with it.

"I have some creamers and sugar," I said and dug them from my pocket.

"Uh, this is fine, sir. Black is fine."

"You want me to go over and make you a sandwich or something?" I asked. "I just grabbed a cupcake because they looked good. I can get you something else if you want."

"No, sir, this is fine, really."

"Okay, I don't want to bug you or anything. I just noticed you were a little empty-handed over here, and, to tell you the truth, I figured the only way I was going to get my hands on a snack and a cup of coffee was to tell one of those old gals over there I was going to take it to one of you." As soon as I said it I realized how selfish my words sounded. "Not that that's the only reason I came over here or anything."

The serviceman smiled nervously and sampled the coffee. There was something odd about him that made our encounter awkward. He wouldn't look at me; his face was void of expression, and even when he drank his coffee he didn't react to it at all. There was nothing. It was almost as if he were one of those insane asylum patients who have a lobotomy procedure and their brain is turned to mush. I'm not naïve. I had a fairly good idea that this guy was probably one of those who had seen some unimaginable violence overseas, and it had messed his head up so badly he didn't know how to be normal anymore. It was sad to watch, and I couldn't let this poor guy sit alone with the living nightmare I was sure was playing out in his head.

"So, where are you guys coming from?" I asked.

"We took off from Ramstein, Germany," the serviceman answered. "It's mostly people coming back from Afghanistan."

"I bet you're glad to be home," I said.

He looked at me for the first time and said nothing.

"Well, we really appreciate your service," I said nervously.

The serviceman nodded an acknowledgment and looked away. There was nothing in his eyes.

I assumed he didn't want to talk, and if he was suffering from some battle fatigue mental illness that was making him crazy, I wasn't so sure I wanted to be the only person sitting next to him. I stood up and offered him my hand and said, "I just want to thank you again for what you're doing."

He took my hand and shook it gently, still not looking at me but forcing a grin to his otherwise expressionless face. I gathered my coffee cup and what was left of my cupcake and returned to my seat across the terminal. My interaction with the young man had been uncomfortable enough for me to decide not to give it another try with someone else. I was suddenly tortured with empathy for the serviceman who had experienced the horror of war that I was sure had ruined him. I could see the back of his head from my chair, so I studied him as he sat erect and motionless, staring out the window.

A few moments later a flight attendant called for the passengers to begin re-boarding their plane. I turned back to the crowd and watched the senior citizen volunteers wrap last-minute treats in napkins and hand them off to takers returning to their flight. I was so moved by what I'd seen that I knew there was no chance of returning to sleep. There are times in our lives when we have reason to be extremely proud of who we are. Even though I was a spectator to it all, I couldn't have been more proud to be an American that night.

I settled back into my seat and began digging in my bag for my phone as the terminal cleared. When I located it, I looked up and noticed out of the corner of my eye that the lone serviceman I'd shared a coffee with was still sitting alone across the terminal. I was sure he'd gotten lost in his thoughts and wasn't aware his flight was about to leave, so I jumped up and ran over to him. "Hey, your plane's leaving," I said.

The young man looked up at me and replied, "I'm not going with them. My flight leaves in the morning."

"Oh, okay," I said. "I just wanted to make sure you didn't get stuck in Bangor like me."

"Are you going to Boston?" the soldier asked.

"Yeah, but I'm not flying," I told him. "Everything north of DC has been shut down and probably will be for another day at least. I have a rental lined up for first thing in the morning. I'm just gonna drive back home. You better check your flight schedule because I bet you've been canceled."

The serviceman stood and looked around the terminal. I pointed toward the electronic arrival and departure boards down the hall. "They'll have your flight status down there. I'll go with you."

We began walking down the hall together. We didn't need to worry about leaving our bags behind. The terminal had returned to its routine early morning emptiness; only a few volunteers were still there folding up the buffet tables. The young man and I didn't talk. I knew he was about to get bad news and he didn't seem to be prepared for it. When we reached the schedule boards, it was easy to see that his flight had been canceled. They'd all been canceled. Nobody would be flying out of Bangor in the morning.

"Fucking winter in New England, man," I said. "Every year. It never changes."

The serviceman lowered his head and rubbed his chin. He was trying to decide what to do next.

"If you're going to Boston, I can take you with me," I said. "It's gonna take a little extra time with this weather, but we should still make it by tomorrow afternoon, easy."

"I can't do that," the young man said without taking the time to even consider it.

"Why not?" I quickly surveyed the sleeves and collar of his uniform to identify his rank so I could address him with something other than "man" or "pal" or "dude." There was nothing I recognized. I couldn't even get a good look at his nametag. "You can sleep the whole way," I said as we walked back to our chairs. "We'll get out of here at first light, grab a bite to eat on me, and have you in Boston by three, four at the latest. Is Boston home, or do you have another connection?"

"Providence," he answered. "I got to get to Providence."

"Shit, man, I can drive you to Providence," I said.

"It's not going to work, sir," the serviceman insisted. "I appreciate it, but…it…"

"Hey, I can tell you got things on your mind. Trying to figure out how to escape this frozen tundra probably isn't something else you need to worry about right now. Let's you and me grab a rental first thing in the morning and go. No questions, no thinking about it, just get in the car and get the hell out of here."

"But I can't, sir," the serviceman insisted again without hesitation.

"Why not?" I asked. I was growing frustrated with the young man who was carelessly refusing my generosity.

"I'm taking someone home. I have a friend with me."

I looked around the terminal to find his companion. Even the volunteer greeters were gone. "Who are you with?"

The young serviceman slowly lifted himself from his chair, stepped to the large window across from us, and pointed toward the tarmac. There, in a large open hangar below us, a single casket was draped in a crisp American flag, resting solemnly beneath the glow of overhead fluorescent floodlights.

Sometimes it's best to simply shut your mouth and just be there. You don't fumble for words, you don't turn and walk away, you just stand there and exist—allow a moment to take its course and then acknowledge that whatever it was just happened. I stood at that window and looked down through all those white flurries at the coffin and said nothing. My thoughts had paralyzed my voice. Time stood still and I suddenly felt as though the world I lived in no longer existed. Long minutes passed as the serviceman and I stood next to each other in silence and watched. I didn't know the identity of the person in the casket, but I knew it was some kid who went to war thinking he was defending his country. He or she likely never saw or knew what killed them. Chances were the body was so ravaged and torn that it was being delivered home in pieces, in far too gruesome a state for his or her loved ones to see. I swallowed hard and tried to look away, but I couldn't. As long as that young man next to me was going to stand at that window, I was going to stand there along with him.

"Do you think they left some of that hot chocolate?" the serviceman asked.

"I can check," I said. "Are you gonna be okay?"

"Oh, yeah," he answered. "I'm fine."

I touched his back lightly and walked across the hall to the storage closet I'd seen the volunteers use. Lucky for us they'd either forgotten to lock it or weren't concerned that anything inside would be stolen. I found a basket full of assorted tea bags and packets of hot chocolate next to a recently cleaned coffee maker. I grabbed the basket and coffee maker and headed back to our chairs, only stopping for a moment to fill the pot with water in the men's room. When I got back to our seats, I plugged the coffee maker into a wall socket next to us and poured the water into the top of the machine. "We'll have some hot water in a minute," I said.

The serviceman returned to his seat and yawned. I didn't want to bother him with questions, but I was wide awake now and I wanted to know everything about him and the person in the casket. "So, are you working a burial detail or something?"

"Not really," he answered. "He's my friend. We grew up together."

"Really?" I said. "Were you together in Afghanistan?"

"Not in the same place, but yeah, we were both there."

"I'm sorry for your loss," I said. "It's been a terrible war."

"What do you do?" the young man asked me.

"I'm a sports columnist for the *Globe* in Boston."

"Hm," the soldier responded. "You like doing that?"

"Sure," I told him. "I get to see a lot of free games and hang out with professional athletes all day."

"Why are you in Maine?"

"Your question should be, 'How the hell did you get stuck in Maine?' It's this weather. Two days ago I started chasing a story in Boston and needed to get an interview with one of the Bruins who's probably going to get thrown out of the league. I tried to catch him in Toronto, missed him there, tried to hunt him down in Montreal and lost him there too, so now I'm going home, where, if I'd just had some patience and waited, I would have been less than a mile from the jackass yesterday morning."

"What did he do?" the serviceman asked.

"He challenged another player to a fight, and when that guy refused, he slashed him across the back of the head with his stick. The other guy is going to be fine, but this guy, Leduc, he's looking at a very long suspension. They may even kick his ass out of the league."

"Interesting."

"It's a big story in sports," I insisted.

"Hm," the soldier grunted. He understandably couldn't care less.

"Not a big hockey fan?" I surmised.

"No. Not really."

"So do you have family in Providence?" I asked, trying to keep our conversation going.

"They're like family. My friend's parents live there."

Here's the thing about me, I'm not a man often at a loss for words. I can talk to anyone. Journalism is all about asking the right questions, being a good observer, and then having enough talent to write about it. Most people don't realize how difficult it is to interview professional athletes. When they're winning and everyone is getting paid, it's easy to find guys on the team willing to give you a few quotes for a story, but when people aren't happy with their contracts and the team isn't playing well, you can quickly find yourself dealing with a bunch of spoiled babies who think guys like me are bottom feeders whose job it is to make things worse. The trick to being good in this business is to look at each player as an individual and find something about him that gives you a connection. Compliment his alma mater or tell him his kids are cute. If he's single and a ladies' man, pump up his ego by telling him there was a flock of beautiful groupies in the team hotel looking for him before the game. If he's trying to be a devoted husband, save him from the pool of skanks who won't leave him alone in the hotel lobby. Whatever it is, if you can get that hook in him, that guy is not only going to answer your questions when the going gets tough, he's going to find you on his own accord and become one of your best unnamed sources.

I tried to think of something the serviceman and I might have in common, but talking to the young man was like finding a sealed tin can with no label. You want to open it, but you don't know if it's full of fresh green beans or something so old and rotten it spoils your appetite.

"Was your friend married?" My question was bait to see if he was willing to talk or if he preferred silence.

"No," he said. "He would have been married one day. He would have been a good husband. He would have been a good dad."

"How long did you guys know each other?"

"A long time. We were little kids when we first met. We basically grew up together."

"And you joined the service together?" I asked.

"We did everything together," he replied. "He was like my brother. He *was* my brother."

Now I was intrigued and the writer in me was awakened. I didn't go to college with plans to someday write about hockey players. I wanted to learn how to write compelling news stories so I could be a respected journalist. I ended up in sports because it was easy, and at the end of the day, that's kind of my thing: find the easy way and take it. Getting an early internship in a local paper's sports department and having a blast spending all afternoon watching baseball and then writing about it was all I needed to forget those dreams of reporting compelling stories. Like anything else, the more I enjoyed it, the better I was at it, and that was how I got the job with the *Globe*.

Listening to this young serviceman tell me who he was and what he was doing, the journalist in me saw a story. Had it not been the middle of the night, I would have called my editor and told him he needed to assign someone to this guy and interview him. Pulitzers were made of this kind of stuff. It was two in the morning however, and no one at the *Globe* was going to get called out of bed to interview a soldier just back from Afghanistan who was stuck in an airport in Bangor. If someone was going to look into the story, it was going to have to be me, and the more I thought about it, the more certain I was that this young man's story, no matter where it led, needed to be told.

As I gathered my thoughts and tried to come up with a pitch to get him talking, he stood up and slung his duffel bag over his shoulders. "I can't sit up here like this," he said.

"Everything's closed," I told him, "and you can't go walking around outside."

"I'm going down there," he said.

"To the hangar?"

"Yeah. I'm going down."

"Can I go with you?" I asked.

"If they'll let you. I don't mind."

"Well, let's find a security guard," I suggested. "You probably need to do all the talking."

We picked up our belongings and walked into the hallway. It wasn't long before we found the security guard sitting on a stool at the terminal entrance. I stood back and let the serviceman approach him. I assumed my lack of involvement gave us a better chance of getting into a clearly secured area. The two men talked beyond my hearing range and then they both walked back to me.

"You going with him?" the security guard asked me.

"If I could, I'd appreciate it." I pulled a lanyard with my press credentials attached to it out of my bag and showed it to the guard.

"I'll need to take your driver's license and switch it with a pass," the guard said after confirming I was a professional journalist.

"Whatever you need is fine, sir," I told him. I was relieved that he didn't ask me anything about why I was following the young man. It was much less complicated if I allowed him to assume I was working on a story.

The guard escorted us to an exit door at the top of a stairwell. We walked down the stairs together, and when we reached the bottom, he warned us that we were about to step onto the taxi ramp and it was going to be cold. We both nodded that we understood and the guard pushed the door open. The stairwell filled with howling wind and freezing air. We could see our destination about fifty yards away across a long stretch of black pavement. The three of us leaned into the furious tempest and rushed toward the hangar, each of us blindly fighting the stinging gales.

Though the hangar door was open, the wind and snow were hitting it broadside, so once inside we were again safe from the elements. A man wearing a neon safety vest over his coat walked out of an office in the hangar and asked if he could help us. The security guard explained to him that the young man with me was assigned to accompany the casket to its next destination and I was a writer from a newspaper doing a story.

The man in the safety vest shrugged and said, "It ain't too warm out here. Guess we could shut them hangar doors a bit, but I'm supposed to leave 'em open unless the snow starts comin' in. Last time it got cold like this and we shut them doors they froze, and the motor got burned up trying to open 'em back up again. There's some folding chairs laying around here you can use. Just don't go wandering around in here, and don't touch anything, and let me know when you leave. I'll be in the office doing some paperwork. The other guys are staying warm in the break room down the way there."

We thanked the man for his cooperation and the security guard left us with a handshake. The young serviceman and I retrieved some folding metal chairs that were leaning against a wall and returned to the side of the casket. "Who are the other guys he was talking about?" I asked.

"I think they're the SPs from Dover," he answered.

"What are SPs?" I followed the serviceman's lead and waited for him to decide where we would sit before I placed my chair next to his.

"Air Force police," he answered. "I think they use them for the honor guard. We're supposed to meet them here in the morning for a flight through Boston and then to Dover Air Force Base. Then we have a National Guard flight to Providence. I guess they're here already."

"So are you in the Air Force?" I asked.

"Yes," he answered indifferently. Then he added, "We all wear the same fatigues now."

I replied, "I guess you learn something new every day." I'd assumed the serviceman was a soldier or a marine.

We sat for a few moments in silence, both of us studying the flag-draped casket before us. I began to question what I was doing and soon felt awkward. The airman didn't appear to be in need of comfort, and he clearly didn't want to talk, not yet anyway. The last thing I wanted to do was disturb him, yet I couldn't leave his side. It was a mixture of selfish intrigue and guilt that drew me to him. There was no way I was going to let that kid sit alone with his fallen comrade, but there was also no way I was going to sit there with him in silence and not ask about the war.

The whole scene turned surreal when the doors of the dimly illuminated hangar began to slowly close to just a few feet of completely blocking out the storm raging on the tarmac. When the doors stopped and the engine operating them was silenced, we found ourselves alone in the cavernous jet shelter; the only sounds were the creaking of aluminum siding being tested by the wind. I was the first to speak.

"My name's Avery, by the way," I said and extended my hand. "Avery Friberg."

The airman looked at me blankly and shook my hand. "Nice to meet you, sir."

"Please, call me Avery or Ave."

The airman nodded and looked back at the casket. Another few minutes passed. I was debating whether he was simply so caught up in his thoughts that he didn't realize I'd just given him the opportunity to formally introduce himself or he thought doing so would suggest he wanted to talk. I really did want to leave the guy alone, but I couldn't. I just couldn't.

"So are you back home for good?" I asked.

"No."

"Are you going to see some family while you're back?"

"Yes."

"Well, good," I said. I looked down at the airman's hands to see if he wore a wedding ring before asking about a wife and kids. There was nothing. "What was the weather like in Afghanistan?" Two questions in and I was already asking about the weather. *Stupid, stupid question.*

"It's the desert," he answered. "Cold at night. Hot and dusty during the day."

"Yeah, I bet." I struggled for a question to segue into a topic that might encourage him to share a little more about himself or his circumstances, but the idea that my question might annoy him held me back. I took a deep breath, leaned into my chair, and decided that if I had to sit there another hour before the guy next to me decided to talk, then that was what I'd do, which is exactly what happened.

After the first forty-five minutes of rather anxious silence, I got up and located a bathroom and then bought two bottled waters from a vending machine. When I returned to my chair I handed one to the young airman without asking if he wanted it or not and then sat back down. He thanked me, opened the bottle, and drank almost half of it before lowering it from his lips. He then sat back in his chair, looked straight up toward the ceiling, thought for a few moments, and then leaned forward again, cupping his chin in his hands, elbows on his knees, thinking. I could sense something was stirring inside him; he'd become restless and was fighting with a thought in his head. Journalists can tell when someone has something to say but they're afraid to say it. I was going to leave the airman alone to fight the demon that was preventing him from talking to me. At some point he'd start to talk; that's just the way human beings are. Anyway, I still had over four hours to kill before the rental car counters opened.

As the airman leaned forward in his chair, I was able to sit back and watch him. I studied the faded patterns in his camouflage uniform and the exposed tan line on the back of his neck and tried to form a picture of who he was. I still had no idea of his rank or age. His head was nearly clean-shaven; enough stubble was present to indicate his near baldness was by choice and not the result of nature. I guessed he was either in his mid- or late twenties, maybe even younger, having had every semblance of his youth drained from him through daily exposure to the horrors of war. I was replaying media coverage in my head of desert village gun battles when the mysterious airman's voice interrupted my thoughts.

"It was nice of you to come down here with me," he said.

"No problem," I answered cautiously.

"I'm sorry I'm not much for words right now."

"That's okay. We're just two guys hanging out."

"I can't believe I'm here," the airman reflected. "It's very strange. My heart feels like, um...my heart feels like I have to try to keep it beating." A tear rolled down his cheek.

I put my hand on his back. "It's all good, man. You're home now."

The soldier brushed the tear from the side of his face and took a deep breath, then another. "I, uh, I apologize."

"For what?" I asked.

"I, uh...I'm uh...I don't know. I'm sorry."

"Hey, it's okay," I reassured him. "It's just me and you, man. You don't have to say anything."

The airman smiled at me and took another drink from his water bottle. After returning the bottle to the side of his chair, he sat up straight and rubbed life back into his legs. "You're a reporter?" he asked.

"Yeah," I answered.

"You ever write about anything other than sports?"

"Naw. I could," I said, "but sports is my thing."

"If I told you a story, could you write it for me?" the airman asked.

"Oooh," I hesitated. "I guess that depends."

"On what?"

"I'm kind of knee deep in alligators right now with the hockey season. I could find you a writer, though." I already had a few in mind.

"I'm not asking you to write a book," the airman clarified. "I'm just wondering if maybe if I told you a story, you could write it down for me."

"Why don't you write it?" I asked.

"I'm a little busy too."

Contrary to what most of my ex-girlfriends would say, I do have a conscience. To continue to suggest that I was too busy chasing meaningless sports stories to help the young serviceman while he was busy fighting a war, struck my guilt nerve like a ball-peen hammer smacking my funny bone. Without considering the consequences, I volunteered my services. "Sure, I guess we could work something out."

The soldier signaled his appreciation with a nod and looked back at the casket. He was clearly gathering his thoughts, and I again allowed him time to himself to decide his next move. After a few moments, the airman looked back at me and said, "You're probably going to want to take notes."

"Oh, sure," I said and dug my voice recorder out of my bag. "Do you mind if I use this? It's much easier."

"I don't mind," the airman answered.

I repositioned my chair so he was to my right and the casket was to my left and confirmed I had a full charge on my recorder. My thought at that point was that he was going to share something with me that I could condense into a brief article that, depending on its content, some newspaper or periodical might actually want to publish. I was a journalist, after all, and a story to me meant a few columns of print. I in no way imagined what was to follow.

"Ready when you are," I said and placed the recorder on the airman's duffel bag.

The serviceman sat for a moment and then got up and walked over to the side of the casket. He gently folded back the flag and carefully lifted the lid. I watched him study the person inside, his expression changing several times, clearly with memories filling his head. After a few moments, he turned and motioned for me to join him. I stood and cautiously stepped to his side.

"I want the world to know him," the airman said. "Can you do that for me?"

"Sure, I can try," I answered. "I've got a few hours to hear all about him."

"Oh, this can't be just about him," the young man said. "It has to be about us. This has to be the story of Patrick Bennett and Robert Debruijn."

We returned to our chairs, I pressed the record button on my recorder, and the two of us then sat together until dawn, the young airman sharing his life with me as I listened, transfixed to his every word like a child hearing a wonderful fairy tale for the very first time.

CHAPTER 2

Before continuing I have to jump ahead to how this story made it to the page. Even though I write about hockey and baseball, I took a lot of English lit in college, so I know a compelling story when I hear one. Sitting there listening to this one, I was already forming an outline in my head of how I would tell it. It soon became clear that any attempt to shove it all into a current event article would be a disservice. What I came to envision was a full manuscript that might someday become a published memoir. I even thought it would be easy. There would be no reason for taking any creative license or embellishing anything for the sake of capturing a reader's attention. This book was virtually going to write itself; I only had to assemble it in some decipherable order, a process I began in my head as I drove back to Boston the next day.

It may have taken a few weeks, but I was happy with my preliminary chapter outlines. There was already a clear beginning, middle, and end. I figured my job was to fill in the blanks while doing my best to capture the true characters and circumstances of the people involved. Simple, right? Well, here's the deal—there are reasons why

I'm not a novelist, and I was reminded of each and every one of those reasons within just a few days of trying to fill the pages beneath those chapter titles.

As I wrote I realized that I lacked the fine details I needed to do this the right way. Those details were certainly out there somewhere; the problem was that the people who could help me were either family members in mourning or they had already returned to the war in Afghanistan. I was committed to not being lazy and making things up simply for my convenience, no matter how trivial an issue might be. That commitment proved a barrier that soon brought a frustrating shadow of doubt over what I was trying to accomplish. I went so far as to pitch the story to a couple of old college friends who were writers to see if they might be interested in running with it. None were. "Great story," they all said, but not their genre or field of expertise.

I'd cautiously reached out to the two airmen's parents by phone and briefly discussed with them my ideas for the book. They didn't know me from Adam, so there was little they wanted to share during that first conversation. I told them that I only wanted to introduce myself and let them know what I was doing in case they heard from another party that something was in the works. I promised I'd write a completely factual account of the two boys growing up and joining the service together. I added not so subtly that their cooperation and input would greatly increase my ability to tell an accurate story about their sons. I also promised to send them a brief outline along with a copy of my résumé for their review. If after looking over the material they wanted to help me, they could give me a call and I'd fly out to their homes and conduct interviews in person. I have to admit neither set of parents seemed eager to proceed, which worried me greatly. I could always survive a case of temporary writer's block, but the project was as good as dead if I didn't have the support of both families.

I went back to work, chasing the Bruins across the country for weeks at a time, writing columns after each game that were so similar to one another I was merely regurgitating the same crap night after night. The only things that changed were the names of the players scoring goals and the final scores. Everything else in my articles was simple fluff, chock-full of death-defying hockey clichés. My articles didn't change much, but my routine sure did. On the road I stopped going out for post-game drinks with the other writers, and I never lingered around the rink any longer than I had to. Instead I headed straight back to my hotel and worked on the manuscript. I did the same during my flights.

An eight day trip to the West Coast that was not only a welcome respite from the northeastern cold but a chance to get some work done on the book actually ended with me reaching a point of surrender. I'd lost all confidence in what I was doing. Although the images were clear in my head, the material I had written was melodramatic and full of gaping holes I was unable to fill because I simply didn't know enough about the boys and where they grew up.

The night we were in San Jose playing the Sharks, I received an e-mail from the office in Boston saying I had just received an unusually large box and it would be in the mailroom when I got back. I called the office the next morning and talked one of the interns into opening it. When he called me back, he said it was a delivery from someone named Bennett, and it looked like it was full of someone's personal journals or diaries. There was also a manila envelope inside with a bunch of letters and copies of e-mails in it. I told the intern to reseal the box and leave it in my cubicle, then called my boss and told him I had a really bad case of the flu and the team didn't want me around for fear I might make everyone sick. Even the local reporters in the press box the night before were giving me the stink eye every time I coughed or blew my nose. My boss gave me the okay to end the road trip and come home as soon as I could find a flight.

I was home the next night and had the box delivered to my apartment the following morning. I opened it while juggling my normal breakfast of a cup of coffee and a bagel smothered in cream cheese. Inside the box were seven notebook journals, some clearly more worn and aged than the others. On the cover of each was written *Property of Patrick Bennett* and a year. There was a journal for every year from 2005 through 2011. Before looking inside any of them, I opened the manila envelope and read the note attached to a small stack of papers:

Hello Mr. Friberg,

I think somewhere here you will find what you are looking for. I have also included copies of some correspondence that might help you.

Best wishes,

P. Bennett

I scanned some of the papers. Patrick, it appeared, had written home while the boys were in basic training and continued writing e-mail home during his deployment overseas. I didn't find anything terribly revealing; Patrick sounded like a young man who was both excited and sometimes oddly blasé about being a member of the armed forces in a war zone.

I moved on to the journals. They began when Patrick was a twelve-year-old sixth grader. Every year after that, until he graduated from high school, there was another journal. He didn't make daily entries, and most were only a few paragraphs depicting an average kid venting about a frustrating day on the baseball field or struggling with a subject in school, but there were other entries that went on for pages and contained astonishingly candid descriptions of everything from trivial teenage angst to personal thoughts about religion and a confusing war in Iraq.

I read all the journals and finished the last letter shortly after midnight. Post-It notes were attached to the entries that mentioned both boys or something that applied to my story. I should have been exhausted, but the journals and letters reignited the fire inside me to get this story on paper. I now felt a connection to both boys. I wasn't just a conduit scribe anymore. The relationship between the two had created its own energy or spirit I guess you could say, and it was inside me. I felt it as surely as I can feel the heat and cold. That was when it hit me—I needed to get out of the way. I needed to stop trying so hard. I needed to abandon my words and my futile attempts at obeying rules of grammar and what I thought were contemporary literary standards for a successful manuscript. The story was in the journals and the letters. There was the unadulterated tale of best friends Patrick Bennett and Robby Debruijn. I needed to stop acting like a writer and think of myself as more of a gardener.

I never got the impression that the Bennetts or Debruijns didn't want to talk to me. I did sense it was too soon, though, which was completely understandable. As much as I understood there was a mourning process involved with the families, I also needed to get this done while the voices in my head were still challenging me. I knew the second those voices stopped talking or began to whisper, I'd lose interest and the project would fizzle out. I was even beginning to think maybe this was a project the families should be doing themselves if they actually wanted their sons' story in print. But at the end of the day it always came back to me, and that was when, in a moment of drunken clarity, I decided not to be a selfish writer anymore, inserting myself all over a manuscript that had virtually nothing to do with me. Instead I was now going to wear the shoes of a landscape artist charged with bringing a once beautiful garden back to life. Nothing new needed to be planted, and no fresh sod needed to be laid. I only needed to trim and shape what was already there. Once I cleared the tangled vines and highlighted the rainbow of perennials that were being strangled by war's tragedy, I could restore that amazing garden to life.

My new approach included the decision to create a manuscript compiled almost completely of excerpts from the journals and correspondence home. I wasn't going to get permission from either family until I was done because I thought it would be much easier for the families to say no to a concept instead of something they could actually examine. The risk was that I'd spend months on a fruitless project that would be ultimately rejected by the very people I wanted most to please. If I got this right and the families did approve, however, I was sure we could share this story with the rest of the world.

The content of the following pages is mostly details of the boys growing up as told in excerpts from journal entries and letters and e-mails home from Patrick Bennett. I later learned that each year

Patrick's parents gave him a new notebook for Christmas. His mother loved to write and she hoped her son would someday share her passion.

I have added my own narrative for time and place perspective and to clarify situations that Patrick mentions yet fails to describe with the thoroughness I think this story deserves. Only a small fraction of the entries were actually used. Early in the journals, Patrick's thoughts wander into some precarious areas that, although they were written by a child, are not particularly appropriate material for juvenile consumption, which leads me to believe he clearly was confident in the security of the journals. His awakening to the charms of the opposite sex is one example of subject matter he freely writes about without fear of his parents' discovery. He is also comfortable with profanity at the age in which boys begin to experiment with the taboos of our culture. I could have edited those instances out but chose not to because doing so would alter who Patrick was at the age when boys associate profanity with adulthood and being cool. Robert's personality appears in stark and significant contrast to that of his friend.

Many of these entries are both heartwarming and heartrending, complex, full of clichés, and sometimes even difficult to imagine they are actually true. I suppose that's the difference between manicured fiction and a story based on the truth. There is no safety net here. There is no protective cloak to pacify the easily offended. This is a story about two best friends who grew up to serve their country and one made the ultimate sacrifice. It is as beautiful a story as it is a tragedy. That's my opinion, anyway, and I'll go a step further. If you aren't touched in some way by what you read here, as a thirteen-year-old Patrick Bennett would say, "There's got to be something fucking wrong with you."

CHAPTER 3

December 25, 2004

We promise to never read the content of these journals. We understand that if we ever read a single page other than the cover, our son will never trust us for the rest of his life, and he will never talk to us again.

Signed,
Col. R. G. Bennett
Pauline Bennett

Every journal begins with an identical family contract. It clearly wasn't enough at first.

January 1, 2005
YOU ARE TOTALLY BUSTED! NICE TRY MOM AND DAD!!!!!!!!!!

Signed,
Your only son who knew this was a trick!

January 2, 2005

It's really cold outside. It snowed a ton and my dad made me shovel the sidewalk. My mom made a totally gross goulash last night that looked like puke. I ate it anyway. It was horrible. I don't think my dad liked it either. He didn't say anything, but I could tell.

January 3, 2005

Me and some friends went to the gym today. My mom thought we were playing basketball, but we were really across the street behind the pool office smoking cigarettes. I didn't like it at first. Now I smoke all the time. We steal the cigarettes from the PX. It's so easy. The dumb adults are so clueless. Did you know it's a proven fact that they used to call cigarettes Fags back in the olden days?

January 6, 2005

I hate this journal. It is the worst Christmas gift any kid could ever get! I already got real school homework I have to do. Who wants to keep a stupid journal? It's like having your parents make up even more homework for no reason. That's what school is for!!! My parents are usually pretty cool. What did I do to deserve this!!!

January 7, 2005

This is your last chance you guys. I'm not going to write personal stuff in here just so you can spy on me. I don't deserve this!!! Confess!!! When is the last time I got in trouble? Why are you punishing me? I can tell when people are lying. I'm not stupid!!!

January 8, 2005

My dad took me to the army surplus off post today and bought me a used footlocker for my room. It has a lock on it so I can put my personal stuff in there like this journal. My mom asked me if I was writing stuff in it last night while we were having dinner and I could tell she didn't know what was in here. I ragged on her goulash! If she was snooping in my stuff I'd be able to tell. Goulash is like her favorite thing to make. If I said it looked like barf, she'd be hysterical and fire would probably shoot out of her ears or something. My dad said he'd get me a trunk with a lock as long as I didn't put anything in there I shouldn't have. I guess he was talking about pictures of naked ladies or drugs. I'm just going to keep my baseball cards and some other junk in there I don't want to get messed up. I kind of trust them now. Tomorrow is my first day back at school. I kind of want to go, but I kind of don't.

January 9, 2005

I went back to school today. My teacher is Mr. Rosales and he's pretty cool. He made us all write an essay about the best Christmas gift we got and the worst one we got. He said to call it our "least favorite," but I know what he means. We had to describe the gift and then tell why we liked it or didn't like it. The best thing I got was a new sled called a toboggan. Me and my friend Robby have been using it every day because we can both fit on it at the same time. He doesn't like to be the guy in front. The guy in front is the coldest because the wind is stronger when you're in front and it makes Robby's teeth too cold. He got his two front ones on top busted out. The dentist fixed them so he looks normal, but I guess his tooth nerves are still messed up. If it gets super cold outside, he sometimes has to go inside because his teeth hurt too much. It's weird, but he's not a sissy or anything. It's kind of my fault that his teeth got knocked out, so I can't be mad. My worst gift wasn't this journal. It was socks.

Over the course of the next few weeks, Patrick writes mostly about menial activities at school and sledding afterward with his friend Robby. He sprinkles his text with short blurbs that reference how he and Robby met and how their relationship was evolving. Personally, I found their first meeting was extraordinary. Because they met before Patrick received his first journal, describing that meeting and the first few months of their budding friendship in detail required some extra work. The journals offered a small amount of help; the rest of it I had to piece together myself with interviews and a handful of visits back to an Army installation in Kansas where the boys grew up.

After my interviews and research were completed at Fort Leavenworth, I spent a few weeks driving around the Sunflower State trying to get a feel for the people there. I was always treated well and didn't meet a soul who wasn't friendly. They do like to stare at strangers, though, which takes a little getting used to. They are without a doubt a religious bunch. My general conclusion is that most of the people raised in Kansas or thereabouts credit God with acts of perceived providence. Whether a turn in their lives is taken as a miracle or some lower level of divine intervention, by the time they grow up, I think most Kansans understand that there isn't a decision they make or a step they take that doesn't in some way change their lives.

Whereas a young adult raised in one of the urban sprawls on our coasts might still be grappling with childish dramas, a keen observer might note that the average Kansas teen is capable of recognizing a significant crossroads approaching their life and even making wise decisions about the approaching challenges. They're not bred smarter or gifted; they don't receive a significantly more intellectual public school experience than the average American child. They're simply raised differently, and it begins with their early exposure to the concepts of a moral code supported by their parents' faith. Certainly with rules of behavior there must also be a standard of discipline for those who fall short of their community's guidelines for behavior. In the case of Kansas, it is shame and guilt that seem to hover above all else in degrees of punishment. "Shame on you," and "You should be ashamed of yourself," means something to a Kansan.

Children too young to understand guilt and shame are still often spanked or receive some other form of corporal punishment, although it is much less likely to occur in public than it once was. This period usually ends as soon as children begin to learn there are repercussions for their actions. It doesn't mean they're going to stop misbehaving simply because they got a few good whacks across the bottom, but it does force them to weigh the value of their behavior against the very real possibility of an unnecessarily painful backside-lashing.

As soon as children begin to ask themselves, "Am I going to get in trouble for this?" what they do next is one of the earliest indicators of a child's developing maturity. What you'll find unique to the children of the northernmost fringes of the great Midwestern Bible Belt is that many don't only consider their parents' reaction to bad behavior—they also consider what God might think. Imagine a world where a little boy staring at a cookie jar full of fresh-baked oatmeal raisin treats refrains from taking one, not only because his mother told him not to or a spanking is sure to come if he disobeys a clear parental order, but because taking a cookie would be a sin and God could very well send him straight to hell for the transgression. That world exists, and it's in the bull's-eye of this country's heartland.

On the other end of the spectrum, most children growing up in Kansas don't fall to their knees and thank God for their fortune when things are going well. They're just content and satisfied. When things go bad because of their poor choices, they still blame everyone else and pout and cry until the next juvenile distraction comes along, like every other kid in the country. There is plenty of daily poking and prodding of authority to see what they can get away with and what they can't. The difference is that most children raised in the small conservative Christian communities of Kansas are almost always held accountable for everything they do. There are no free passes—not from their parents, not from their God or community, and once they learn to feel shame, not even from themselves.

On the day Patrick and Robby first met, the wheels of providence weren't powered by a great prayer or a reward for some outstanding act of grace. It was the hand of something much simpler that reached down to that tiny corner of northeastern Kansas and planted the seed of destiny with the commission of a sin—the telling of a lie. Not a big one, at least not for the eleven-year-old who concocted it. This lie was more within the fib category, complex in its execution and supporting malfeasance, but lacking almost altogether in lasting result. God and Santa Claus wouldn't care. No one was going to get hurt, no reputations sullied. That was the plan, anyway.

The scenario was simple. A sixth grader rises from his slumber and his head is immediately filled with two thoughts: *Man, I need to pee,* and *I really don't feel like going to fucking school today.* And that's the exact vernacular of the thoughts as they appeared in this particular young boy's head. Absent of any significant forethought, the boy soon arrived at the breakfast table with complaints of an upset stomach and the feeling he might vomit at any moment. This was of course a strategic choice from a lengthy catalogue of available ailments carefully evaluated during a morning bowel movement. To choose something associated with fever, for example, could be investigated with a thermometer. A morning headache could warrant nothing more than a few words of sympathy and two children's aspirin, and he'd still have to go to school. The prospect of throwing up, however, changed the illness paradigm completely. You can't confirm or disprove a stomachache, young Patrick Bennett thought, and his mother wouldn't want to hassle with having to go back to school and pick him up if he actually did vomit in class. You could punch another kid or get caught scratching profanity on the bathroom wall, and all they'd do was make you stay after school for a couple of weeks, but when you hurled, they handed you an E ticket and sent you straight home: case closed, no more discussion.

There was always the chance of a hiccup in this particular plot, though. You might get caught forgetting to act like you're sick, which would not only foil your current exploit but also draw into question any future attempts to miss a day of school due to illness, legitimate or otherwise. Subterfuge is always accompanied with a certain level of risk; the challenge is to recognize and evaluate those risks and then determine if the anticipated reward significantly outweighs the repercussions of failure. Cunning children learn this lesson early. The problem is that they have yet to grasp the idea that almost every adult is smarter than they are, and more times than not parents can smell a bamboozle coming even before it has been fully implemented. In the case of young Patrick, he wasn't sure if his mother was on to him when she told him they were going to the hospital to get checked out if he was too sick to go to school. That wasn't a big deal—lying to a doctor he didn't know was a hell of a lot easier than lying to his parents. Patrick figured they could knock out a quick visit to the children's clinic in an hour and he'd be home playing video games in his room before his classmates finished their first recess. To counter the possibility that his mother might be setting him up, Patrick even agreed that it was a good idea. *Genius,* he thought—*pure genius.*

The hospital at Fort Leavenworth is named after Brigadier General Edward Lyman Munson, a Yale School of Medicine graduate who became the military's expert in preventative medicine during the early twentieth century. The way it worked at Munson when Patrick was growing up was you walked in the door and told a receptionist in the lobby your child felt sick, and as long as it wasn't an emergency you sat and waited no more than thirty minutes in the pediatric clinic until you saw a doctor or a nurse practitioner. The hospital only services about forty thousand people and a handful of military retirees who live nearby outside the fort's walls. There are no issues with insurance. You simply show the people at the counter your military dependent I.D. card and you're in. The system was so easy back then, and because it was also free, the hospital routinely filled each morning with mothers and their children who were often in need of nothing more than a day of rest and refraining from junk food. Patrick and his mother were regulars at the hospital. Got a sore throat? Off to the pediatric clinic to make sure it isn't strep. Sprained ankle? Let's go get some x-rays and make sure it isn't broken. Tummy hurting you? How about we go make sure it isn't the result of a bad virus or food poisoning? It was just too easy.

So off they went to Munson, Patrick embracing his stomach and doing his best to look ill. The waiting room was already filled with sick kids and their mothers. Patrick studied the others, trying to determine who else was faking it. He knew there had to be at least one or two. After a short wait his name was called and they were escorted by a nurse to an exam room. The nurse checked Patrick's temperature and blood pressure and then she left. Patrick and his mother were discussing the possibility that he might be coming down with the flu when the doctor entered the exam room. With him was a boy about the same age as Patrick. Both wore matching lab coats. The doctor shook Mrs. Bennett's hand and then Patrick's. He then introduced the boy with him—he was the doctor's son. The doctor asked the Bennetts if they minded having his son in the room. Patrick's mother looked at him to make the call and he answered with a shrug. "It's fine," Mrs. Bennett replied, and the doctor began his examination.

A few questions were asked: Do you think it was something you ate? How long have you felt this way? Does your body also ache? Patrick knew better than to embellish his lie by compounding it. As far as he was concerned, he simply woke up feeling like he was going to throw up. He had no idea why. The doctor declared his discomfort was probably the result of a virus and his body would fight it off within the next few days. He then asked Mrs. Bennett if they could talk outside the room, which left Patrick momentarily alone with the doctor's son.

Patrick told the other boy it must be nice to be able to miss school and hang out with his dad all day at the hospital. The boy answered that he went to school at home and got to visit the hospital with his father as much as he wanted as long as his studies were taken care of first. Patrick had never heard of kids being able to go to school at home. *That would be sweet!*

The doctor's son then asked Patrick, "Have you pooped yet?"

What the fuck kind of question is that? Patrick thought, again indulging in his recently acquired vocabulary of profanities. "You want to know if I took a dump yet today?"

"Feces can clog your bowels and give you bad cramps and indigestion. Maybe that's why your stomach is upset," the boy said.

"What the hell are feces?"

"It's poop," the boy answered matter-of-factly, "but it could also be parasites or food poisoning, or maybe you just have the flu. I know all about it. I'm going to be a doctor myself someday," the boy bragged. "My dad let me sew up a Great Dane's scrotum once after his friend cut off its testicles."

Patrick sat up straight like a hound dog alerting on a coon and insisted on clarification. "You gave stitches to a dog's ball sack?"

The doctor's son answered proudly, "After my dad's friend removed its testicles. They do that so the dog can't make more puppies."

"I know why they do it," Patrick answered. "That's gross, dude."

"No, it's not gross at all," the boy disagreed. "There isn't much blood, and the dog is sedated—"

"Where did you do it?" Patrick interrupted. He was picturing the whole thing going down on a picnic table in someone's backyard.

"At the veterinary hospital—my dad's friend is the head veterinarian."

Now that at least made sense. "Hmm," Patrick reflected for a moment, "that's kind of badass, actually."

"It was the first time I ever sutured a live animal before," the boy added. "I usually just practice on chickens and turkeys."

"Ooohkay," Patrick said and suddenly wished his mother and the kid's father would come back to the room. *This kid is a fucking freak.*

"Yeah, they're good to practice on," the kid continued. "My mom gets them at the commissary and she lets me slice them and then practice stitching the cut back together. It's pretty fun. I like it."

"That's weird, dude." *Mom, get me out of here!*

"Then we eat them."

"You eat the chickens?"

"I take the stitches out and then my mom cooks them."

"So your mom goes to the commissary and buys chickens, and when she brings them home you play doctor with 'em, and then when you're done you eat 'em for dinner?"

"Sometimes they're turkeys. Turkeys are better because they're bigger and their skin can hold a stitch better. I could show you sometime."

"Um…" Patrick stumbled for a way out. "I don't know, man. That's kind of weird."

"No, it's normal," the kid corrected him.

Just then the doctor and Mrs. Bennett walked back into the room. Patrick's face was flushed with fear and his mother noticed it. "Are you okay?" she asked.

"I'm not feeling too good," Patrick answered. "I'm ready to go home."

The doctor said, "We're going to assume this is some kind of virus. That means plenty of liquids and bed rest. You may throw up sometime today, and if you do, that's fine. As long as you only throw up once or twice; people usually start feeling better right after that." The doctor looked back at his son and winked. "You know, my son Robert is your age. Did you two introduce yourselves?"

The two boys acknowledged that they had.

"Do you go to school together?" Mrs. Bennett asked the boys.

"Robert is homeschooled," the doctor interjected.

"Oh, that's nice," Patrick's mother said. "You boys should get together sometime."

Oh geez, c'mon, Mom. Was it too much to ask for a simple courtesy inquiry on how he felt about it first?

The doctor agreed with Patrick's mother, and they exchanged phone numbers as Patrick stewed over the idea that he was no longer going home to enjoy a leisurely day of playing hooky as originally planned. Instead he would spend the day preoccupied with the anxiety of having had his mother just commit him to a play date with a weirdo. That was God's act of providence on the day young Patrick Waties Bennett first met fellow sixth grader Robert Duncan Debruijn.

Patrick went back to school the next day and told his friends about the dopey kid he'd met at the hospital the day before, but a funny thing happened while he was telling them the story. What the weird kid was doing to grocery store poultry actually made sense. He said he wanted to be a doctor. How cool was it that his dad let him follow him around at the hospital and even let him practice how to give stitches? The more Patrick thought about it, the more it seemed like a perfectly reasonable thing to do. It still didn't mean he wanted to be friends with the kid. There was something odd about him. He didn't seem retarded or anything, but something just wasn't right. He was kind of scrawny and didn't seem like the type who would want to play sports or wrestle around. He looked more like one of those kids who read a lot and are a lot smarter than everyone else. Patrick figured that was why he was being homeschooled. Robert was probably one of those boy geniuses who go to college while they're still teenagers.

About a week later, Patrick's mother told him Robert and his parents were coming over for dinner the following Saturday night.

Patrick was indifferent to the idea—he wasn't nervous about seeing Robert again, and he didn't have other plans. When the dinner date was discussed over the next few days, Patrick's parents gave him several reminders about how to properly behave with guests. Patrick's father was a colonel and professor assigned to the Command and General Staff College on the fort, and it was common to have other officers and their families over for dinner. Patrick always used good manners and never spoke unless spoken to, so he was suspicious about what he perceived as unnecessary lecturing about appropriate behavior. In his defense, even at eleven he was about as well versed in formal dining etiquette as he was in the rules of baseball, and he loved baseball. What were they so worried about? His parents didn't know he knew how to swear yet, and he sure as hell knew better than to utter an unutterable in front of guests. The punishment for something that egregious would surely be so severe he couldn't even imagine it. He was always polite and chewed with his mouth closed. He even managed to keep his elbows off the table. Patrick could also take a hint and knew when it was time to excuse himself so the adults could have some privacy. He never wanted to stick around any longer than he had to, anyway.

When the Debruijns arrived for dinner, the Bennetts greeted them like it was a really big deal to have them over. Dr. Debruijn was a lieutenant colonel, and he and Colonel Bennett hit it off immediately. Mrs. Debruijn had been looking forward to the opportunity to meet some new friends and was particularly excited about the prospect of finding a new friend for Robert. After introducing herself to Patrick, she told him he could call her Katy, but Patrick's mother warned him, "You'd better not."

Patrick replied, "That's okay, Mrs. Debruijn, but you can call me Pat."

"Well, thank you, Pat," she replied, "and of course you remember our son, Robby."

Robby was almost cowering behind his parents, causing Patrick to have to bend around his mother to see his face. "Hiya," Patrick said and waved nervously.

Robby raised his hand, gave a single limp-wristed acknowledgment, and then looked down at the floor.

When the mandatory foyer greetings and introductions were completed, the adults moved straight to the living room for drinks and appetizers while Patrick led Robby to his bedroom. He knew he had about thirty minutes to kill before dinner was served, so he thought he'd use the time to see what his peer was into for the specific reason of ascertaining whether they could be real friends. Robby was clearly anxious and stood in the middle of the room with his hands clasped behind his back.

"Relax, dude," Patrick told him.

"I'm fine," Robby answered as his eyes scanned the contents of the recently cleaned and organized bedroom.

"You like baseball?" Patrick asked. "I got some baseballs signed by a couple of the Royals. George Brett signed one of 'em. You know who George Brett is?"

Robby responded by shaking his head no.

"George Brett—he's in the Hall of Fame. He's only the greatest Royals baseball player who ever lived. Do you like video games? I got a PlayStation."

Again Robby responded with a silent gesture: not interested.

"Do you like any sports?" Patrick asked. "Games...anything?"

"I like reading," Robby replied.

"Reading?" Patrick repeated for clarification. "Like books and stuff?"

"I like reading medical books."

Patrick sighed. There was no way he and this nerd were going to be friends. He looked around his room one last time for something they might have in common but saw nothing. Robby continued to stand in the middle of the room as if he were waiting for some instructions.

"I guess we can go see what our parents are doing," Patrick said in frustration and gestured for his guest to head for the living room. There the boys sat quietly next to each other on a couch and watched the adults talk about nothing important between sips from highball glasses until dinner was finally served.

The boys sat across from each other at the table in the formal dining room and nervously avoided eye contact. Robby was behaving nothing like he had when the boys first met at the hospital, and Patrick was beginning to think maybe something really was wrong with the kid. After grace was offered by Colonel Bennett and everyone's plates were filled, the mothers started talking about their boys and prodded them to join the conversation. Patrick talked about the parts of school he liked and how he was excited about moving on to junior high school next year. Mrs. Debruijn said Robby would also be going to junior high school on the fort next year. When Patrick's mother asked him if he was looking forward to it, Robby mumbled almost inaudibly, "I guess," and that was it.

A few more attempts were made to get the boys interacting, but everyone could tell Robby preferred to be left alone. The adults decided to change the subject to the topics military families always talk about, which was also Patrick's cue to disengage from the adults and finish eating so he could be excused. Normally the next few minutes would consist of Patrick shoving food into his mouth as fast as he could chew it and then make room for more with no consciousness of what the adults at the table were talking about. He didn't care and had nothing to offer. He just wanted to get back to kid stuff like watching television or playing. That was what was normal, but this was not a normal dinner, and the kid sitting across from Patrick was the reason everything was off-kilter.

Patrick had experienced feeling sorry for people before. Those were mostly the elderly or people with obvious disabilities. Feeling sorry for a kid his age who wasn't handicapped was completely new to him. Instead of racing to finish his meal, Patrick slowly studied Robby during the rest of the dinner. His final conclusion was that Robby must be really sad about something, which would explain why he seemed so pitiful. Still it was none of his business, and when the night was over, he would insist that his parents discontinue their attempts at bringing the two boys together. They just weren't a compatible fit.

After dinner Patrick volunteered to clear the table and fill the dishwasher. The gesture appeared to be random, but it was actually a pre-assigned task that provided the elder Bennetts with an opportunity to show their guests how skilled at parenting they were. Patrick didn't mind. He saw how proud his parents were when their guests commented on how impressive it was that he did the dishes without being asked. The truth was it was just another example of how a Bennett family dinner party was a totally choreographed event. As was typical of many military families, having guests for dinner included a timetable for the dinner's procession, and as a member of Team Bennett, Patrick had three major responsibilities: entertain the guests' children, clear the table after dinner and start the dishwasher, and all the while do absolutely everything within his power to portray himself as a perfect child, which he did with significant success. It was all an elaborately orchestrated hoax.

Mrs. Debruijn asked Robby if he would like to help Patrick with the dishes, and he answered, "No." It wasn't the kind of *no* you get from a belligerent child who is being a pain in the ass. It was just an honest answer. Patrick's eyes widened. *Can he do that?*

Dr. Debruijn said calmly, "Hey, Robby, the Bennetts just treated us to a very nice dinner. The least we can do is thank them by cleaning up. What do you say?"

Robby didn't say a word. He simply scooted his chair away from the table, filled his hands with dirty plates, and sauntered off to the kitchen with a stunned sixth grader trailing right behind him.

Patrick waited for some warm water to begin flowing and then rinsed the dishes as Robby delivered them to the sink. Robby cleared the rest of the table by himself fairly quickly and stood in the kitchen watching Patrick fill the dishwasher and put away the pots and pans that were washed by hand. Patrick made a few more feeble attempts at conversation with his guest to no avail. It was bizarre. Something had to be really wrong with the kid. When the dishes were put away and the kitchen counters were wiped clean, Patrick asked Robby if he wanted to go play some video games. His response was a shrug and, "Not really." It was already dark outside, which eliminated the prospect of going out to find something to do.

After dinner was when Patrick's father brought out his good liquor and, even though it was fun to watch the adults slowly become intoxicated, it wasn't included in Patrick's dinner mission, and it was impossible if he was responsible for entertaining someone himself. Patrick decided that if the adults were going to drink awhile before their dessert of ice cream and cheesecake, he and Robby might as well start on theirs. He walked over to the refrigerator, opened the door, and there was the answer to his problem—a defrosting whole chicken.

Patrick took the chicken out of the refrigerator and plopped it down on a cutting board on the center island cook's table. "So, this is what you use to practice giving stitches?"

Robby's eyes got big and he took a deep breath and smiled wide as if he'd just received a fantastic gift.

"Are you going to show me how you do it or what?" Patrick challenged.

"Okay," Robby answered and followed with an extensive list of supplies they needed to assemble first.

What followed was a flurry of two boys running around the house looking for a sewing kit and tweezers, searching the garage for a smelly tackle box where they might find some fishhooks, and getting into a cabinet for some leftover rubber gloves and protective masks Colonel Bennett bought when he restained an old coffee table. Robby even went out to his parents' car and got two white lab coats out of the trunk. Within ten minutes the kitchen was converted into an operating room. The boys even set up a desk lamp to illuminate their patient during the operation. They suited up in Robby's small lab coats, and then Robby carefully instructed Patrick on the finer points of suturing a three-inch laceration on the side of a chicken breast.

Patrick began referring to Robby as Dr. Debruijn, which he clearly enjoyed. He noticed Robby liked showing him how to sew the stitches a lot more than he enjoyed actually doing them himself, which was strange to Patrick. He'd never been taught how to do something by another kid before, and it was during that realization that Patrick made his final assessment of his new friend. Robby *wasn't* normal. He wasn't a freak and he wasn't retarded. He was just different in a very odd way. He didn't laugh, but he could manage a smile if he understood the joke. He didn't say much, but when he did Patrick could tell whatever it was Robby had to say, it was important to him. He wasn't overtly friendly, and he wasn't the type to want to talk for the sake of being social, but all those things that made him different also made him fascinating to Patrick. He needed to figure him out. He had the sense that Robby was mysteriously fragile and needed to be protected. It was the strangest feeling Patrick had ever had.

When the adults eventually ran out of things to talk about, the Debruijns decided it was time to go home. By then the poor chicken had been sliced up and sewn back together so many times it was almost unrecognizable. The boys only stopped when there was no space left on the chicken to operate and Robby's parents insisted it was time they go. While the two families were all standing at the front door saying their goodbyes, Patrick told Robby he should come over again sometime and they could hang out. Robby blushed, was suddenly shy again, and looked down at the floor. "Okay," he said, and then without a *see you later,* or *give me a call sometime,* Robby, in all his weirdness, turned around and walked out the door.

Dr. Debruijn and his wife offered a final thanks to the Bennetts for dinner and met Robby at their car. The Bennetts watched them leave. Colonel Bennett then asked his son to meet him in the kitchen, a recognized precursor to a serious family discussion or revelation of some kind. Patrick didn't think he was getting in trouble for anything; he'd been a perfect gentleman during the dinner and he and Robby made themselves scarce right afterward, which was his primary objective after cleaning up. Nope, this was about something else and Patrick was safely curious about what it might be.

He sat down on a stool next to the kitchen cook's table as his father refilled two cocktail glasses with a mixture of tonic and gin and a slice of lime. Mrs. Bennett checked the dishwasher and then went to the refrigerator. Colonel Bennett took a sip from one of the glasses. "So what do you think of Robby?"

"He's okay," Patrick answered. "He's kinda strange. Maybe he was nervous because he didn't know me. After dinner we had a pretty good time."

"Do you think you two might be able to be friends?" Mrs. Bennett inquired. She placed a small glass of milk in front of her son and accepted the second cocktail glass from her husband.

"I guess," Patrick answered nonchalantly. He had plenty of friends already. It wasn't as if he needed more.

His parents looked at each other and smiled with relief.

"What's going on?" Patrick asked. *Why is it so important to you guys whether I like Robby or not?*

"Robby's a special kind of boy," Colonel Bennett answered. "He's not the type of kid who is going to make friends easily at your age. It's nice that you're willing to give him a chance."

"I don't see what the big deal is," Patrick answered. "He's just shy and kind of…I don't know—it's like if you pushed him too hard he might break."

"Well, Son," his father began, choosing his next words carefully, "Robby has a condition that makes it difficult for him to be emotional about things. He probably has trouble understanding what you think is fun or funny, and he's probably very uncomfortable with some things that you don't even think twice about."

"Like what?" Patrick asked. He had no idea what his father was trying to tell him.

"I'm not even sure," his father answered. "We've all just met him. I just want you to know there are probably some things that he's very uncomfortable with and even afraid of that you aren't. If you two are going to be friends, you're going to have to understand that or he's going to be very hard to get along with."

"I think he's shy," Patrick said with confidence. "He's probably nervous around people he doesn't know, that's all. I know kids at school who are goofier than Robby is."

"Honey, we just want to make sure you are careful with him," his mother said. "You're going to have to give him a lot of second chances to be your friend, and there are going to be times when you think he doesn't want to be your friend anymore when he actually does. Can you do that?"

"I guess," Patrick answered. *Man, they are making way too big a deal out of this.*

Patrick finished his glass of milk and went to bed without another thought about Robby. He believed he understood what his parents were trying to tell him and it made sense. Robby was clearly a nerdy kid who probably had no friends and needed one. It didn't help that his parents kept him out of school. How was he supposed to find anyone to hang out with if no one his age knew him? If he wanted to come over every once in a while and even meet some of Patrick's friends, that was fine with him.

The next day Patrick and his father spent much of the afternoon watching an early September Royals game on TV. Even though the season was as good as over for the local Royals, watching baseball together was the one activity the Bennett men always looked forward to. Summer was the best time of the year for Patrick, and playing baseball was the one thing that made it that way. The fort had a spring and summer league for kids, and when it was over Patrick and his friends continued to play in one way or another until the harsh, chilly winds of autumn and the subsequent bitter cold of northeast Kansas winter made it impossible. Football then took over, but it was never as important as baseball.

As the game progressed, Patrick began to daydream about next year's Little League season. He thought about who he hoped would be his teammates and what the competition would be like to get selected for the All Stars. By the seventh inning, the Royals were getting blown out by the Milwaukee Brewers and Patrick lost interest in the game. He hadn't lost interest in baseball, though—quite the opposite.

He asked his father if he wanted to go out and throw a ball around, but Colonel Bennett had to go to the college and do some work. Patrick called some friends, thinking at least one would be available for a round of catch or even a quick game if he could muster enough people together. Not a single friend was home. He could always go out to the backyard with his glove and bounce a tennis ball off the side of the garage by himself, but that wouldn't be much fun. All the guys were probably at the basketball courts—he could walk over and join them there. That idea just wasn't in the cards either. He wanted to play catch.

"Hey, mom!" Patrick called to the kitchen where his mother was putting away some groceries. "Do you have the phone number for those people who came over last night? I want to see if that kid wants to come over and play catch!"

"I thought you said he doesn't like baseball," Mrs. Bennett said as she entered the living room and handed her son a piece of paper with a phone number on it.

"I can change that," Patrick said with an eager smile. He took the paper from his mother and headed for the phone. After dialing the number, he held the phone to his ear and waited a few moments, then said, "Hi, Mrs. Debruijn. This is Pat from last night. Can I ask Robby if he wants to come over and play some baseball?"

"Why, sure," Mrs. Debruijn replied happily.

Robby's voice came on the phone. "Hello?"

"Hi, Robby, it's me, Pat. I wanted to ask you if you wanted to come over and play some catch."

"Catch?"

"Throw a baseball around for awhile," Patrick clarified.

"That's okay," Robby said and returned the phone to his mother.

"If you don't know how to play, I could teach you," Patrick offered, having no idea Robby was no longer on the phone.

"Hi, Patrick, this is Robby's mom again. I guess he doesn't want to play."

"Does he know how? I could teach him."

"I think he has an idea what the rules are, but he's never wanted to play. Let's ask him again."

The sound of the Debruijns' phone being jostled filled Patrick's ear and then he heard Mrs. Debruijn say, "Robby, Patrick is being very gracious in asking you to go over and play with him. I'm sure he could have asked a lot of other boys, but he chose you. What do you think? Should we give it a shot?"

"That's okay," Robby answered.

Patrick interjected, "Tell him I'll teach him how. I even have an extra mitt he can use if he doesn't have one. It's already broken in and everything."

Mrs. Debruijn repeated Patrick's offer to her son.

"That's okay," Robby insisted.

The phone jostled again and Mrs. Debruijn said to Patrick, "Can Robby meet you and you two can discuss it together?"

"Sure," Patrick answered. "How about in ten minutes at the old fort wall next to your house?"

"He'll be there," Robby's mother said. "Thank you, Pat."

The fact that these two boys met and grew up in Fort Leavenworth, Kansas, is as important to this story as the characters themselves. Of course I didn't realize that until I visited the place for myself. Several things stood out during my first of several trips back there. One is the location of the fort. High on the bluffs overlooking the massive Missouri River, Fort Leavenworth is situated at a wide bend where large cargo ships are often seen lazily drifting south with the current to some destination far beyond the imagination of the young eyes watching them. This is not the flat Kansas plain I had expected. This is uneven, rolling hill country covered with green pastures and trees. Outside the gates of the military post is the small town of Leavenworth, established long after the fort became a permanent fixture on the landscape. Other than a plethora of prisons in the area, the city of Leavenworth seems quaintly average and unassuming. No major highway runs through it and there is no claim to fame that might attract seasoned tourists. It is a town entirely unremarkable and, at the risk of offense, forgettable—the perfect place to grow up.

At the north border of the city are the gates to the fort. As a first-time visitor, I found the instant contrast between the military installation and its civilian counterpart my second most intriguing discovery. There are no long columns of soldiers marching through the streets, nor are there neat rows of drab government barracks everywhere. On the contrary, beyond a central hub location for a contemporary Post Exchange shopping area and a large grocery store still referred to as a commissary, the rest of the fort consists of small, peaceful neighborhoods of mostly historic two- and three-story homes, each surrounded by carefully groomed lawns and mature, indigenous trees.

The Bennetts lived on Scott Avenue in a two-story brick house nearly a hundred and fifty years old, with a wide porch on each floor. Across the street is an open park covered with giant elm, oak, and walnut trees, with a freshly painted gazebo in the center where brass bands play traditional patriotic tunes in the summer. Behind the Bennett house, there is a small yard and a driveway that runs parallel to the rest of the homes on the street. On the other side of the driveway is a steep, grass-covered hill, perfect for snow sledding in winter or cardboard box sledding in summer. At the bottom of the hill begins a flat delta that leads to the mighty Missouri River about two miles east, clearly visible in the distance. At the bottom of the hill, still in the Bennetts' backyard, you can see the remains of the pathway worn into the hillside by covered wagons that had just crossed the river and were beginning their adventure westward on the Santa Fe and Oregon Trails.

To the south are five similar old homes, also occupied by the families of officers stationed on the fort. North and directly next door is an old stone chapel that was one of the first permanent structures built on the fort in 1842. Not many people actually attend regular Sunday morning services there. It is small and museum-like, musty smelling and creaky. Between the large panels of stained glass, the walls are covered with various-sized memorial plaques more likely to be seen in a mausoleum at a cemetery, thus explaining why this is known as the Memorial Chapel. Some find the tiny chapel depressing, whereas others are so captured by its solemn character they choose to wed there. The regular Post Chapel is big, bright, and contemporary, and this is where most of the fort's Protestant worshippers assemble on Sunday morning. A large choir accompanied by the power of a bellowing pipe organ is the highlight of the service. Even civilians come on the fort to go to church just for the music. It is also why the Bennetts and Debruijns went to services there, even though they both lived within walking distance of tiny Memorial Chapel.

At the corner next to the historic church, five different two-lane streets come together. At their intersection is a large statue of Ulysses S. Grant in a worn and weathered Union officer's coat studying a battle map. North of the intersection behind Grant's statue is a long stone wall. The two landmarks, particularly the Grant statue, were the logistical centerpieces of young Patrick Bennett's and Robert Debruijn's world. Everything they did as children was within walking distance of the statue and the old fort wall. The post movie theater, the community pool, the baseball fields, their personal playground, all of it was right there in a tiny Norman Rockwell neighborhood within an Army fort in northeastern Kansas.

Robby and his family lived nearby in a house on Sumner Place, right off of Kearney Avenue, which was the street that ran parallel to the long stone wall. The wall itself isn't particularly imposing, considering its original purpose. It's only about forty feet long. The east end stands only about six feet high and gradually grows to about ten feet as it follows a gentle slope to its western end. Strategically placed along its face are openings for cannon and rifle placements. There's a plaque on the wall that says it was built in 1847 to help protect the fort against Indian invaders. For children in the area, it now serves as a school bus stop. It was also the place where Robby and Patrick were about to meet so Patrick could teach his new friend how to throw and catch a baseball.

Stepping out his front door and walking across the street, Patrick could cut behind the old fortress and be in Robby's yard, which was adjacent to the back side of the wall. The trip took less than a minute. Robby's yard was flatter than the small park across the street from Patrick's house, so they played catch at Robby's house behind the wall that conveniently also served as a backstop for Robby's many errant throws.

Patrick met Robby behind the wall with a baseball and two gloves in hand and tried fiercely to convince his new potential friend that playing baseball was *the* thing to do over summer break. He'd have fun and meet all the guys, and it would also give them something to do together. Robby remained uninterested. Patrick assumed it was because he'd never given the game a chance and finally insisted they throw a ball around a few times so he could gauge his friend's skill level. It was immediately clear that teaching eleven-year-old Robby to throw a baseball was going to be like trying to teach the same thing to a five-year-old girl. At first Patrick thought Robby might be trying to throw with his weak arm, but when he switched, his delivery was even more vexing. Patrick was befuddled. To him a boy throwing a baseball was about as natural a thing to do as walking across the room, yet Robby couldn't figure out a single thing about the mechanics of a throw. He stepped into it with the wrong foot, his elbow either flailed wildly or was tucked against his side, and he flicked the ball when he threw it with a floppy hand motion, a total sissy move.

It was a good thing the boys were so young and Patrick didn't know anything about homosexuality. If Robby's rather feminine attempts at throwing a baseball had been associated with the possibility that he was gay, Patrick would have ended the budding friendship out of adolescent ignorance. Instead of getting frustrated and giving up, Patrick remembered what his parents told him about Robby needing some extra chances. At that point Patrick felt he knew exactly what his parents were talking about, so he kept working with Robby, even joking with him to lighten the mood, yet at the same time teaching him how to catch and throw the same way his father had taught him.

Robby never could figure out how to throw a baseball, or football, or anything. He certainly tried, but he just couldn't do it. It wasn't that he wasn't smart enough to figure it out; if anything, he was too analytical about it. At the end of the day, the motion of throwing, or any athletic activity, was simply unnatural for him. He was like a dog trying to walk on its hind feet. It just wasn't his thing.

It didn't really matter to Patrick if Robby was going to be a baseball player or not, but it would matter in a few months if Robby wanted to spend time with him during the summer. Patrick lived and breathed Little League Baseball, and if he wasn't at practice or playing in a game, he was hanging out with the other guys on the team at the public pool, which was right behind the row of houses across the street. That's just the way it was and, though Patrick was willing to give Robby a chance, he already had plenty of friends who had much more in common with him and were actually fun to be around.

This first meeting between the boys occurred several months before Patrick received his first journal, so there isn't any record of his thoughts about that first meeting from the perspective of an eleven-year-old. Both families agree that Patrick took it upon himself to teach Robby how to throw and catch a baseball and even swing a bat almost every day after school and on weekends until the weather simply didn't allow it. When that happened they continued their friendship, but it was an unusual relationship from the start.

The boys had no mutual friends and didn't go to school together. Robby knew nothing about sports. Patrick liked to rough-house and emulate the moves of professional wrestlers he saw on television. Robby coiled with apprehension when he was playfully grabbed or pushed or even touched unexpectedly. During football season the boys in the neighborhood traditionally played a game they innocently called Smear the Queer. The rules of the game are fairly simple. A football is thrown up in the air and everyone fights for it. When someone gains possession of the ball, he runs around in circles to avoid being tackled by the other kids. When the kid with the ball is brought down, he throws it back up in the air and another fight for the ball ensues. Robby's first invitation to meet Patrick's other friends came during the occasion of a game of Smear the Queer.

One Saturday morning the two boys walked to the nearby Gruber football field together to meet a small group of Patrick's friends. There had been torrential rains the night before and the air was still thick with the frigid mist of late autumn. The field had already been scarred from its overuse during the recent junior league football and soccer seasons. The grass was dead and in most places unable to sustain its grip to the soil. Gruber Field was now one big, beautiful mud pit—the perfect arena for an epic battle of Smear the Queer. Robby took one look at the field and the boys already rolling and sliding around in the muck and decided the best place for him was in the bleachers.

Patrick made a few attempts to get Robby on the field, but he wouldn't budge. That was acceptable to Patrick. He hadn't really thought his new friend would dive right in with the other kids, particularly if they were piling on one another in the mire. It wouldn't be acceptable if Robby didn't give it a try the next time or maybe the time after that.

The game lasted about an hour and then some older kids started showing up. They wanted to use the entire field for a regular game of football, and even though they told the younger boys they could play, Patrick and his crew decided it was best to move on. The boys separated, all but one sopping wet and completely covered with dark, rich Kansas soil.

When Patrick and Robby started walking across the field to return home, Patrick suddenly stopped and said, "It's going to look funny if we get home and I look like this and you look like that."

"No, it wo—" Robby tried to say before the first pile of sludge smacked his chest. He froze in shock as his friend rearmed himself.

"Sorry, dude," Patrick said and raised another handful of mud.

Robby turned his head and shielded his face just as the second scoop of muck slopped onto his bare neck and the top of his sweatshirt. He gasped and shook with terror. "That's enough!"

"Not until you look just like me, brother." Patrick paused for a moment to see how his friend was reacting. The two boys stared at each other, daring, until Patrick broke a smile. "Lighten up, dude. It's just wet dirt."

Robby looked down at his filthy shirt and then surveyed the open space around him. There was no escape—no adult to call out to for help, nowhere to run and hide. He looked back at his friend and took a deep breath. "Please don't get it in my face," he begged. He turned his head again and braced himself.

"C'mon, dude," Patrick pleaded as his shoulders drooped. "Have some fun. I'm not messing with you."

Robby didn't respond.

Patrick wasn't a bully and hated those who were. He knew that resuming his present course would be mean—certainly not fun, but Robby wasn't going home clean, either. An idea came to him and he darted off toward one of the end zones, far from where the other boys were assembling for their game. Just before reaching the goal line, Patrick dove forward and slid across the field, leaving a wake of freezing rainwater, saturated earth, and dead grass behind him. When his body came to rest, he sat up and yelled across the field, "C'mon, you big pussy!"

There aren't many eleven-year-old American boys who don't understand the context of that challenge. Robby understood that Patrick wanted him to also run and slide in the mud, but part of the message was confusing and didn't really compute. *What does a big pussy have to do with anything?* It made no sense.

"Dude!" Patrick yelled again. "Either you do it or I come over there and drag you!"

Robby looked down at his still salvageable sweatshirt and khaki pants. Would his mother get mad if he ruined his clothes? More important, might there be some virus or parasite lurking at his feet just waiting to find some open portal to his bloodstream where it could then fester and multiply until he landed in the hospital? "No, thank you!" he yelled back to his friend.

Patrick slammed his hands down with a splash and lifted himself up. "Goddammit, Robby! You know what? I'm just going home by myself!" Patrick then spun around and started to walk away.

He'd only taken a few steps when he heard Robby trying to catch up with him. Patrick was willing to forgive him and accept that this was just another activity that Robby wasn't going to participate in. It didn't mean he wasn't disappointed, but he was running out of things they could do together.

As Patrick slowed his pace so Robby could catch up, he heard a thud behind him. When he turned to see the cause of the sound, there was Robby, face down in the end zone, his face and chest covered with mud. Patrick turned and ran back to his friend with the glee of a father whose son had just performed his first bicycle ride without training wheels. Robby rolled over on his back and stared into the gray, cloudy sky, spitting debris from his mouth and wiping his face.

"Now wasn't that fun?" Patrick asked as he stood over his buddy.

Robby frowned and stuck his finger in his mouth. When he withdrew it, the finger was covered with blood.

"Oh, shit!" Patrick exclaimed. Kneeling to help his friend, he asked, "Are you okay, dude?"

Robby opened his mouth, exposing two cracked front teeth and a small cut on the inside of his upper lip. He tried to say something, but what came out was unintelligible babble. Patrick pulled off his filthy sweatshirt and removed the long-sleeved shirt he was wearing beneath it. "Put this on there for the blood," he said. "It's not that bad, dude, but we need to get back to your house." Patrick then helped his friend to his feet and they began walking home.

Patrick was ashamed of himself for forcing Robby to do something he didn't want to do that resulted in his friend getting hurt. As they walked together, Patrick asked several times if Robby was in pain or needed some other assistance. Robby continued to hold the now bloody shirt to his mouth and answered by shaking his head. He certainly looked fine, other than having a blood-soaked shirt hanging out of his mouth. There were no tears or grimaces of pain, no rushed attempt to scramble home for help. Patrick was relieved his friend didn't appear to be hurting. He wasn't so confident in what was to come when they got home. Was Robby going to snitch on him and say he made him slide in the mud even after Robby insisted he didn't want to do it? Would the Debruijns call his parents and say he was no longer welcome to play with their son?

By the time the boys reached his house, Robby's lip had stopped bleeding. The two boys walked up the steps to the front porch and Patrick stuck his head in the door and called for Robby's parents. He was in enough trouble. Traipsing into his friend's house covered with mud would only make things worse. Mrs. Debruijn appeared at the top of the stairs. Halfway down Patrick opened the front door, revealing two boys caked in brown sludge. At first sight Kathryn Debruijn's heart warmed to see her son finally being a boy with another boy at his side. Those warm feelings only lasted about three steps. As she grew closer, she saw the very bloody shirt in her son's hand.

"Are you okay?!" Robby's mother ran down the remaining stairs and crossed the foyer before either boy could answer. When Robby opened his mouth and displayed his damaged front teeth, Mrs. Debruijn gasped, "Oh, my Lord." She turned her head toward the living room. "Honey! You need to come see this!"

A moment later Dr. Debruijn appeared. When he first saw the boys, he began to laugh and said, "Well, well. Am I supposed to hose you two down?"

Mrs. Debruijn found much less humor in the situation. "Look at your son's front teeth," she demanded.

Dr. Debruijn stepped closer to his son, who again opened his mouth wide, peeling his lips back so his father could examine his injury. "Oh, boy," Dr. Debruijn said. He put on a pair of glasses he kept in his shirt pocket and looked closer. "Yep, yep," he said as he conducted his preliminary examination. "Not going to need stitches, but those teeth might be a problem. At least what's left of them. How do you feel?"

"Okay," Robby answered.

Dr. Debruijn turned to Patrick. "Are you okay?"

"Yes, sir," Patrick answered. "I'm just dirty."

"I'll say," Dr. Debruijn said with a smile. "What happened?"

"We were running around in the mud over at Gruber Field and he hit his face on the ground," Patrick answered. "We came straight home. I'm really sorry this happened."

"Aaah," Dr. Debruijn said, brushing aside the unnecessary apology. "Better than a broken arm. Thanks for bringing him back home."

Mrs. Debruijn was already showing some relief on her face when she told Robby to run upstairs and clean up so they could go get his teeth fixed at the fort's dental office. Before Robby stepped inside the house, his father told him to wait just a minute. He hurried off to another room and quickly returned with a camera. "We need a picture of this," he said.

The boys were then ushered back into the yard for a photograph. Patrick was relieved he wasn't in any trouble. Dr. Debruijn didn't appear to think it was a big deal at all, and Mrs. Debruijn was even smiling as she stood beside her husband while he directed the brief photo shoot.

Robby had his broken teeth capped and never blamed Patrick, although Patrick always felt directly responsible. It was his challenge that had set the wheels in motion, except that wasn't the truth at all. Robby hadn't gathered the strength to try sliding in the mud like his friend. He was only trying to catch up with Patrick as he was being abandoned and slipped during his sprint across the slippery wet football field. What came to be one of the first pivotal moments in their relationship was insignificant to Robby. It was a simple accident, not a breakthrough in his apprehension about almost anything physical. Patrick saw it completely differently, and it became the foundation of his instinct to always protect Robby.

In the next two months both boys had twelfth birthdays and the holiday season came and went. During that time the boys solidified their friendship after school and on weekends, often visiting each other to do nothing more than talk. Other times, when weather permitted, they spent the afternoon throwing a baseball or football around the yard or performing outdoor chores together. No one remembers when the boys became best friends. It's likely that Patrick realized they were best friends by the time he made these two journal entries.

January 13, 2005

Friday is one of my favorite days. It's always the easiest day at school and then when it's over you feel free. Me and Robby went over to Suicide Hill across the street from the old fort wall and did some sledding before it got dark. The snow is really packed now and we were flying. There were some other people there who wanted to know where I got my toboggan. I told them my dad gave it to me for Christmas and they said that was cool and I agreed. Robby is probably my best friend, but we don't even go to school together. He's so smart they don't let him go to school with the rest of us. I'm smart too, but I guess Robby is like scientist smart. His dad is a doctor and I know those guys are super smart. The only thing wrong with Robby is he's not very good at sports and he's super shy. He's okay around me. Other people make him nervous. I can't really hang out with him when my other friends are around because he gets too quiet and just stands there. Then I start to feel bad for him and no one has any fun. We're going to rub butter on my new sled's skids tomorrow to see if that will make it go even faster.

January 14, 2005

The sun came out today and the wind stopped. Me and Robby got to Suicide Hill around ten and almost had the whole place to ourselves. The butter idea didn't really work. It was warmer than usual and we could have stayed all day, but these older kids got there and started hogging the best part of the hill like a bunch of assholes. I can't wait to get bigger. I'm going to try to get to be a little over six feet tall when I'm done growing. I'm going to have lots of muscles too. Robby is probably going to stay super skinny. I'll have to make sure and lift a lot of weights so I can protect him.

CHAPTER 4

My mom signed me up for spring league baseball today. I'm so happy I can't sleep. I'm going to call Robby tomorrow and see if he's going to sign up too. It would be cool if we're on the same team. He sucks at baseball, but he'll never get better if he doesn't try. Everyone sucks the first time they play. I don't think I sucked that bad, but I don't really remember. It's probably going to take a guy like me who doesn't suck, to teach a guy like Robby who does suck really bad, to not suck so bad.

March 24, 2005

I called Robby today and he doesn't want to sign up for spring league. He's going to change his mind as soon as he sees one of our games. My job is to get him ready for the summer league that starts later in summertime. I don't think we can be best friends anymore if he doesn't like baseball. That would make me kind of sad.

P atrick confided in his father that he thought Robby might also refuse to join the summer youth baseball league. Colonel Bennett suggested they take Robby and his father to a professional baseball game in nearby Kansas City to see if that might spark his interest. Seeing a Royals game was always a treat—Patrick thought it was a great idea. The season had just begun and there were plenty of seats available, so Colonel Bennett called Dr. Debruijn and they settled on the next Saturday afternoon for Robby's first real Major League Baseball game.

April 2, 2005

Our dads took me and Robby to a Royals game today. Robby never saw a real baseball game with real baseball players before. We had a blast! The Royals beat the Angels 6 to 2. I taught Robby how to keep score. I like going to games with my dad, but I think it's going to be cooler if the Debruijns start going to games with us. Awesome, Awesome, Awesome!!! I would write more, but I'm tired and my stomach is kind of upset. I think the hotdog or the nachos I ate at the game gave me the squirts.

The first time I read this entry, I didn't think much of it. During the course of my interviews, though, I learned this was a much more significant event than was portrayed by Patrick's short journal entry. Patrick not only took his leather glove to Royals games in case a foul ball came his way, but he also used to take a scorebook with him. The book allowed him to keep track of how the players from both teams performed at the plate throughout the game. When the later innings rolled around, Patrick would look at his book and tell his father how the batter had done during his previous at bat, and they would discuss it as if it were fairly important. Eventually the people sitting around them would take note of what Patrick was doing and they would begin to make scorebook enquiries, which made Patrick feel very grown-up and important.

The game that day was played on a beautiful, breezy, late spring afternoon. Their seats were along the third base line, high enough to see the entire field, but low enough to hear the pop in the third baseman's glove when he caught the ball. The Bennett men went to several games a season—Mrs. Bennett appreciated the opportunity for some private time—and the best game was always their first one of the year. There was something wondrously magical about a perfectly groomed professional baseball field and the carnival atmosphere before and during the game. Patrick was excited to share the experience with his friend.

After settling into their seats and placing an order with their fathers for the pregame run to the concession stand, Patrick revealed his scorebook to Robby, who had absolutely no interest in it no matter how much Patrick insisted on its importance. All Robby seemed to care about was getting a corn dog and making sure he had enough sunscreen on.

The Bennetts made a point to arrive at games extra early so they could watch the players take batting practice. On this day Patrick spent that pregame time trying to explain the fundamental rules of the game to Robby. He assumed his friend knew nothing about batting averages or pitchers' earned run averages, and there was no way he knew there was an actual duel being played out between the pitcher and the batter. By the game's first pitch, Patrick had painted baseball not as a simple game of throwing a ball back and forth until someone eventually hit it with a bat. On the contrary, baseball was a complicated sport that required constant strategy and a great deal of skill.

As the first inning progressed, Patrick showed Robby how he was logging the players' statistics with each turn at bat. Robby didn't ask any questions. When the top of the second inning started, Patrick asked Robby if he'd like to give it a try. Robby said, "That's okay," but he continued to watch how Patrick made entries in the book.

When the bottom of the second inning started, Patrick asked Robby again, "Do you want to give it a try?"

Robby repeated his first response, "That's okay."

The fathers had been eavesdropping on the boys while they talked. Dr. Debruijn decided he would stay out of the boys' conversation, although his instinct was to step in and insist his son at least try to keep the game's statistics for an inning or two. Colonel Bennett was proud of his son's attempts to get Robby involved even if they were unsuccessful.

When the second inning ended and the Royals ran out on the field to begin the top of the third, Patrick handed the scorebook to Robby and said, "I got to pee. You keep the stats until I get back." Patrick then rose and skipped up the stadium stairs toward the men's room without waiting for a response from Robby, who looked over at the fathers.

"I don't know how to do it," Dr. Debruijn said with a shrug.

"Me neither," Colonel Bennett lied. "That's always been Pat's thing. Sorry, I can't help you."

The men leaned back in their seats and returned to a conversation about their memories of attending their first professional baseball games. Robby put his soda down and opened the book. He checked the large scoreboard above center field and made sure the visiting team's lineup hadn't changed. When the first pitch of the inning was swung on and missed, Robby checked the strike box on the score sheet and waited for the next pitch.

Patrick went to the bathroom, stopped at a souvenir stand, and watched the rest of the inning from the top of the stands. When the inning was over he hopped back down the stairs to his seat with a plastic bag in his hand. "Well, did you do it?" he asked as Robby returned the closed scorebook to him.

"Yes," Robby replied.

Patrick opened the book to the game's score sheet page and looked over Robby's entries. They were perfect. "Nice job, dude," Patrick said. "Here, you win a prize for that." Patrick withdrew a Royals baseball cap from the plastic bag and handed it to Robby.

"Thank you," Robby said, totally lacking any evidence of enthusiasm. He held the cap in his lap and studied it.

"You gonna put it on?" Patrick asked.

Robby placed the oversized cap on his head without first removing the manufacturer's sticker from the bill. The tops of his ears jutted clumsily outward with the sides of the cap pushing against them. Patrick looked at his friend and chuckled. "C'mon, you big dork," he said. "Give me that thing."

Robby removed the baseball cap and handed it back to Patrick, who immediately removed the sticker from the bill and then resized the cap with the adjustable strap on the back. He gave it back to Robby. "Now try that."

Robby took the cap and placed it on his head, this time it fit perfectly and didn't make his ears protrude like those of a chimpanzee. "Look at me," Patrick said, and when Robby turned to face him, he reached up and carefully bent the corners of the bill downward. "This'll help keep the sun out of your eyes." When he was satisfied the hat had been adjusted properly, Patrick smiled and said, "You look like a real baseball player now."

Robby nodded in agreement. "I'll keep score the next inning if you want," he said.

"Sure," Patrick replied. "How about you take the top of the innings and I'll take the bottom?"

"Okay," Robby answered.

Patrick felt a nudge from Dr. Debruijn, who was sitting next to him. When he looked to see what he wanted, Robby's father winked at him and tried to nonchalantly pass him a twenty-dollar bill. Patrick frowned and shook his head. Dr. Debruijn mouthed the words *Are you sure?* Patrick reiterated his position with a slight wave of his hand. Dr. Debruijn then mouthed, *Thank you*, and they all returned to watching the game.

Robby quickly mastered the score sheet and even corrected Patrick's work a few times throughout the day. This was when Patrick learned that his new friend was a perfectionist, though he didn't display it with a "Do it right, or don't do it at all" attitude like a parent or a teacher. It was simpler than that. It just didn't make sense to Robby to not want to do something to perfection, and Patrick figured that was why there were so many things his new friend didn't want to do. He knew he couldn't do them well, so why waste his time trying?

After the game the Bennetts dropped off the Debruijns and returned home for debriefing. Patrick told his father that Robby was pretty good at keeping an accurate score sheet and maybe he could do it for his Little League team when the season started. All the coaches kept their own scorebooks, and most of them handed the recordkeeping off to some poor kid on the bench who wasn't playing. If Robby liked doing it, everyone would be happy as long as he didn't screw it up. Colonel Bennett thought it was a great idea and suggested he run it by Robby's father to see if he concurred before they mentioned it to Robby. No one remembers how the arrangement played out, but before Patrick knew it Robby was on his baseball team, not as a player but as the assistant team manager, whose sole responsibility was to keep record of the game's statistics and score during games. They even gave him a uniform.

April 7, 2005

It's a miracle!!! Robby is on my baseball team!!! Go Pirates!!! My best friend, the King of All Dorks, is going to be our scorekeeper. They gave him a uniform and everything. We are going to totally kick some ass this year! Pirates Rule!!!

Robby didn't actually join the team until the last practice before their first game. At the conclusion of the previous practice, Dr. Debruijn showed up and stood next to the head coach as he informed the team that a boy their age was going to be joining the team as a coach's assistant and the players needed to be nice to him and treat him like a teammate. Patrick knew exactly who the coach was talking about, but he was puzzled when the coach alluded to his friend as having some "special needs." To a twelve-year-old, that translated to "crippled," or "retarded," which wasn't Robby at all. When the words were spoken, Patrick looked at Dr. Debruijn and waited for him to dispute the coach. He didn't.

When the coach was finished, Patrick looked down the bench in the dugout where the other boys on his team were seated and said,

"I know this kid and he's cool. He's really shy and not very good at sports, that's all. It's probably because he's super smart like those brainiacs that everyone thinks are weird when they're a kid, but then they grow up and turn out to be smarter than everyone else. He's going to be a doctor someday." Patrick then looked at Robby's father, who smiled gratefully back at his son's friend.

That was the first time Patrick stood up for Robby and it felt good. It never crossed his mind that he had a choice about it. Their new coach was making Robby out to be different from the rest of the boys before he even met him, setting him up for failure before he even got a chance to try to be a normal kid. *You can't tell people some other guy is a retard when he isn't,* Patrick thought, *and then expect those people to not treat the guy different from everybody else.* Patrick understood his coach was trying to do the right thing by preparing the other boys for their new overly timid teammate, but the way he was going about it rubbed him the wrong way.

Patrick never left Robby's side when he started showing up to practice and games. He wasn't going to let anyone tease or bully him, and he made it very clear to Robby when they talked before his first day with the team.

"You let me know if anyone tries to fuck with you, dude," Patrick said. "Anyone messes with you, they're messing with me."

Robby wasn't exactly comforted by his friend's gallantry. The thought of other boys "messing with" him had never entered his mind until Patrick warned him it might happen, and that word—that F-word. It really bothered him.

Patrick was already a popular kid and a good ball player, and he'd been in a few after-school scrapes with some boys who thought they could bully him. Patrick's solid reputation among his peers meant that when Robby was around the team the other boys treated him well because that was what Patrick did, and Patrick was certified cool. For those boys still on the cusp of popularity, a little of that coolness rubbed off on them from being friendly with one of Patrick's friends was a sure way into his circle and obtaining their own Cool Club cards.

As for Robby, he always sat at the far end of the dugout to make sure he wasn't in anyone's way. He also didn't like to be in the middle of all the cheering. Loud, sudden noises bothered him. He didn't talk much either, but he was quick to give his teammates and coaches information from his stat book when they wanted it. Sometimes kids would ask Robby a question just to make him feel like he was a part of the team. Patrick knew it was going on and appreciated the effort.

When something good happened Robby was included in the high fives. When the team won and headed toward the opposing team's side of the field to shake hands and offer the mandatory, "Good game," Patrick always stayed behind and gave Robby a playful pat on the butt before he joined the rest of his teammates. Robby never left the dugout to shake hands with members of the other team whether they'd won or not. What good could come out of touching the hands of seventeen filthy rivals who had just been playing in the dirt and grass for the last hour and a half?

During that first season the boys' parents became close friends. They would sit in lawn chairs away from the other parents and drink lemonade spiked with vodka or gin from an Igloo cooler. The two families also sat together at church, where the music was always the highlight of the service. Robby's mother enjoyed the choir as much as

Mrs. Bennett did. Unfortunately neither could carry a tune, so joining the popular choir wasn't an option.

May 24, 2005

We got creamed today by the Red Sox. I hate those guys. They're killing everybody. I know almost everyone on that team from school. That makes it worse. I was really mad after the game, but then Robby cheered me up. Me and Robby drank a bunch of soda on the way home and had a burping contest in the back of his dad's SUV. We had to stop when Robby ripped a really long one and it grossed our moms out. I was laughing so hard I had snot and root beer coming out of my nose!!! That was probably the funnest time I ever had after losing a game. We play those guys one more time. Revenge will be mine!!! Go Pirates!!!

May 25, 2005

I got in trouble today at church. I used to go to Sunday school while my parents were in church, but I stopped because it was boring. Church isn't any better. It just goes by faster. Me and Robby were just sitting there and then everyone got up to sing and Robby's mom is such a terrible singer I just couldn't stop giggling. I put my hand over my mouth and everything. My mom at least knows she's not a good singer. She just kind of fakes it when it's time to sing. She'll stand there and look like she's singing, but she's really not. My dad sings and Robby's dad sings. Me and Robby just stand there. After the service my mom and dad were kind of mad at me for goofing off in church. I told them that burping contest popped into my head from yesterday and I couldn't help myself. They said if it ever happened again I'd have to go back to Sunday school. That can't happen. The only thing good about Sunday school is they have free doughnuts.

Patrick spent most of his summertime afternoons at the Grant community pool across the street and less than an additional block from his house. Robby didn't like to swim or the idea of stripping half naked and baking in the sun all day, so he spent his days continuing his home studies and visiting his father at the hospital. Almost every night when they weren't at practice or playing a baseball game, the two boys would meet behind the old fort wall and catch fireflies, or climb the trees, or sometimes go across the street and sit in the gazebo and do nothing more than talk amid the nightly chorus of locusts and cicadas.

By the end of the summer of 2005, the tiny neighborhood around the intersection of Grant, Riverside, Pope, and Kearney was all that existed to Robby and Patrick. Their entire world was within that serene little gated corner of northeastern Kansas that was completely devoid of danger or anything significant to fear. The only thing to worry about was getting home on time for supper and not being outside of earshot when it got dark and parents called them home for bedtime. It was a place to grow up with complete ignorance of the world outside, where you could play all day and let your imagination run wild without any kind of boundaries whatsoever. There wasn't a single thing they lived without, except knowing what their futures might bring.

That summer would be the last of its kind for the boys. Patrick had topped his social food chain in elementary school, and his friends all stayed the same through the summer. Robby now had a real friend, which presented its own challenges, the most basic being that of having to learn how to communicate with someone his own age. Just as he was getting the hang of it, summer ended, and it was time to begin his first experience with public school.

CHAPTER 5

L uckily for the boys there was a junior high school on the fort. Other than having a different class to go to every period and being assigned his own private locker to keep school supplies in, junior high wasn't that big a transition for Patrick. George S. Patton Jr. Junior High School wasn't significantly larger than the elementary school Patrick attended, and he already knew most of the members of the new seventh grade class. During that first semester, the only time Patrick had to interact with older kids was between bells in the hallway and in Beginning Home Economics, which included a few eighth graders.

The only classes Robby attended were a second period English class and a third period algebra class, which the boys had together. Patrick would finish his first hour class and Robby would already be waiting at his friend's locker during the period break. Patrick would then switch out his books and the boys would walk together to their next two classes. When algebra was over, Robby went home to continue his studies there while Patrick completed the rest of the day at school. It was as if Robby's parents were sneaking him in and out at

Patton, and if you didn't know any better, you'd never know he was even there.

One of the benefits of junior high over elementary school was that Patton had extracurricular sports. Patrick joined the football team, although he spent almost the entire season practicing and rarely got a chance to play. He was too small for the varsity team, and the junior varsity team was crowded with seventh and eighth graders. He almost quit when it became clear early in the season that he wouldn't be playing much, but a wise coach noticed he was becoming discontented with his lack of playing time and he pulled him aside and explained that all the coaches noticed and admired his efforts, and if he kept it up, he was going to be a great player in the future. That was all Patrick needed to hear.

When the football season ended, Patrick joined the wrestling team and then ran track in the spring. The older boys' skills and size mostly prevented him from participating in matches and meets, but when there was a competition designated just for the seventh graders, Patrick excelled and drew the attention of his coaches.

No matter what sport he was participating in, Patrick was usually home on school days by four thirty. He'd take a shower, have dinner, and then call Robby to see how he was coming along on their homework. When the school year started, Robby always had his homework completed by the time Patrick got home, but as the year progressed and their studies became more difficult, Patrick would ask Robby to hold off on their homework until he got home so they could do it together. On those nights, depending on the weather and amount of daylight left, the boys would select a location to meet and spend an hour or two finishing their homework together.

Robby was a whiz at algebra. Math with letters often made Patrick's head spin. When the problems they were sent home to solve became too difficult for Patrick, Robby would patiently dissect the theory behind the solution and try to make sense of it for his friend. Most of the time, Patrick eventually got it. Sometimes he never did. When that happened he pretended he understood for the sake of moving on and then simply copied Robby's work. He didn't dare tell Robby he was cheating. Robby couldn't understand why someone would want to copy someone else's work instead of learning how to do it right themselves. In his mind if you cheated on your homework, that wasn't only dishonest, it also defeated the entire purpose of going to school.

September 18, 2005

I totally blew it on my algebra test. I've been tricking Robby into giving me answers to the quizzes. He thinks he's been showing me how to do stuff, but all I've been doing is pretending to understand what he's talking about and then I just copy his work. I never thought about what I'd do on a test. Thank you Jesus for not making me have to show my parents this grade. Robby really is super smart. I have to start paying attention or I'm going to get in big trouble. Me and Robby collected two boxes of cans for the hurricane Katrina fundraiser at school. If we collect the most cans we win some free movie tickets and a couple of Applebee's gift certificates. I don't think we have a chance. We saw Caroline Bailey and Beth Harper standing in front of the commissary begging for cans right there where people walk out. They already had a full grocery cart and were halfway full with another one when we saw them. That's kind of cheating in my book, but I wish we had the idea first. All I know is, I hope they like chili and Chunky soup in New Orleans because we're about to send them a whole buttload of the stuff.

On an average school year weekend, Patrick would get a call from a friend or he'd make the call to his buddies to find something to do after his chores were completed. If he thought there was a chance Robby might like to participate, Patrick would then call him and play up that day's activities in a manner designated to entice Robby from his medical books and dead chicken suturing. Sometimes it worked and sometimes it didn't. On Sundays the two families continued to attend church services together and then have brunch at the Officers' Club on the fort. The fathers and their sons might then watch an afternoon football game depending on who was playing, while the mothers continued visiting in another room or went shopping together.

When Robby wasn't doing homework or wasn't busy with Patrick, he spent most of his time at the hospital with his father. The idea of becoming a doctor himself some day was firmly cemented in his mind. Robby rarely initiated a conversation unless he had a question about something, but when he did it was almost always on the topic of practicing medicine or something he'd done or seen at the hospital. Patrick enjoyed hearing about some of the incredible things his friend was getting to see and he often envied him.

October 8, 2005

Robby got to see a guy who got his fingers cut off with a chainsaw today. How awesome is that! They landed a helicopter at Munson and flew the guy to a hospital in Kansas City to get them reattached. I want to see that kind of stuff and I kind of don't want to see that kind of stuff. I want to see it because it's probably totally gross. I don't want to see it because it might be too gross and it could give me an aneurism. It's a proven fact that you can see something gross like a bone sticking out of your arm and if you're not prepared for it, it doesn't make any difference how badass you are, your brain could blow a fuse and then you shit your pants and just drop dead. It's why they say you can have the shit scared out of you. It can really happen. I confirmed it with Robby. He knows all about that kind of stuff.

October 17, 2005

Robby got to see another dead person today. He is so lucky!!! It was a guy who had a heart attack. Robby said he was already dead by the time they got him to the hospital. If he was still alive they probably wouldn't have let him look at the guy, but I guess no one really cares once you're dead. I wonder if the guy looked down while he was floating up to heaven and wanted to know who the goofball was looking at him.

The remainder of the boys' seventh grade year passed quickly. Patrick got his act together academically and finished the year with a handful of As and two Bs. Robby had successfully navigated his limited exposure to public school for the first time, giving him and his parents the confidence to enroll again part-time at Patton for eighth grade.

When spring and summer baseball leagues resumed, Robby's father arranged for his son to be the scorekeeper again on Patrick's teams. Robby was much more comfortable being around the guys on the team this time and did much less cowering alone at the end of the bench. He still wasn't comfortable with all the yelling and wouldn't shake hands with the other team's players after the game. Patrick continued his postgame tradition of giving his friend a big smack on the behind when they won. Robby pretended to be annoyed by it, but Patrick could tell the team's statistician actually enjoyed the gesture—it was a welcome reaffirmation of their special friendship. No one else got a congratulatory slap on the butt from Patrick.

June 19, 2006

We kicked the crap out of the Yankees today. I got two singles and laid down a bunt that was a thing of beauty. The guy keeping the official scorebook got the lineups all screwed up so the coaches from both teams had to come over to our dugout to see if Robby's book had it right. It did and that made Robby feel pretty good. He saved the day!!! I gave Robby a big noogie and messed his hair all up. He hates when I do that, but he didn't today. I like to see him when he's proud of himself. My mom let us eat dinner in front of the TV so my dad could watch the hockey finals. My dad used to play hockey where he grew up back east. No one plays around here. I'd probably be a good hockey player. The only problem with hockey players is they all get their teeth knocked out. The Carolina Hurricanes won. You should see how big their trophy is—it's fucking huge! My dad says Canada is probably really mad at us right now because we beat their team from Edmonton. I didn't think people from Canada ever got mad at anybody. My dad said I was mostly right, except for when it comes to hockey.

The summer passed as the previous one had, and before the boys knew it, it was time to go back to school. Robby continued to take two classes at Patton and shuffle in and out before anyone could see him. Patrick continued the same schedule of school and sports. Although he was only an eighth grader, he made the varsity football and wrestling teams, which elevated his popularity among not only his peers but the students a class ahead of his. Nowhere was that increased stature more valuable than when girls made a serious entry into Patrick's life. Soon he had his first girlfriend.

The kids were still too young to drive and go out on regular dates. Because Patrick's new girlfriend lived within walking distance of his house, he'd go over to her house and they'd watch TV and make out for hours on end in her basement. He didn't need a car for that. Cindy Kravits was her name, and she was a cute and very popular cheerleader. Patrick was quickly smitten. There was still room for Robby in his life, just not anymore on Friday and Saturday nights.

November 11, 2006

My mom dropped me and Cindy off at the movies in Leavenworth and we saw Night at the Museum. *We sat in the back row and basically made out the whole time. Cindy has this lip gloss that tastes like a mix between bubblegum and cherries. I told her I liked it so she wears it just for me. I guess she's officially my woman.*

November 13, 2006

After church Mrs. Debruijn asked me and Robby if we wanted to go see a matinee off post and we both said yes, but then Robby said he wanted to see Night at the Museum. *Since it was kind of a secret that I already saw the movie without him, I went and pretended I had no idea what was going on. I don't tell Robby a lot about what I do with other friends, to make sure he doesn't get his feelings hurt. So we were sitting there eating popcorn and the movie started and I remembered a dinosaur comes to life and kind of roars really loud like a lion and starts chasing people around. I didn't think Robby was going to be scared or anything, but he totally hates loud noises and if it's a loud enough noise, he can totally freak out. That's why he usually has earplugs with him when we watch movies. So I whispered to him that it was about to get real loud and the next thing I know, my goofball best friend shoved the napkins we got with our popcorn and sodas in his ears. Except he didn't tear off the extra part! He just let it hang out the side of his head!!! I think every-one behind us thought he was just being a silly kid. I didn't realize the loud dinosaur part wasn't coming up for another ten or fifteen minutes because I was too busy kissing my girlfriend the first time I saw the movie, so now I had to sit there with Robby looking all goofy until that part of the movie was over. Also what I didn't remember about the first time I saw the movie was that it just keeps getting louder and louder the whole time, so Robby had to keep those napkins in his ears the whole rest of the movie. I wasn't embarrassed or anything. That's my boy and if he has super hearing capabilities like a hawk, you don't make fun of that kind of stuff.*

Patrick's journal entries are nearly identical over the course of the next several months. Cindy becomes the focal point of his short writings, yet there are few revelations worth mentioning. About the only thing clear from the entries made between December 2006 and June 2007 is that Patrick and Robby seemed to be enjoying the stereotypical lives of virtually carefree fourteen-year-olds. Patrick was learning how to sustain a relationship with a member of the opposite sex, and Robby was right behind him, learning the difficult skills of becoming an average teenager.

Girls were now the main source of distraction for Patrick's entire crew of male friends from school, and there was a perfect place on post where you could always find a flock of them. Hanging out at the Grant pool between eighth and ninth grade subsequently transitioned to more of a social scene than just a bunch of boys horse-playing around all day. There was a staple group of about twenty kids, boys and girls, and they'd arrive shortly after noon, take over a handful of tables and reclining lawn chairs, and loiter together until it was time to either go home for dinner or go to baseball practice or a game. The girls mostly sunbathed and only got in the pool occasionally to cool off. There were already two or three of them who understood perfectly well how horny the boys were and what they were thinking as they watched the girls slather their tan bodies in baby oil and lie out in their bikinis.

June 12, 2007

OMG! The funniest thing happened today at the pool. Kim Bowers was there in an orange bikini with her boobs all hanging out and her boyfriend Sam Del Bagno got a boner and didn't even know it. We all started cracking up and when Sam figured out we were capping on him, he ran off and dove into the pool, but the lifeguard made him get out because it was adult swim period. Classic! If that ever happened to me I'd fucking kill myself. Seriously, I'd blow my fucking brains out. If you're reading this and it's because I'm dead because I shot myself in the head, it's because my friends saw me with a boner at the swimming pool. I told Robby what happened and he's so weird he didn't think it was funny. Instead, he starts telling me about how a dick works and how you can get boners for no reason. Sometimes I wish there was someone else around when Robby tells me this stuff. I can't tell if he's messing with me or he's serious.

The entire crew, minus Robby, paired up early in the summer if they weren't already going steady. Patrick had to make a conscious effort to include Robby, which sometimes interfered with his time with Cindy, who never understood why her boyfriend spent so much time with a nerd like Robby. He was so weird. The night Cindy shared as much with Patrick, she was summarily broken up with. No one was going to bad-mouth his buddy. There were plenty of other girls around.

July 1, 2007

I broke up with Cindy yesterday. She was trashing Robby and I couldn't take it anymore. I'd call her a bitch, but she really isn't. I think she's just really really immature. She's probably going to want to get back together in a few days. I told my mom and dad to tell her I'm busy if she calls. I'm going to ignore her if I see her at the pool. If she thinks I'm still mad at her maybe she'll leave me alone.

As soon as word spread that he was back on the market, a girl named Linda Gowers was happy to step in and fill Cindy's place.

July 5, 2007

I went to the fireworks show at the golf course last night. Robby didn't want to go because he thought there would be too many people and it would get too loud, so I met some other guys there. We were just walking around and this girl named Linda started talking to me. She lives on post, but she went to a Catholic school in the city last year. She's really hot and she said she's seen me before but I don't remember seeing her before. Bye-bye Cindy Kravits, hello Linda I don't remember your last name!

The two began dating immediately, if you can call it that. Linda's parents didn't like their daughter and her new boyfriend going into her room together or going down to their basement all by themselves. Linda's father was a kind man and he liked baseball so he and Patrick had something in common to talk about, but there was no way Linda's dad was going to let Patrick touch his fourteen-year-old daughter on his watch, no matter how much he liked him. Little did he know that the idea of Patrick having intercourse with Linda was more petrifying to Patrick than it was to her father.

July 20, 2007

Linda is a total horndog! We were making out on the patio of the old Girl Scout building by my house and she totally put her hand on my you know what. She even started to rub it a little! What if someone saw us doing that? If the MPs came by and saw that, we could probably go to jail for minors having sex. My parents would kill me if we got caught. I liked it though. I'm not going to tell anyone. If I do they'll think she's a slut and all the older guys will try to steal her from me.

In actuality none of the kids were having sex or even trying. The farthest anyone went was an occasional hand up a shirt, and if a boy got that far, he was pretty much a hero. Patrick was completely satisfied with passionate necking. Anything beyond that really did scare the hell out of him. When Linda and Patrick started seeing each other, Linda's family already knew they would be moving at the end of August to Fort Campbell, Kentucky. Patrick understood he only had two months with Linda and he was going to make those two months count. During that period Robby fell almost completely off Patrick's radar. The boys saw each other at games and practice, but there were few interactions other than on Sundays when their families went to church and brunch together. Robby wasn't the type to pick up a phone and call Patrick just to talk, and Patrick would much rather spend his phone time with his girlfriend. The boys still considered themselves friends—they just had more important things to do.

When their ninth grade year started, Patrick was one of the most popular kids in school and a starting linebacker on the varsity football team. He got over Linda moving within a few weeks and began another short relationship with one of her friends after she invited him to the first school dance. The boys didn't share either of the two classes Robby attended at Patton their freshman year, so Patrick never saw him during the school day. Because they no longer shared homework assignments, there wasn't any compelling reason to meet after school. That logistical separation allowed Patrick to become even more engrossed in being popular and playing football. On game days Patrick's parents picked up Robby and took him with them. When the games were over, Robby and Patrick sat in the backseat of the family's SUV, where Robby quietly listened to his friend rehash the game. Afterward, they parted until the next Sunday.

The boys' parents realized their sons' friendship was waning but decided to let it run its course, hoping Robby wouldn't get his feelings hurt. The Debruijns understood there would be times when it was best for Robby to learn life lessons by experiencing them. To shelter him from uncomfortable situations that he was sure to encounter for the rest of his life was a disservice, no matter how difficult it was to stand by and watch. Mrs. Bennett offered to talk with Patrick about it and encourage him to reserve more time for Robby, but the Debruijns felt it might actually tarnish Patrick's feelings toward their son. It was best to just let the boys be boys. By the end of football season, Patrick and Robby's relationship was reduced to two kids who met once a week with their parents because they had to, not because they had any interest in each other. Robby had his own full plate with his studies and preparing for medical school, which continued to include following his father around the pediatric clinic at Munson. Patrick was consumed with juggling his schoolwork, sports, and busy social calendar.

A few weeks before Christmas break, Patrick started to feel sick at school. As the day progressed, his minor nausea grew into severe cramps. By the time his fifth-period biology class ended, Patrick was doubled over in pain at his desk because his lab partners, who were supposed friends, spent the entire class trying to make him laugh, which made the cramps worse. The teacher was also Patrick's wrestling coach—it was wrestling season by then—and Patrick told him as the students filtered out of the room that he wouldn't be able to practice that day because his cramps were so bad. He then went to his final class of the day, which was choir.

The music teacher had the choir members stand while they sang, but Patrick was in so much pain he couldn't do it. She recognized something was wrong with Patrick and sent him to the office to be examined by the school nurse.

Patrick discounted his pains to the nurse once he knew his mother was on her way to pick him up. When she arrived Mrs. Bennett asked Patrick if he thought he needed to go to the hospital or if he'd rather go home and take some Pepto-Bismol. Patrick had no idea what was wrong with him and didn't feel like waiting around in the hospital, so he elected to go home. There his mother gave him a capful of the pink antacid and sent him to bed. When Colonel Bennett got home a few hours later, he discovered him curled in a fetal position and moaning.

"How you doing, chief?" he asked.

"I feel like I got stabbed."

Patrick's father called his friend Dr. Debruijn and told him Patrick was very sick with painful cramps that weren't reacting to medicine. The next thing Patrick knew, he was in the back of the family SUV headed for the Munson Army Hospital emergency room.

Dr. Debruijn arrived at the hospital with the Bennetts and met them in the parking lot. Patrick was embarrassed that Robby's father had come from home to examine him. Sure he was hurting, but he didn't want to look like a sissy in front of his friend's father. The hospital was full of other doctors; there had to be someone else just as capable of fixing him who he'd never have to see again. Patrick had yet to realize how embarrassing that examination would become.

Dr. Debruijn ushered the Bennetts into an exam room and asked Patrick some preliminary questions. He checked his heart rate and blood pressure and asked if he'd ever had a rectal exam before. Patrick had no idea what his friend's father was talking about. He looked at his mother, signaling she would know. Mrs. Bennett answered that she didn't think so, and then she and her husband left the exam room. Patrick got very nervous as he watched Dr. Debruijn put on rubber gloves and squirt lubricant on his fingers. "I need to go in and see if you're inflamed in there," he told his young patient.

"In where?" Patrick asked.

"In your behind," Dr. Debruijn answered. "It shouldn't hurt. It's going to feel kind of like you do when you take a big poop."

Patrick's mind raced in panic mode. *Is there anything more humiliating than having your friend's dad stick his finger up your ass?*

Dr. Debruijn positioned Patrick on the exam table and conducted the examination. It was brief, but he touched something that made

Patrick wince. As soon as Patrick confirmed that something inside him was tender, Dr. Debruijn stepped away from the table and removed his gloves. He asked Patrick's parents to reenter the exam room and told them Patrick's appendix was inflamed and needed to come out.

The diagnosis of appendicitis didn't immediately register with Patrick. He only knew the pain in his abdomen was excruciating and he wanted someone to make it go away. Dr. Debruijn explained the details of the surgery, assuring Patrick that he would sleep through the whole thing and wake up a little sore but good as new. That was fine with him, particularly when Patrick learned they wouldn't be accessing his innards from the same location as the exam.

The surgery was performed that night to prevent the possibility of a rupture. They were too late. Patrick arrived at the hospital in worse shape than previously thought. In the recovery room, Mrs. Bennett got her first taste of her son's personal repertoire of profanities, which under the fog of anesthesia he shared with wanton abandon. Patrick was aware of the fact that he was recklessly dropping assorted F-bombs, including a handful of rather R-rated references to the residual pain caused by a catheter that had been temporarily inserted into his penis. "My dick is on fire," he moaned. "Mom, my fucking dick is killing me. What did they do to my dick?" He simply couldn't stop talking.

Mrs. Bennett handled the scene quite gracefully. She understood full well her son was drugged up and not in control of his mouth. Patrick apologized when his head cleared and he had to face the terrifying truth that his spewing of vulgarities hadn't been a bad dream. Mrs. Bennett told her son not to worry about it, though she'd never forget it. Colonel Bennett was quietly tickled by his son's antics and accepted Patrick's knowledge of profanity as a sign that he was truly growing up. It was an oddly proud moment for him.

When Dr. Debruijn came into the recovery room and explained how the surgery had gone, he told Patrick's father that, had they not taken him to the hospital that day, Patrick could have died. It was that close. Unfortunately, with the rupture, Patrick's recovery was going to be more complicated than was originally expected. He would have to remain in the hospital indefinitely for observation and to take a regimen of antibiotics. Patrick was far less concerned with the prospect of having been near death than the pain that was growing in his abdomen as the painkillers wore off. Before leaving the room, Dr. Debruijn ordered a sedative in Patrick's IV drip. The doctor's young patient was back to sleep and being wheeled to his new hospital room a few minutes later.

Before dawn the next morning, Patrick was awakened by a nurse who checked his vital signs and gave him a foul-tasting liquid to drink. She explained that his parents would be allowed to visit him in a few hours and he needed to stay in bed and not try to walk around. Though he still felt pain, Patrick fell back to sleep as soon as the nurse left his room. The next time he opened his eyes, Robby was standing over him in a white lab coat. "Oh, hey, dude," Patrick said in a gravelly voice as he stretched and cleared his head. "What time is it?"

"Six thirty," Robby answered. "Your mom and dad will be here in a minute. How are you feeling?"

"Sore, man. Very sore. Holy shit!" Patrick said. "How long have I been asleep? What day is it?"

"You had your surgery yesterday," Robby said calmly.

Patrick's head continued to clear. "Oh, man," he said as he tousled his hair and rubbed his face. "Those drugs they gave me really fucked my head up. Tell your dad thanks for everything. Sorry he had to come from home and do an operation last night."

"That's okay," Robby said. "He likes surgeries. You have to stop cussing, though."

Just then Dr. Debruijn stepped into the room with a nurse. "How you doing, slugger?" he asked.

"Sore."

"Well, you're gonna be sore for a while," Dr. Debruijn told him. "Tell me what hurts."

"Almost everything from my chest down to my privates," Patrick answered.

Dr. Debruijn pulled Robby's bed sheet and blanket down to his knees and examined his surgery wound, pushing gently on different areas of his abdomen each time and asking, "Does this hurt?" or "How does this feel?"

It all hurt, only some parts hurt more than others. Robby stood quietly in the corner and watched.

"Come on over, Robert," Dr. Debruijn said to his son when his examination was completed. Robby stepped up to his father's side and looked down at Patrick. "Pat's appendix may have actually ruptured while we were prepping him last night," Dr. Debruijn said. "There were no signs of infection, but we're going to put him on some antibiotics to make sure. What would you suggest we start with?"

Robby frowned for a moment, thought, and then said, "I'd start him on two grams of Unasyn."

"Side effects?" his father asked.

"Chills and diarrhea. Maybe some tingling in his legs and feet as long as he's not allergic."

"Alternative if he has a poor reaction?" Dr. Debruijn asked.

"I'd try Ceftriaxone. It might make him a little weak and feverish. If it does, we can give him something else for that."

"And what about the pain?"

"Start with Dilaudid until he starts to feel better. Then we can put him on Tylenol 3."

"What do you think, Patti?" Dr. Debruijn asked the nurse standing next to him.

"Sounds good to me," she answered.

"I concur," Dr. Debruijn said. "Nice job, Robert."

Even with his pain and discomfort, Patrick was impressed. *That was fucking cool.*

A few minutes later Dr. Debruijn and the nurse left the two boys alone in the room. Patrick asked Robby what exactly happened to him, and Robby explained how the appendix is basically a useless organ that can get infected, and when it does you have to remove it before it leaks and fills the abdomen with toxic pus. In Patrick's case his appendix had actually ruptured, but he would be as good as new in a week or two, and he'd probably even be able to wrestle again before the season was over. That was good news.

At exactly seven, Patrick's parents walked in and sat with him as he sipped his liquid breakfast. Colonel Bennett only stayed for a few minutes because he needed to go to work, but he assured his son he would be back later in the afternoon. Patrick didn't really care. All he wanted was a television with a remote control. Mrs. Bennett wasn't about to leave her only son's bedside during visiting hours. She arrived that first day after the surgery with comic books and sports magazines and even snuck in a Hostess cupcake in case her son needed it. Patrick appreciated the care being offered him, but by the second day of his hospital stay he was already irritated with his mother. She talked too much and kept trying to help. No kid wants to crap in a steel pan and hand it off to his mother.

Robby also stopped by frequently, although he didn't linger, especially when Patrick's parents were there. To Patrick, his friend always seemed to be at the hospital even before and after regular visiting hours. Patrick came to look forward to Robby's brief visits. During the next few days, he entered Patrick's room around six thirty and looked at the chart that was always left hanging from the end of his bed. From the entries on the chart, he'd tell Patrick what his schedule of medications and diet was going to be for the day. When a nurse walked into the room while Robby was there, they talked like co-workers and the nurses often asked Robby to help with some menial task like he was an actual assistant. It was fairly clear to Patrick that while he was spending all his time goofing off with other friends and playing sports, Robby had been at the hospital truly learning how to be a doctor.

Patrick appeared to be getting better over the course of the next three days. Then he woke up on the fourth day shivering and covered in sweat. Somehow he'd become infected with a new virus. His parents hadn't looked terribly nervous when they first went into the hospital with Patrick; they were concerned but not scared. Most people don't think a routine appendectomy is any more dangerous than having tonsils removed. This infection wasn't appendicitis, however; it was sepsis, and the fear in Patrick's parents' eyes couldn't be hidden from him, no matter how encouraging the words from their mouths. For the first time, Patrick was scared.

His core temperature soared, and when his brain started to swell they sedated him into a coma. A vigil was held at his bedside—visiting regulations were lifted—and everyone waited for him to either get better or die. This lasted seven agonizing days.

When Patrick finally woke up he discovered his room was covered with Christmas decorations. His parents were there and sure enough, there was Robby right there with them. The worst was over and Patrick's prognosis was positive. He was still in a fog, but he was going to recover and walk out of the hospital someday with a clean bill of health.

Patrick was in the hospital for a total of four weeks, which included Christmas. As he recovered Patrick noticed his mother left when Robby showed up, so he asked Robby to come by more often. After that conversation, Robby began to visit Patrick's room more frequently, and the visits lasted much longer. Some of Patrick's other male friends came by on the weekends, but because of their age they had to be with their parents, which probably had a lot to do with why they never stayed for more than a few minutes. Patrick didn't like the guys seeing him in such a weak condition, and all they did was tease him while he lay sick and defenseless in his hospital bed. A couple of girls came by, too, and that was even worse. Patrick knew he looked like he felt, and that was "like shit."

Many families have a favorite Christmas that is ingrained in their memory for one reason or another. The Bennetts and Debruijns would never forget the one they spent in Munson Army Hospital. Dr. Debruijn arranged for them to use one of the staff lounges on Christmas Day. It had some sofas and easy chairs and a small kitchenette, and it was decorated with garland, colored lights, and a real Christmas tree with wrapped and beribboned gifts piled beneath it. Patrick's mother and Mrs. Debruijn made a feast and turned a simple folding table into a beautiful banquet setting. They all opened presents first and then stuffed themselves with their special Christmas meal. When they were full, they watched a video of *A Christmas Story* on a hospital projector used for training films and then sat around and talked awhile longer. It was perfect. It even snowed outside.

January 7, 2008

You will not believe what just happened to me. I just got home from the hospital because my appendix blew up! Robby's dad took it out in an emergency surgery and everything. I almost died!!! I was in there for almost a whole month. It felt like I got stabbed in the gut. My parents and Robby visited me every day. Robby was very cool. My mom was kind of bugging me, so whenever she was in my room for more than an hour or so, he'd come in and most of the time she'd leave and come back later. That was a lifesaver. I have to be really nice to my parents for a while, especially my mom. When they drugged me I said some really bad things I wish I could take back. At least now I know why I can never do drugs. We totally had Christmas with the Debruijns right there in the hospital. This is the most secret thing I've ever written in any of my journals. I was so happy when everyone came to the hospital for Christmas it made me cry. No one saw me. I went to the bathroom when I felt it coming. I got in there and just started bawling my eyes out!!! I couldn't believe it!!! I had to turn the water on in the sink full blast just so no one would hear me. My stomach is still sore where they had to cut through the muscle. The rest of me is completely healed. The scar is pretty cool.

I learned an interesting side note about that Christmas night of 2007 and Patrick becoming so overwhelmed with joy that he had to hide in the bathroom to conceal his tears. He wasn't hiding anything—everyone knew.

Patrick was released from the hospital and returned to school having only missed two weeks of classes because he'd been sick over the holiday break. He was far too weak to return to the wrestling team, so he spent his after-school time catching up on homework assignments he'd missed. As his energy slowly returned to him, he decided to start getting ready for the spring track season.

The fort had a large gymnasium full of every modern fitness contraption available. Patrick asked Robby if he wanted to go to the gym with him after school so he'd have a partner to work out with. All his other friends were busy with either wrestling or the basketball team. Robby didn't want to go to the gym. In his mind the only reason to work out was to train for a sport, and he had no interest in anything athletic. Patrick didn't need a workout partner and could have easily let it go, but Robby was growing into a scrawny kid, and Patrick knew if he didn't put on some weight and at least a little muscle, Robby was going to start getting bullied. His remedy was to basically kidnap his friend one day and insist he go with him to check out the gym.

February 23, 2008

I made Robby go to the gym with me today. It's like every other kid in the world is growing except for him!!! He's getting a little taller, but he's the skinniest kid I ever saw. They're going to kill him next year at high school if he shows up being so skinny and shy. Dr. Debruijn says I can start working out with weights now. I'm going to start running too, to get ready for track season. Robby's going to hate working out with me. I'm going to make him do it anyway. It's for his own good. I had to call him a big dork today just to get him to try some of the machines out. Sometimes I call him a big dork because that's kind of his nickname I guess. I don't call him that all the time. Sometimes when we're kidding around I'll call him that and he knows I'm just kidding around. Then there are times like today when I call him a big dork and he knows I'm really thinking he's being a big dork. He knows the difference. Of all the smart people I know, he's probably still the smartest and that's including girls. That doesn't mean he can't be a big dork sometimes.

Robby had never used any kind of fitness machine before, but on that first gym visit when Patrick led him into the area where new Pro-Fitness machines were lined in neat rows, Robby was suddenly curious—not about getting fit, but about how the machines worked. Each piece of equipment had a picture of the various muscle groups the machine targeted, along with a diagram of how the machine should be used. Anatomy was a subject Robby associated with the medical field, so he was very interested in the mechanics of how a machine could strengthen muscle or help them heal faster. Patrick demanded his friend try the machines out instead of standing there like a big dork and watching everyone else. That was the day Robby became a fitness nerd.

There are a handful of masculine titles young men have for those who incorporate a steadfast fitness routine into their lives: gym rat, animal, beast, to name a few. You couldn't apply any of those to Robby, though, without seeming to mock him. He was simply too uncoordinated and skinny. Almost every physical activity Robby took part in, from throwing a baseball to lifting a dumbbell, looked awkward and unnatural.

Most people beginning a new fitness routine set goals for themselves and then figure out some workout regimen that will help them achieve those goals. If you want to be big and muscular, you lift a lot of weight and add a lot of protein and carbohydrates to your diet to sustain energy. If you want to be lean and strong, incorporate more cardiovascular exercise into your workout and do more isometric lifting with lighter weights. The average person working out in a gym doesn't make their fitness routine any more complicated than that.

Robby couldn't have cared less about growing muscles and getting stronger. He wanted to use the machines so he could gather a better understanding of what a muscle felt like in motion. He wanted to experiment with what happens when you push a specific muscle group to exhaustion, and then he wanted to experiment with different ways to help that group of muscles recover. Improving the size of his biceps muscles so girls would be impressed or bullies would be less likely to pick on him not only never entered his mind, that thought pattern was beyond his scope of reality. He would exercise those biceps so he could better understand how the tendons and muscles worked together to lift and carry and push. Patrick didn't care what Robby's motivations were. He was just glad, though initially shocked, to have a friend who was also a motivated workout partner.

February 24, 2008

Me and Robby went to the gym again. He actually worked out!!! After we worked out on the machines for a while, we did some bench presses in the free weight room. Robby couldn't even lift the bar!!! Man, he has a long way to go. After we lifted weights we went in the sauna for about two minutes and then we had to leave. It's kind of weird sitting around with a bunch of strange men sweating your ass off in a tiny wood room that's like 150 degrees. I don't think we'll ever do that again. Robby kind of started to freak out. It was hard to breathe in there and I think he's a little claustrophobic. All my other friends are on the wrestling team or playing basketball after school. I don't miss hanging out with those guys. I don't even want a girlfriend right now and that's the truth.

The two boys spent the entire second half of ninth grade going to the gym directly after school before all the parents got off work and the place became crowded with adults. Neither of them got more muscular, but working out accelerated Patrick's recovery and helped Robby become more coordinated. The boys went to the gym together and worked out in the same room, but their routines were completely different. Patrick broke his regimen into three different routines: a chest and triceps day, a back and biceps day, and then a whole day designated for legs. There was no real tracking of his progress. When the weights started to feel lighter and he was able to do more reps, he increased the weight he was lifting and considered that an achievement.

Robby, on the other hand, based his workout on the muscle group he was interested in on that day. He always had a three-ring binder with him to keep notes, but he didn't use it to track whether he was getting stronger, although he did include that information. His notes were for the more important purpose of documenting his findings. *When I do overhead pull-downs, I notice there is a point when my elbows work harder than my deltoid muscles. When I use the abdomen machine, I also feel tension in the back of my neck.*

To prepare for the approaching track season, the boys also began jogging around Gruber Field near their homes. Robby started out with no stamina whatsoever and had to be constantly pushed. Patrick was accustomed to having to motivate his friend to try new things, but this was the first time he felt like he had to yell at him. Although it was more in the spirit of coaching than being angry, Patrick constantly yelling across the field, "C'mon, dude, don't be a lazy ass!" was upsetting to Robby, and he reacted with pouting and silence. There was nothing interesting about running circles around a football field. It didn't feel very good, either.

Patrick knew he sometimes hurt his friend's feelings when he yelled at him, so he was careful to try to use the same methods and words his coaches used when they were trying to motivate him. Still there were many times when Patrick felt guilty for selfishly forcing Robby to do things he didn't want to do.

March 11, 2008

I feel really bad right now. I feel like I'm yelling at Robby all the time when we go to the track. Why is it that every other person in the world gets the difference between a coach yelling at you and some asshole just being an asshole? Robby won't complain, but I can tell I'm hurting his feelings. I told my parents at dinner that I was feeling bad about yelling at Robby so much. My dad said as long as I don't call him names, maybe it's good for Robby to have someone to yell at him a little to keep him moving and toughen him up. Robby's seen me get yelled at by our coaches during baseball games. He knows how it works. I probably shouldn't care but I do.

This was the difficulty in being Robby's friend. Patrick had to always find a balance between what he wanted to do and what Robby was unwilling to try. If he wasn't interested, then Patrick had to decide whether he really cared if Robby joined him or not. As the boys grew older and closer once again, Patrick wanted to include Robby in the things he got to experience as a new teenager. He was having fun and wanted Robby to share in some of that fun.

With track season around the corner, Patrick attempted to talk Robby into trying out for the team. Robby was smart enough to know he wasn't ready and flatly refused, which was rare. The only thing he could do was run, and he knew he wasn't fast enough to keep up with the other kids. He would have been even worse as a distance runner. When the squad was set, Patrick was glad his friend had declined an attempt to join the team. Though he was satisfied his heart was in the right place, Patrick also understood that he'd almost set his friend up for certain failure.

Patrick ran the third leg on the one-mile relay team and was both a long and high jumper. The relay team never broke third place at any of the meets, but Patrick's natural skills at the long jump and his mastery of the Fosbury Flop technique in the high jump were twice rewarded with first-place medals. Robby attended every meet with Patrick's parents. When Patrick stepped onto the track right before his event, the three stood—Patrick's parents whistling and cheering while Robby stood silent, his arms folded across his chest, fists clenched with anticipation. When Patrick sprinted off from his mark, his parents cheered even more wildly, but Robby remained silent, his fists now braced against his mouth, body rocking, about to explode. In just moments it was over. The Bennetts waved their congratulations to their son while Robby dropped to his bleacher seat, emotionally drained. Once the meets were over and the winners were formally recognized, the Bennetts took the boys to an A&W restaurant in town for chili dogs and root beer and the compulsory belching contest on the way home. It never got old.

Ninth grade went out with a whimper and summer came with a new spirit of anticipation. The only thing the boys could think about was starting high school in the fall. Patrick played baseball and Robby kept stats again, but there was no more time for endless hours of socializing at the pool every day. Robby's father arranged a part-time job for Patrick at the hospital, although it came to light several years later that Dr. Debruijn was actually paying Patrick out of his own pocket.

May 15, 2008

Robby's dad is the coolest!!! He got me and Robby actual jobs at the hospital. We get paid and everything!!! I think we're going to be the people who put stuff away and run errands and junk like that. Fine by me. I got a job!!! That was so easy. The news says everyone is getting fired because the economy is so bad and there's no more money, but me and Robby were just sitting there at his house and his dad just gave us jobs. We didn't have to apply or anything. I'm tired of hanging out all day at the pool anyways. I'm probably going to save my money to buy a car next year. I can get my driver's license when I turn sixteen in October. That will be sweet.

Patrick worked in the physical therapy clinic, where his initial responsibilities were to put things away and wipe down the tables and rehab equipment between patients. After a few weeks, Patrick was assigned the task of staying with the patients and counting out their exercise reps for them. The patients were mostly old retirees or very young soldiers, and all were sociable with Patrick and made him comfortable with his increasing responsibilities. Patrick was initially bored with his first real job, but after the therapists let him get involved with the patients, going to work was fun.

The boys' workday began with their arrival at the hospital at nine, after the various clinics had already been open awhile. At noon the boys met and took a lunch break together. They ate their sack lunches in the cafeteria and talked about their day for thirty minutes, and then they went back to either the physical therapy clinic or the pediatric clinic for another four hours.

Robby was now also on his father's private payroll, in lieu of an allowance, but his responsibilities were much more involved. He greeted people, helped them fill out paperwork, kept the pediatric exam rooms clean between patients, and, as usual, tagged along with his father when he made his rounds. Both boys were very respectful of the medical staff at the hospital and did everything they could to avoid getting in anyone's way, yet they were very comfortable there, as if they were regular staff. Many of the nurses remembered Patrick from his extended stay during the holiday season. Of course everyone, and to be clear here, *everyone*, knew Robby.

Robby was still too young to be in the operating room during surgeries, even when his father was operating. If someone in the ER was getting sutures or some other low-risk procedure, Robby could watch, as long as the patients didn't mind, and they usually didn't.

A month into summer, Robby's father told him that another doctor had invited him to observe a colonoscopy procedure if he was interested. Was he ever! Robby only wanted to know if Patrick could come too. Dr. Debruijn called his colleague and the approval was granted. Robby bolted to the physical therapy clinic. "Pat, Pat come here," he whispered loudly when he spotted his friend across the room.

Patrick rarely saw his friend so excited. *This has to be good.* "What's up?" he asked.

"My dad says one of his friends is going to let us watch him do a colonoscopy," Robby said with a grin.

"A what?"

"A colonoscopy. It's a colon exam, but it's a real operation."

"With the patient knocked out?" Patrick asked.

"Yeah. You get completely sedated. It's in an operating room and everything."

"Cool," Patrick declared. "Let me see if I can go."

Patrick skipped across the room to his supervisor and told him about the opportunity to watch a real operation. "Do you know what a colonoscopy is?" the supervisor asked.

"Sure," Patrick answered confidently. "It's a colon exam." Patrick had no idea what a colon was.

"Okay by me," the supervisor said. "Just come back when you're done."

The boys returned together to Dr. Debruijn's office and he walked them to the hospital's outpatient surgery center. He made a brief call from a phone on the wall and then showed the boys how to wash their hands and put on surgical gowns and gloves properly. After a final warning to "stay out of the doctor's way and be very quiet," Dr. Debruijn helped the boys place surgical masks over their faces and led them into a small operating room.

A patient was already lying fast asleep on his side on a steel operating table. At his head was an anesthesiologist monitoring his breathing, and beside him was another doctor seated next to a small video monitor. A nurse stepped over to the boys and asked, "Are you our observers?" The boys nodded their heads.

"Okay," she said. "I need you to stand right over here. That way you can see the doctor and the monitor. Are you familiar with the procedure?"

Robby raised his hand like an elementary school kid who knew the answer to a teacher's question.

"Good," the nurse said. "We need you to stay very quiet. The doctor might point some things out to you, but don't interrupt with any questions until we're finished. Okay?"

The boys nodded.

The doctor stood up and acknowledged Patrick and Robby and then stepped behind the patient, partially out of view of the boys. As he inserted a scope into the sedated patient, he motioned for the boys to watch the video monitor across the room.

"Wohhhh," Patrick whispered. "Is that the guy's intestines?"

"Yes," Robby whispered back.

Suddenly Patrick realized the scope had been inserted into the patient's colon via his anus. "Oh, dude, that's crazy," Patrick whispered beneath his mask.

Robby nudged him to be quiet. "Shhhh."

"Jesus, dude. How far does that thing go up there?" Patrick asked as he watched the probe on the monitor moving through the patient's cavernous bowel.

"Shhhh," Robby repeated.

The doctor continued his exam for another fifteen minutes and then removed the scope. "He looks good," the doctor said to his nurse and anesthesiologist and his two young observers. "No polyps, no bleeding—that's a healthy colon. Sorry, boys."

Patrick leaned over to Robby and whispered, "What's he sorry for?"

"If the man had had any polyps, we would have been able to watch them get removed," Robby answered.

"Oh, man, that would have been choice," Patrick answered.

"Yeah," Robby agreed.

The nurse ushered the boys out of the room and stood by as they removed their surgery attire.

"Ma'am, could you please tell the doctor thank you?" Robby asked the nurse as he removed his operating gown.

"Yeah, tell him we really appreciate it," Patrick added. "That was radical."

"I'll pass that along," the nurse said warmly. "Are you boys good to find your way back to the clinic?"

The boys answered that they were, and after another *thank you* stepped into the hallway.

"That was totally badass," Patrick declared and raised his hand for a high five.

Robby gently slapped his friend's hand and said, "I'm going to do that someday."

Patrick wrapped his arm around his friend's head and playfully rubbed Robby's hair with the knuckles on his other hand. "You can do me right now if you want, Dr. Debruijn."

Robby pushed Patrick off of him with little effort, smiled, and straightened his tousled hair. The two boys then returned to their regular assignments having witnessed their first real surgery.

June 26, 2008

I got to see the craziest thing I've ever seen in my life today!!! Me and Robby got to watch a doctor stick a rod thing with a tiny camera on the end of it up this guys ass!!! The guy was knocked out and everything!!! How totally crazy is that? I guess it's common to get cancer in your butt when you get older. Robby says everyone has to get the same exam when they turn 50, unless you get ass cancer before that. Of all the places to get cancer, in your butt? That would totally suck. It's not like you can tell anyone. No girls are going to want to go out with you if you have tumors growing all over your cornhole. You probably can't even sit down anymore. Whatever happens to me, I'm going to make sure I do everything to make sure I never get cancer in my butt. How embarrassing.

Toward the end of summer the real Dr. Debruijn called Patrick to his office. Patrick didn't think he'd done anything wrong, but he was still nervous about the mysterious reason his friend's father wanted to talk to him privately. When Patrick arrived at the office, they shook hands and Patrick sat in an oversized leather chair in front of the doctor's desk. Robby's father began by asking Patrick what he thought of his job in the physical therapy clinic. Patrick answered that he was having a blast and thanked him again for the opportunity to make some money during the summer. There was more brief small talk, enough for Patrick to realize he wasn't in trouble, and then Dr. Debruijn started asking questions about his son.

Before Patrick answered any of the questions, Dr. Debruijn assured him that their conversation wouldn't leave the room. Patrick knew what he meant, but it didn't make him any more comfortable with talking about Robby behind his back. None of the questions were specific or embarrassing. Dr. Debruijn just wanted to know how the boys were getting along, and then he thanked Patrick for taking the time to be a good friend to Robby.

Patrick always thought it was strange how adults seemed to think it took a significant effort to be Robby's friend. Robby was a better friend than anyone he'd ever known. Robby would never betray him or lie to him. He'd do almost anything for Patrick, although Patrick understood that he'd probably have to ask Robby to do whatever it was first. To top it off, Robby was about the nicest kid Patrick had ever known. In his book, if you didn't want to have a friend like that, then you were probably an asshole, and nobody would want to be your friend anyway.

Dr. Debruijn asked Patrick if he thought Robby was ready to go to regular school full-time. Patrick wasn't sure how to answer that. How should he know if Robby was ready or not? Dr. Debruijn and his wife were the ones who were homeschooling him. Patrick knew Robby was smart, but he didn't know how good he was at American history or social studies. Dr. Debruijn then explained that he wanted to know if Patrick thought Robby could blend in with the other kids and whether the other students would accept him.

Patrick reminded Dr. Debruijn that the upcoming year was also going to be his first year of high school, and they'd be going off post to a civilian high school where neither of them would know many people. Patrick had no idea how civilian kids would take to Robby. Dr. Debruijn then shared the idea that he and Mrs. Debruijn really wanted to get Robby in regular school full-time for at least two years before he graduated, and they were hoping he was getting closer to that being feasible. Patrick told Dr. Debruijn that no matter what happened, he'd look out for Robby, and if he could arrange for all of their classes to be together, Patrick would make sure no one messed with his son. Robby's father shook Patrick's hand and thanked him again.

August 11, 2008

Robby's dad called me into his office today and I was really scared I'd done something wrong. It turns out he just wanted to ask me if I thought Robby would be okay going to LHS full time next year. I kind of get why he's so nervous about it. The smarter you are, unless you're also really cool or good looking, everyone thinks you're a big geek. I guess we both know Robby's kind of nerdy. I told Dr. Debruijn I could watch over him if he got all our classes together. He seemed happy with that. Two more weeks, baby!!! High school!!! Go Pioneers!!!

The Debruijns ultimately decided not to enroll Robby in school full-time during the boys' sophomore year. It proved to be a wise decision. Fort Leavenworth doesn't have a high school, so the teenagers on the post either go to Leavenworth High School, or they attend a much smaller private Catholic high school which is also off post. LHS is a large school by Kansas standards, and it was Patrick's first introduction to what he referred to as "dirtbag kids." Of course not all of the Army brats coming from the fort were angels, but they were all mostly being raised in two-parent families, their fathers were mostly educated military officers, and they all had been taught a healthy respect for adults and rules and regulations. Very few of the post teenagers arrived at LHS already doing drugs or sneaking out in the middle of the night and spray-painting graffiti all over town. They certainly didn't do anything that could get them locked up. That kind of behavior would be scandalous, and besides, there was no need for it.

Patrick began the school year with a plan to lay low and see how things played out awhile before he tried to make new friends and get into high school life. It helped that he had a wild card in his back pocket—his above-average size and ability to play football. He knew he'd never get to play as a sophomore, but he joined the football team anyway and fought through the grueling humid late summer practices without a complaint. The payoff was that he met and impressed a lot of the school's older jocks and quickly became one of the boys. He might be a sophomore, but he was a sophomore with a lot of heart.

Being on the football team also scored him some points with the ladies, and he landed a new girlfriend, Karen Wilicott, in the first month of school. She was a sophomore yell leader, which was a sort of cheerleader intern. She got to wear a cheerleader uniform, but her job was to sit in the bleachers with the other yell leaders and act as a chorus for the regular cheerleaders. Karen was also a military brat, which gave them something in common. The only caveat was that Karen's father was a US Marine colonel in charge of a small contingent of Marine military police that served as guards at the military prison on the fort. He scared Patrick with his big muscles and constant scowl and his flattop haircut. Patrick did everything he could to avoid being around him.

September 17, 2008

Karen's dad is totally freaking me out. I think he may be way too hard-core for me. He's like one of those G.I. Joe guys who looks like he's probably killed a bunch of people in Iraq and might snap at any second. I don't know. I really like Karen, but I'm not going to keep going out with her if I think her dad is going to stab me in the neck just because I'm not sitting up straight or

I'm sitting too close to his daughter. Me and Robby decided we're going to get a car together as soon as I get my license. He says I can be the main driver. We haven't told our parents yet, but they'll be glad they won't have to drive us around all over the place. I think we have close to two thousand dollars saved up. We probably only need to double that for a good used car. There's no way our parents are going to just buy one for us. Our parents aren't like those kinds of parents.

Patrick got his driver's license a few weeks later when he turned sixteen, so Karen was the first girl he was able to take out on a real date. When he arrived at Karen's house to pick her up, Colonel Wilicott rarely said a single word to him. Patrick tried to initiate a conversation a few times, but the colonel was stalwart in his attempts to intimidate him. Patrick didn't dwell on it. He assumed Colonel Wilicott had gotten wind of how big a slut his daughter was and could picture the things she'd be talking Patrick into doing during their dates.

October 5, 2008

It's official, the Chiefs are the worst team in the NFL. They got smoked by the Panthers today 34–0. That's 5 straight loses and 2 of those were to the Raiders and the Broncos!!! How do you trade away the guy with the most sacks in the league and then expect to win with a quarterback like Brodie Croyle!!! I think Karen would do it if I tried. All we do is make out all the time. Last night we actually got in the back of the car for more room. I'm beginning to think she's already done it with other guys, but I'm not going to ask her. She keeps wanting to sneak out in the middle of the night. Wrong!!! If she wants to sneak out with other people and go do stupid shit in the middle of the night and get busted by the MPs then that's fine with me. I'm not going to be the guy her dad blames for corrupting his daughter when she gets caught. That man is a fucking beast. Get caught in the middle of the night on the hill behind their house with his daughter, you might as well just go kick a grizzly bear in the balls. You know who really needs a good kick in the balls? Whoever hired Brodie Croyle.

Patrick never went all the way with Karen, but they sure went every other way together. Soon they were telling each other they were in love, which only heightened the passion between them. Unfortunately Karen was telling Patrick she loved him on Friday night, and on Saturday afternoon she was parked by the river doing things with a senior Patrick was too afraid to even try. And it wasn't just one guy—it was two or three before Patrick found out what was going on.

It hurt Patrick to lose Karen, but he learned some valuable lessons during their short relationship, the most important being that he needed to be more careful about whom he trusted. Because he was starting most of his new friendships from scratch, Patrick felt like he had the opportunity to look for clues to his new friend's shortcomings and then not expect things from them that were obviously beyond his or her capability. If he discovered significant character flaws in people he was hanging out with, he just stopped socializing with them. It was easy. There were more than five hundred kids attending Leavenworth High School. It wouldn't be a problem to find a handful he liked.

Patrick and Robby didn't see much of each other the first part of their sophomore year other than on Sundays at church. Their families continued to sit together and go to brunch at the Officers' Club afterward. Patrick shared with Robby how exciting high school was and often talked about how cool it was going to be when they started going together. Patrick even took his friend to one of the varsity football games one night, hoping he'd see how all the kids their age were together having fun without a bunch of adults around. Robby hated it.

October 17, 2008

I took Robby to his first LHS game tonight. I really miss playing!!! Only one sophomore gets to dress out with the varsity team. That's because he's the best kicker in the whole school. I introduced Robby to a couple of people, but he just stood there like a big dope and wouldn't talk. Then when the game started, it got too loud and we had to leave. We got our asses kicked by Shawnee Mission South so we didn't miss anything.

Robby having problems with the crowd noise didn't surprise Patrick. In the past they either avoided or simply walked away from anything that was loud enough to bother him. That first high school game, though, was when Patrick saw how a noisy crowd could cause Robby to panic. Unlike the Royals games, where there was lots of open space for the sound to dissipate, being sandwiched together on stacked bleachers with people talking constantly around them was a major distraction to Robby, and it didn't help when something on the field caused the crowd to suddenly erupt with screaming and yelling.

Being seated close to the school's marching band was the final straw. Every time they started to play, Robby would cover his ears with his hands. Patrick assured him they weren't that bad, although he understood it was the volume that was bothering Robby and not their lack of talent. When the home team Pioneers scored, or someone made a great play and everyone stood up to cheer, Robby flinched and recoiled as if he'd been violently startled. Then his face turned white with terror in anticipation of the next outburst from the crowd. Robby did want to see the game; it was the rambunctious crowd around the spectacle that he couldn't handle—something inside his head just wouldn't allow it.

The boys left the game at halftime and Patrick took Robby to a small diner in town called Homer's for a couple of cheeseburgers and sodas. Robby was candid about how the loud noises at the game bothered him, but his description of how the noise made him feel seemed more like he was someone with a keen superpower instead of a disability. Patrick knew some people had the ability to see farther than others, and some people were naturally stronger. Robby's superior ability to hear things was no different. It was a gift, not a problem. The case was promptly closed, and the boys were now free to talk about Robby joining Patrick at school and the two of them getting that car.

From the outside that night at the game might seem like a dismal failure in Patrick's attempts to integrate Robby into his new world as a high school student. What Patrick didn't know, because it was so rare that his best friend would ever outwardly display excitement or anticipation, was that Robby saw all those kids having a good time and he wanted to be just like them. He was tired of feeling different. He wanted to go to school and be like everybody else his age. He wanted to be a Pioneer, just somewhere where it wasn't so loud.

Every dinner conversation at the Debruijn house turned to the laundry list of things Robby would need to do quickly over the next two months to get into LHS for the second semester. He had to study for some class placement testing required of homeschoolers.

He had to work on his atrocious handwriting, and he needed to practice reading out loud in front of other people. Those were just some of the things the family discussed in preparation for Robby's high school career. Patrick never paid any attention to what Robby was doing in his home studies, so he was completely unaware of how hard his friend worked to get ready for the second semester after Christmas break.

After Robby completed his general studies testing to determine where he was academically, the Debruijns met with a school counselor and charted a course for Robby's slow indoctrination into full-time public school. One of the classes suggested by the counselor was the school's Junior Reserve Officers' Training Corps (JROTC) program, referred to by the students as simply ROTC.

Not every large high school in the country has an Army, Navy, or Air Force JROTC program, but they are far from rare. Leavenworth High School's program is unique in its size and popularity—six different classes each identified as a separate company. Of course that can be easily attributed to the large number of students from military families on the fort, but it's supported by the school's policy of allowing students the option of foregoing the school's otherwise mandatory physical education class if they enrolled in JROTC.

Patrick thought of JROTC as a prep class for joining the military and that wasn't exactly in his plans, so instead of enrolling in JROTC the first semester of his sophomore year, he took a PE class because he knew it would result in an easy A. When Robby told him he was going to take a JROTC class during the second semester, however, Patrick decided he might as well join him. Gym class was boring anyway.

The second semester started right after Christmas break. Robby and Patrick joined a JROTC class during fifth hour—E Company. Afterward the boys separated and Robby attended a special general studies class to make sure he met the school's sophomore level of academic competence. If he was successful, he could then start his junior year in sync with the rest of the students in his graduating class. Patrick took biology.

On his first day of high school, Robby's mother dropped him off in the student parking lot where Patrick was waiting for him. The boys went to the JROTC building together and were immediately issued uniforms and some training manuals that showed them military rank structure and some explanations of general military etiquette.

Leavenworth High School starts at the ninth grade and because the boys were starting the JROTC program in the second semester of tenth grade, neither of them had a clue what was going on. Everyone else already knew how to march and wear their uniforms properly once a week for Wednesday inspections. The other students also had some level of rank that the boys didn't, and it seemed the second they walked in the classroom they were doing something wrong and there were far too many people who felt it their responsibility to correct them. It didn't take long to figure out some of the juniors who were cadet sergeants, and seniors who were cadet officers, took the class very seriously and felt it was their responsibility to keep in line the knuckleheads who were only there to avoid PE.

January 10, 2009
I think I have totally fucked myself over!!! I changed my easy A gym period to ROTC just so I can take a class with Robby and I can't

fucking stand it. They actually put other kids in charge and they're all sergeants and captains and shit, and all they do is walk around telling the freshmen and sophomores what to do. What the fuck, man!!! Robby just takes it. It's like everything else with him. He just stands there and takes it. Well not me. I got a feeling something bad is going to happen in that class. I hope it's not me smacking the shit out of someone who gets in my face because I have a piece of thread loose on my uniform. I'm going to tough this one semester out and then I'm out of there. Sorry Robby, but I can only handle so much. He's got the rest of this year to get his shit together and then he can take ROTC by himself if he likes this abuse. I say fuck this bullshit. I guess I do cuss a lot sometimes. I'm just frustrated. AAAAAHHHH!!!!!!

Luckily for Patrick, he knew some of the E Company upperclassmen from the football team and, ignoring his own distress, he asked them to take it a little easy on Robby until he got used to the way things worked. As he had years before, Patrick described Robby as a kid who was intelligent beyond his years, so intelligent that he'd had to be homeschooled, but his smarts also made him nervous around people. You could take one look at Robby and understand, or think you understood exactly what Patrick meant.

Patrick then offered himself as a sacrifice. "I know you guys have to yell at us every once in a while. If you feel like you have to yell at Robby, just yell what you got to say at me. I can take it and I'll make sure whatever it is he did wrong gets straightened out." Patrick spent the rest of the week seemingly being picked on by the leaders in the class. Robby felt sorry for him, having no idea he was the reason for the constant barrage of criticism.

January 22, 2009

I'm getting the hang of this new ROTC class. I still don't like it, though. Robby was getting touched up almost every day by his squad leader and platoon leader so I finally had to ask them to ease up a little. His platoon leader is a jock so we kind of have a jock respect for each other even though he's older than me. I think that's how the school Jock Code works. We're all one big family, until someone fucks around with someone else's girlfriend. I'm sure getting yelled at more. It used to really piss me off. Now it kind of makes me laugh. I'm sorry, but I think that class is a big joke.

It didn't take long before the class leaders and adult staff instructors began cutting Patrick and Robby a great deal of slack. Patrick never voiced his displeasure with the JROTC program anywhere other than his journal. The relationship between the two boys wasn't lost on their peers in JROTC. Robby was weak, quiet, and defenseless, and Patrick was his caretaker. They couldn't help but respect Patrick for what he was doing. The easing of criticism helped the boys figure out how to march and get their uniforms together, and soon they fit right in with the rest of E Company.

February 1, 2009

It was so cold today the gas totally froze in my mom's car. I was sure we were going to get a snow day because of all the ice and sleet. Didn't happen though. Me and Robby did really well on a uniform inspection in ROTC. It was so cold outside we had the inspection in the gym while a PE class was going. Those sorry bastards were running around getting all sweaty while us guys in ROTC only had to stand around and get our uniforms inspected. That was the whole class! Sometimes I love ROTC. Robby is totally getting off on it now. It turns out he's the best necktie tier in the company so he's got guys lined up before inspections, begging him to tie their ties for them. I can't even kid around with him anymore once class starts. Such a serious little lad, my boy Robby.

Robby had never experienced an academic class like JROTC in junior high or with his home studies. His mother and a series of tutors usually allowed him to work at a pace that was comfortable, and he never moved on to the next level of anything until he was competent and had a firm grasp of what he'd been studying. His parents were always patient with him and never raised their voices at their son in anger or frustration. The first time he witnessed kids his age being yelled at by adults was during summer baseball when a coach unloaded on the players for a stupid mistake or not trying hard enough. Because Robby wasn't actually a player, he was never the target of scolding, although it still made him nervous to be around it. The only person who had a license to yell at Robby was Patrick.

Patrick understood the art to motivating his friend. If Robby was already interested in doing something, he didn't have to bother, but when he needed to be pushed, Patrick knew exactly where Robby's button was and how hard to push it. The method was simple: when Robby needed a spark lit under him, Patrick began with a nagging tone. "C'mon, dude," or "Dude, don't wuss out on me now." It was a signal to Robby that Patrick wasn't going to let him pout his way out of something. It was also a sign that Patrick thought whatever they were doing was important or at least important to him. The nagging usually worked, but not always. When it didn't, Patrick pulled out his big guns—profanity.

As Patrick matured so did his skills with the English language. There was no more shock value in spewing obscenities among his friends when he was in high school. It just wasn't cool anymore. You were a dirtbag if you couldn't complete a sentence without cussing, but there was a time and place, according to Patrick, and the best place for it was when Robby was whining and being lazy. "What the fuck, dude?" Patrick would say. "C'mon, Robby, this shit should be easy. Robby, are you fucking kidding me? C'mon, dude. What the fuck is wrong with you?" Patrick never actually attacked his friend by calling him names, even when he was most frustrated with him. Robby wasn't the kind of kid who could brush that off and Patrick understood that. If he truly wanted to get his attention and let him know he meant business, Patrick raised his voice a little and lobbed a profanity grenade Robby's way. "Put some hot sauce on it," as Colonel Bennett would say.

Profanity was only one on a list of things that made Robby uncomfortable. There were a few things that truly irritated him. Loud noises, being in direct sunlight on a hot muggy afternoon, and wanting to do one thing but having to do something else were all examples of things that could ruin Robby's day. There was something else that only Patrick knew, and he used it like an ace up his sleeve: Robby could not handle cuss words.

Like every kid growing up, Robby first heard "dirty words" from other kids, movies and television, and sometimes even in the music the boys listened to. Robby's parents never used the forbidden words and made sure their son knew they were not only rudely inappropriate but sinful. Subsequently, as Robby grew older, when he registered a word as a profanity, it was somehow stored in the same brain file as all the other things that made him anxious and upset, like finger-nails scratching the surface of a chalkboard. Patrick was afraid Robby would react similarly when he was yelled at by the JROTC staff members, but Robby was able to recognize the difference between a verbal attack and a voice raised to motivate him. His best friend had taught him that.

As soon as the boys figured out how to march and survive their weekly uniform inspection, Robby was ready to learn how to be a good cadet. Patrick was quickly bored—the class was too easy. Absent now the fear of the unknown in their new JROTC class, Patrick's boredom often manifested as goofing off when the company was assembled outside for drill practice and an upperclassman officer was charged with conducting the drill. Patrick gently pushed Robby to make him lose step or made faces when a command was shouted to the company. Robby glared at his friend as if he were an immature child and then ignored him. Without an audience Patrick had nothing else to do but pay attention, which bored him even more. He began to miss gym class again.

As for the JROTC homework, Robby couldn't have taken it more seriously. Everything military was new to him, and he'd never learned about things like citizenship and leadership before. He'd never really thought of his father as a soldier, although he saw him in uniform all the time. He was a pediatrician, not a soldier. Dr. Debruijn enjoyed helping his son prepare his uniform for inspections and used the time to try to teach his son about duty and honor. There were many things Robby's parents didn't talk about in front of him until they thought he was old enough to understand them. Dr. Debruijn was glad that he could finally begin to share the military aspect of his career with his son. Being a soldier was a proud position for Dr. Debruijn. He wanted to make sure his son understood that someday.

Robby breezed through his general studies class. Most of the other kids in the class were troublemakers being disciplined, which gave Robby another reason to keep to himself. The way the curriculum was designed, he was able to do his homework right there in school and accelerate at his own pace. The program teacher and the two college interns assigned to the class appreciated having a student in the room who wanted desperately to succeed. Their positive attitude toward Robby made him enjoy the class almost immediately, but what he came to love was E Company and JROTC.

About the only thing Robby didn't want to do in that class was be in charge. He learned quickly, and he was happy to sit with another kid and show him how to do something, but standing in front of the class for any reason was completely out of the question. Robby could get away with that as a sophomore, but if the boys went back the next year they would be eventually promoted to cadet sergeants, and that would mean having to make oral presentations and help teach the freshmen and sophomores how to drill. Patrick assumed their experience with JROTC was going to be a one and done kind of thing, and they'd move on to something else during their junior year. Neither of them had any ambitions of joining the service. Patrick assumed they'd ended up in the cadet program to help Robby come out of his shell before he got too far along in school. PE was boring, but marching around the neighborhood surrounding the school was even worse.

That second semester of tenth grade, the first semester of high school for Robby, flew by and then it was summer again. The boys were both sixteen and could legally be employed. Dr. Debruijn arranged for them to work at the hospital again, but this time they would be working a regular eight-hour shift five days a week. Their salary came from a student worker program on the fort that was supposed to introduce high school students to the world of medicine. There was no specific job associated with the program within the hospital, so they went right back to the same thing they'd done the previous year—Patrick worked in the physical therapy clinic, and Robby worked upstairs in pediatrics and sometimes helped in the walk-in clinic. Patrick walked to the Debruijn house in the morning, and then he and Robby and Dr. Debruijn carpooled to work. When the boys' workday was over, Robby and Patrick walked home while Dr. Debruijn stayed another hour or two to finish his shift. The boys changed and either headed right back out to baseball practice or to a game; if there was nothing baseball-related going on, they went to the gym. Summer days are long in northeastern Kansas, so after a workout, the boys spent hours sitting on the old fort wall or in the gazebo across from Patrick's house talking about nothing in particular. As long as there was still daylight outside, the boys felt like they had to be doing something. The last thing either of them wanted to do was go to bed before it was dark. That was kid stuff.

The physical therapy staff at Munson Hospital was nearly the same group as the year before, and because Patrick looked more like a young man than a child by the summer of 2009, he was entrusted with more responsibilities. He still had to clean up and put things away, but his maturity and eagerness to do more resulted in the regular therapists allowing him to help patients stretch and do some of their rehabilitation exercises, particularly when the patients were old men who liked to talk a lot. The staff was glad to hand them off to Patrick so they wouldn't have to listen to the same old war stories over and over again. Patrick enjoyed it. Having some old guy talk to him like they were sitting next to each other at a bar made him feel like an adult.

Patrick's inclusion that summer sparked a heightened interest in the physical therapy field. He learned that a therapist could specialize in sports injury rehabilitation, and he could picture himself doing that as a career. He would love to be a professional baseball or football player, but he knew he wasn't good enough and probably never would be; he'd be lucky to walk onto a small college team if the opportunity arose. If he got into sports medicine as a therapist though, he might get hired by a professional sports team, and then he'd get to rub elbows with the pros and go to all the games, and it wouldn't matter if he was a good athlete or not. The thought was pea-sized in June—by August it was his dream.

August 5, 2009

I think I decided I want to be a professional sports trainer when I graduate. I know I'll never be good enough to be a pro athlete. I'm too little for football and I'm not good enough at baseball. Kansas is the worst place to grow up if you want to be a pro baseball player because you can only play a few months out of the year. Just when you start getting good it gets cold and rainy and then it snows, and by the time it gets warm again, your timing is all jacked-up and it's like you have to go back to sucking for a while before your swing comes back. If you look at where most of the pros are coming from now, they're from places like California and Puerto Rico where they can play all year. Guys like me don't stand a chance.

Reasons why I should be a professional sports trainer.
1. I get to go to all the games, even the away ones.
2. I won't ever have to retire just because I'm getting old and slow.

3. *I get to hang out with the players.*
4. *If my team wins a championship they'll probably let me get a championship ring too.*
5. *Some sports trainers are doctors. That means I could be really rich and buy a Corvette.*
6. *Me and Robby could be partners. When some guy tears his ACL, Robby could be the surgeon who fixes it and I can be the guy who does all the rehab.*
7. *We could live somewhere like LA, where it never snows and you can just walk down the street and pick oranges and coconuts right off the trees.*

Reasons why I shouldn't be a professional sports trainer.
0.

Robby was pleased to hear his best friend talk about how much he liked working at the hospital. For once his interest was at the forefront of their relationship, not Patrick's addiction to sports. He was particularly comforted to hear Patrick making plans for them to be together beyond high school. In the meantime Robby continued to spend his days at Munson doing the same things he'd done the year before and the year before that. He tagged along with his father during his routine rounds and walk-in appointments. When his father suggested it, Robby helped the administrative staff by assisting patients with their paperwork and giving people directions within the hospital. The only added responsibility he was given that year was going up to the inpatient pediatric ward and checking on any child who was staying overnight. Robby went up to the kid's room, introduced himself, and looked over the patient's chart. He would then ask the patient how he or she felt and maybe comment on the kid's medication and empathize about the pain, but he was also quick to add that his father was a great doctor and he was going to make things better for the patient, although it might just take some time to heal. Robby never overstayed his welcome. He was still clumsily antisocial. Once the patient's chart was reviewed and Robby commented that he was sure the patient would feel better soon, which was what he thought his father wanted him to do, he moved on to either the next patient or a new task. As long as he didn't touch the patients or offer significant medical advice or any kind of diagnosis, Robby remained a fixture of the hospital's pediatric care team.

Patrick didn't have a girlfriend to occupy him that summer, so he took Robby with him to a few weekend house parties. They usually ended up spending the evening in the party-thrower's backyard because it was too noisy and crowded for Robby inside. Robby tried his first beer at one of the parties and hated it. Hard alcohol was out of the question. He thought it madness that anyone could enjoy drinking something that tasted like antiseptic mixed with gasoline.

Patrick wasn't a stranger to beer, but that summer was the first time he got drunk. It happened during a party on the fort, not far from the boys' neighborhood. Someone's parents were out of town and when word got out, stolen and otherwise illegally obtained miscellaneous forms of alcohol flowed freely. Some upperclassmen were chugging beers from a hose attached to a funnel and Patrick was compelled to give it a try. He gulped the first one down and was celebrated wildly for his ability to siphon an entire beer from the funnel into his belly in only a few seconds. "Do it again!" a small crowd shouted. "Chug it, chug it, chug it...!"

Patrick had room left in his stomach and didn't feel at all intoxicated. "Load another one up, bitches." They did, and once again Patrick sucked down a beer in a matter of seconds. After absorbing a second round of cheers, he asked Robby if he wanted to try it.

Robby looked at his friend with a scowl and said, "No," as if the question was ridiculous. He didn't like what he was seeing.

Patrick decided he needed to sit down when suddenly he began to feel light-headed. The boys took two empty seats at a picnic table where other kids were challenging one another to take shots from bottles of Southern Comfort and Bacardi. As newcomers to the table, the boys were immediately challenged to participate. Robby was firm in his commitment not to drink—he was perfectly fine with the can of soda in his hand. Patrick, on the other hand, saw that everyone else was having fun and he wanted to have fun too. "Let's do it," he said.

A shot of Southern Comfort was poured for him, and again a chorus of "chug it, chug it, chug it," filled the backyard. Patrick raised the shot glass to his lips and slung the alcohol down his throat like a desert-thirsty cowboy. The burn made him cough and gasp for air while his peers cheered his success. Robby wasn't at all entertained. He patted Patrick on the back and handed him his soda, which Patrick emptied in a short series of gulps.

"Can you get me another one?" Patrick asked as he put the empty can on the table.

Robby gave Patrick a steely glare and got up to retrieve two sodas from a cooler across the yard. As he walked back to the picnic table, he heard cheering again and saw Patrick lean back and pour another shot of alcohol down his throat.

"What are you doing?" he asked his now glassy-eyed friend when he sat back down next to him.

"Oh, relax," Patrick answered with a heavy tongue. "I'm just having some fun."

"Here." Robby opened one of the soda cans and handed it to Patrick. "You can't drink any more alcohol. It's going to make you sick."

"Dude, relax," Patrick slurred. With a drunken smile he reassured Robby, "It's all good, brother."

"If you can't walk, how are you going to get home? I can't carry you."

"Yes, you can," Patrick said with a belch. "You learned in ROTC. Just throw me over your back like that wounded warrior carry they taught us. Wounded warrior!" Patrick shouted and raised his soda can. Half the crowd raised their drinks and shouted back, "Wounded warrior!" although they had no idea why.

"You're drunk," Robby declared with disgust.

"Yes, I am," Patrick replied, "and chances are I'm gonna get a whole lot drunker."

Patrick only had one more beer and a shot of rum that night before his stomach had enough. He could feel the bile churning in his belly and whispered to Robby that he thought he was going to throw up. Robby took his friend's arm and led him straight out the backyard gate toward an open field that was used for soccer. There were no exchanges of *good-bye* or *see you later*. No one even noticed the boys leave.

They made it to a small set of bleachers before Patrick began to projectile vomit. Robby stood next to him, holding their sodas and keeping an eye out for anyone passing by who might discover one of them was a very drunk teenager. When Patrick's stomach was finally empty, and he was able to stand up straight without another episode of dry heaving, Robby handed him his soda and asked if he thought he was going to be okay. Patrick shook his head and threw up the sip of soda he'd just taken.

"You need to sit down," Robby said and ushered him to the first row of bleachers. There the boys sat quietly while Patrick tried to catch his breath.

"I'm never doing that again," were Patrick's first intelligible words.

Robby was glad to hear it and added dryly, "You know you can die from alcohol poisoning."

Patrick looked at his friend and started to chuckle. It was perfect Robby.

"I promise I won't do it again," Patrick said. He looked up into the starry Kansas sky and shouted, "I promise, God. I'll never do it again!"

The boys still had an hour before they had to be home. After a few more minutes of allowing Patrick's head to clear, they decided to walk around the soccer field until he was sober enough to attempt a discreet reentry into his house. As they walked, Patrick devised a plan that began with having Robby spend the night with him. The idea was built on the premise that if the boys arrived home together and went straight to Patrick's room, there was much less chance of Patrick getting stuck all by himself in front of one of his parents.

There was already a fairly sound probability that only Mrs. Bennett would still be awake when they got home at their ten thirty curfew. If the boys walked in together, they could offer a quick good night and then rush off to bed with Patrick's condition undiscovered. If one of Patrick's parents tried to engage in conversation with the boys, Patrick would quickly dismiss himself by saying he had to go to the bathroom and Robby would handle the conversation solo. They'd rendezvous in Patrick's bedroom when the coast was clear. Robby reluctantly agreed with the plan and advised his parents of the overnight arrangements from a pay phone in front of the swimming pool which they passed on their way home.

When they got to Patrick's house, his mother was lying on a sofa in the living room watching television. The boys greeted her and when she sat up, signaling she wanted to talk, Patrick made a beeline to the upstairs bathroom saying, "Can't talk. Really got to go."

Robby hadn't objected to the plan, although he was never confident in his abilities to snow Mrs. Bennett. Per Patrick's instructions, all he had to do was explain that the party was dull, so they left early and hung out awhile on the soccer field before coming home. Leaving the part out about Patrick getting drunk wasn't a lie unless he denied it. He wouldn't have to deny it if it never came up. All Robby had to do was stick to the story with short answers and not under any circumstances mention that there was alcohol at the party. If he could manage it, they were sure to get away scot-free.

Mrs. Bennett asked about the party and how Robby was enjoying high school off post. Robby shuffled his feet nervously and offered his answers without looking directly at his friend's mother. If he had been any other teenager, his demeanor would have sounded enough alarm bells to wake up the entire neighborhood, but this was Robby. He never looked anyone in the eyes, and trying to engage him in small talk was like trying to pull teeth that didn't want pulling. Lacking the telltale signs of teenage shenanigans, Mrs. Bennett had no idea she was the victim in a juvenile conspiracy in which the innocent boy standing before her was actually a participating culprit. "Okay, well..." Mrs. Bennett concluded when it was clear that Robby had nothing to say. "I'll have breakfast on the table around eight. Would you like pancakes or waffles?"

"Thank you, Mrs. Bennett," Robby said and turned and ran toward the stairs.

"Robby, wait!" Mrs. Bennett called over her shoulder from the couch.

It was loud enough for Patrick to hear from the commode in the bathroom. *Oh, shit. She's on to us. Don't blow it, Robby. Please, please, please, buddy. Don't blow it.*

Robby froze and slowly turned back around.

"Do you want pancakes or waffles?" Mrs. Bennett repeated.

"Pancakes, please," Robby answered. "Do you have real maple syrup and real butter?"

Mrs. Bennett smiled. "Yes, I think we do."

"Can I go now?" Robby asked.

"Yes, Robby. Good night."

Mrs. Bennett never had any idea what her son had gotten into that night and how Robby had successfully covered for him. I guess she does now.

August 12, 2009

Me and Robby went to a party at Bruce's last night and I got totally wasted. It was really hot and we were all outside and there was a beer bong and I tried it a couple times just for fun. It sure is easier drinking beer when it's hot outside. It's like you taste the cold more than the beer part. I did the beer bong a couple of times and got a little buzzed and the next thing I knew I was doing shots with a bunch of people I hardly know. Robby looked like he was having a good time at first, but then he started getting mad that I was drinking so much, and then I got kind of pissed off at him for being such a downer. Then I started to get really sick and I puked a couple times. I didn't pass out or anything. I just don't remember leaving the party. I remember being at the soccer field for a while just me and Robby, and then I remember leaving Robby downstairs at my house to deal with my mom while I hid out in my room. As soon as we turned off the lights, the room started spinning and I puked again on the carpet next to my bed. I was so wasted I didn't even try to clean it up. That's when I did pass out. When I woke up this morning, Robby had already cleaned my carpet. You can still smell it a little. I'm trying to cover it up with a candle I took from the bathroom. I had a really bad headache this morning and was still a little dizzy. We had pancakes that were pretty good, but then my dad sat down with us and started drinking coffee while he was reading the paper. I took one whiff of that nasty stuff and puked again. At least I made it to the bathroom that time. It was a total waste of some really good banana pancakes.

August 13, 2009

I went to the mall in KC with my parents after church and bought Robby a metal clipboard that is also a box to keep your paperwork in. I've seen some of the nurses carrying them around. It's not his birthday or anything. I was just thinking in church how he really saved me from getting busted Friday night. If he hadn't been there I would have probably drank myself into a coma. I hear if you get too drunk and have to go to the hospital, they make you chew on a piece of charcoal until you puke all the booze out. It's weird that of all things they could give you to make you puke, they came up with charcoal. That's probably because it's not actually poisonous, just really really rank. I already thanked Robby for being such a good wingman, but you can't just say thanks when your best bro spends all night watching you make an ass out of yourself, and then he cleans up your puke for you while you lay there passed out like a drunk hobo. Sometimes I feel sorry for Robby. He sure is a much better friend to me than I've been to him.

The opportunity to abuse alcohol was always present for the boys as teenagers. None of the people in their crowd indulged in heavy drugs, although they certainly had plenty of marijuana around. Patrick didn't like the idea of smoking anything, particularly filling his lungs with unfiltered pot smoke and then holding it in until his body screamed for fresh air. Sure it was illegal, and his parents would kill him if he ever got caught smoking weed, but not getting high was more the result of Patrick being an athlete and wanting to stay healthy. He did try a hit from a hookah pipe once and that was it. As soon as his lungs began to reject the smoke and he felt light-headed, he knew it wasn't for him. Robby wasn't there for that experiment; when Patrick revealed that he'd tried marijuana and it was a bad experience that he wouldn't repeat, Robby was still angry and disappointed. He respected Patrick and in many ways wanted to be like him. Watching his role model get drunk and then admit he took illegal drugs was a traumatic development in their relationship.

August 19, 2009

I told Robby I smoked some weed once last year with a couple of guys from school and he totally flipped out. I wasn't bragging or anything. I totally hated it. I was just letting him know I tried it. We were sitting in the old chapel talking about how Catholics have to confess their sins once a week to their pastor and I was saying how I could never be Catholic if that was a rule, and then I said, if you had to confess to something what would it be. Robby couldn't think of anything because he's pretty much a parent's wet dream, and the first thing that popped in my head was that time I smoked some pot. Robby looked at me like I'd just confessed to killing someone and then he walked out and left me there. He totally bailed on me! I'm not going to call him. If he's going to be a big baby, that's his problem.

For several days after Patrick's revelation of his experiment with marijuana, Robby didn't have anything to say to him. At first Patrick thought his friend's reaction was silly, and he wasn't going to get down on his knees and ask to be forgiven for doing something that all teenagers did at least once. After two days of being ignored, however, Patrick began to understand what had happened. It wasn't about getting drunk or getting high. It was about knowing something was the wrong thing to do for a multitude of reasons and doing it anyway. Robby trusted Patrick not to be that kind of person. Violating that trust was the worst thing Patrick could have done. When that was finally clear to him, Patrick met Robby behind the old fort wall after dinner and asked to be forgiven. That was all Robby needed.

Taking Robby to some parties that summer was good for him. He didn't have much fun, but it exposed him to their peers and they got used to seeing him around. He remained shy and would rarely talk. Girls petrified him. No one dared bully or tease Robby because they knew Patrick was always nearby to protect him. "If you fuck with him, you fuck with me," Patrick said on numerous occasions. Within a few months, that commitment would be tested.

CHAPTER 6

Robby passed all his general studies assignments and was able to enroll full-time at LHS his junior year. A guidance counselor arranged for the boys to have four of their six classes together. Patrick was taking more advanced English and math classes, and Robby took a biology class that Patrick had completed the year before. Robby was also allowed to stay in the general studies class, where he was able to complete most of his homework while still at school. The boys' mothers rotated carpooling duties and the school again assigned Patrick and Robby lockers right next to each other. They had become nearly inseparable.

By the end of the first quarter, just about everyone knew who Robby was and that he had some quirks. Patrick reinforced the idea to his friends and whoever else wanted to know that Robby actually had a genius IQ and that was what made him seem different from everyone else. No one asked Robby if it was true. They just accepted it as fact.

One day in late September, Robby and Patrick were sitting in social studies and a senior who sat behind Robby started making fun of his name. Robby's ancestors were Dutch and the J in his last name is silent. The teacher mispronounced it as almost everyone does when they read it. This wasn't particularly funny, but the idiot sitting behind Robby thought it was. He was one of the dirtbag city kids Patrick figured by the way they spoke and carried themselves, were destined to grow up and work their whole lives in a gas station convenience store or the bowling alley.

The senior repeated the mispronunciation, snickered to himself, and said it again to make sure Robby knew he was being teased. Robby didn't react, which only made the bully mad. He wadded up a small piece of paper and bounced it off the back of Robby's head. Patrick was already locked on to what was happening and leaned over to the senior who was sitting in the row next to him, whispering sternly, "You'd better knock that shit off." The kid responded by asking Patrick what he was going to do about it. Patrick answered, "How about I kick your ass into next week?"

The senior smiled smugly and started wadding up an even bigger piece of paper. Patrick warned him again, "Dude, I'm telling you. Knock it off or I'm going to fuck you up." The senior answered by lifting the harmless projectile he'd crafted and reaching back as if he was going to throw it at Robby. Patrick wasn't going to let it happen. He launched himself from his chair and lit into the senior with a flurry of punches.

The victim of Patrick's assault had no way to protect himself from the attack because he was stuck between his desk and the attached chair. He was also caught totally by surprise. The senior may have been older than Patrick, but they were the same size. Patrick was an athlete, however, and the kid he was pummeling lived on fast food, cigarettes, and energy drinks. Patrick was connecting with every punch before the senior's desk fell over on its side. The kid, still wedged between the seat and desk, continued his struggle to ward off blows and escape his attacker. That should have been the end of it. Patrick stood over the senior still tangled in the tipped over desk on the floor. He had to quickly decide whether to walk away having made his point, let the kid stand up so they could continue the fight toe to toe, or finish him while he still had an overwhelming advantage.

The teacher was a gray-haired woman in her fifties who made no attempt to physically restrain the combatants. She could only order Patrick to stop and then flee the classroom to find a male teacher who could physically intervene. Until the arrival of that physical intervention, Patrick knew there was nothing to stop him and he wasn't done yet. He started kicking the senior anywhere he could get a clean shot, only yielding when his victim screamed for mercy after one of Patrick's kicks caught him square in the teeth. The sight of blood pouring from his victim's mouth woke Patrick from his rage. A male teacher entered the room and grabbed Patrick from behind as he stood over his victim threatening him furiously, "If you ever fuck with my friend again, I'll fucking kill you!"

Patrick quickly found himself in the principal's office. His knuckles began to feel like they were broken. He knew he was in far more trouble with his father than he'd ever been before and assumed he was going to get put on a very long restriction and have his driving privileges taken away. He also knew he was going to get suspended from school and kicked off the football team. He was worrying about how long his suspension would be when he heard two distinctly separate sirens approaching. Patrick prayed that the sirens would pass by the school, but they kept getting louder until they stopped right at the front entrance to LHS. Patrick's fears turned to shock when a Leavenworth police officer walked in and put him in handcuffs. He wasn't just getting suspended—he was going to jail.

There were fights at school all the time, but no one ever called the cops before. Patrick had no idea of his adversary's condition other than a cut mouth, but if an ambulance had been called, that explained why the cops were there too. *Are the cops here because I really fucked that guy up?* That was exactly what had happened. Patrick had given the other student a concussion and knocked several of his teeth loose. The kid was also bleeding severely enough for the school to think he needed an ambulance to take him to the hospital. The police officer took Patrick out to the parking lot and locked him in his squad car, from which Patrick watched two paramedics load the other kid into the back of the ambulance. He closed his eyes tight and prayed for God to make the other kid okay and to forgive him for what he'd done.

Patrick was transported to the police station and handcuffed to a chair in an interview room. He was never actually put in a cell. His father showed up in uniform straight from work. The first time Patrick saw him was when he and the officer who'd arrested him came into the room and conducted a formal interview. Patrick was read his rights, which he interpreted as confirmation that he was in super big trouble. All that was left to do was cooperate with the authorities and take his lumps, even if that meant juvenile hall. There was nothing to hide. It was fairly obvious what had happened and there was a classroom full of witnesses. Patrick told his side of the story, all the while imagining he was about to be carted off to some civilian youth prison with a bunch of dirtbag city kids. He knew he deserved it. This time he'd gone too far.

Patrick was interviewed, fingerprinted, and released with a citation ordering him to court the next month. The whole process took a little over three hours and then he was released to his father. Patrick was relieved he wasn't going straight to prison, but it was clear he was far from being let off the hook. Now he'd have to wait a whole agonizing month before he went to court and a judge decided what to do with him.

Colonel Bennett didn't say a word to his son during the drive back to the fort. When they got home, Patrick's father told his wife everything and explained that Patrick had to go to court later. Mrs. Bennett cried.

September 3, 2009

I think I may have ruined my life today. A senior was messing with Robby and I literally went ballistic!!! I totally turned into a psycho!!! The fight wasn't even a real fight. The other guy got stuck in his desk and couldn't fight back. I basically had free shots at him the whole time. My big mistake wasn't kicking his ass, because he deserved it and I don't take that part back. I fucked up when he fell over and I kicked him a couple of times in the head. The city cops came and arrested me and totally took me to jail!!! They didn't make my dad pay a bail or anything because I'm still a minor. I have to go back to court next month and see what they're going to do to me. The worst thing about this whole deal is I made my mom cry. Her only son is a convict and it's my fault. I should probably just fucking kill myself.

Patrick learned the next day that he had been excused from the football team and suspended from school for a week, which was the least of his problems. The car keys were also taken away from him indefinitely. He was forbidden from using the phone; his video game console was put in storage in the basement; he couldn't watch anything but the news and PBS on television; and he was on house arrest after school and on weekends until his parents decided otherwise.

Patrick's parents had a private conference with an attorney in the Leavenworth County district attorney's office right before they went to court. Dr. and Mrs. Debruijn were there too, which was a humiliating surprise for Patrick. While the conference was held behind a closed door, Patrick sat alone in the second-floor hallway at the old downtown county courthouse and awaited his fate. When the meeting was over, no one came out of the attorney's office smiling or looking relieved. Patrick feared the worst and dared not open his mouth to ask what had happened. His parents let him suffer by not discussing the meeting with him.

The Bennetts went to court a few days later; Patrick had no idea what was about to happen. Robby was also there with his parents. The boys hadn't seen much of each other since the fight. Having a parent in the car while they were carted back and forth to school made it impossible to have a private conversation. The only time they could talk was during lunch break. The kid who'd been beaten up wasn't in the courtroom. Patrick was relieved because he was afraid to see his victim's condition.

The judge called Patrick's name and he stood in front of the jurist's raised desk and prepared to be sentenced to juvenile prison. There would be no need for a preliminary hearing or trial. The judge asked Patrick a few questions and then asked if he had anything to say before his punishment was given. Patrick told the judge he felt terrible about what had happened, he'd never done anything like that before, and he promised he'd never do it again. He added that he would like to apologize to the other kid if he ever got the chance. The judge told him that was good because that was exactly what he was going to do. Patrick was then sentenced to thirty days in juvenile detention, but the sentence would be suspended if he successfully completed a probation program that would end on his eighteenth birthday. He also had to enroll in court-certified anger management counseling and submit a written apology to the student he assaulted, which would be forwarded to the victim through the district attorney's office. That was it. He wasn't going to prison after all. Patrick knew better than to smile or make any outward gesture of relief, but he was ecstatic inside. So was Robby. Anything was better than going to jail.

October 1, 2009

I finally went to court today and got sentenced. I probably looked like a big pussy to the judge. He asked me if I had anything to say and I basically begged for mercy. The judge scared the shit out of me at first. When he said thirty days in juvy I almost had a heart attack!!! Then he said he would suspend the sentence if I finished my probation without screwing up again. That means if I fuck up one more time before I turn eighteen, I'll have to do the time. I'd do just about anything to keep from going to jail. If the judge wanted me to go to the other kid's house and wash his feet every morning before school, I'd do it. I'm still on restriction. I'd be pushing my luck if I asked my parents when that's going to be over. The best thing for me right now is to keep my fucking mouth shut for a while. It's good I didn't get so depressed that I tried to kill myself. I was never really going to do it, but when you get those kinds of crazy thoughts running around in your head and you're already scared shitless, I guess that's how that stuff happens.

October 3, 2009

Me and Robby were brainstorming today during lunch and we came up with a plan. We're going to quit church and join the youth group. Those guys have their own bible study while the adults are in the regular service and then they have another casual meeting at night. It's not much, but at least I'll be able to hang out with some friends on the weekends. They have some cute girls in that group too. Robby is all in, our parents are all in, we're good to go. FREEDOM!!!

Patrick's implication that joining the church youth group might help steer him back to the straight and narrow wasn't lost on his parents. A teenage-specific weekly dose of Christian virtues was probably a good idea, but Colonel Bennett wasn't ready to ease the other punishments he'd given his son. To address the anger management counseling ordered by the court, Patrick had to see a psychologist on the fort once a week for the next six months. He didn't suffer from any mental illnesses, and getting angry had never been a problem other than that one day at school, so he and the psychologist talked about sports, school, and mostly about what Patrick was going to do when he graduated. It was a total waste of time, according to Patrick.

October 20, 2009

We talked about the Chiefs game against the Broncos and being gay almost the whole time during counseling today. I think my psychologist has finally realized I'm just a normal guy and there's nothing wrong with me. My psychologist played rugby in college and he was telling me how similar football and rugby are. It sounded a lot like Smear the Queer to me and that's what I told him. Then we got in this whole thing about the word "queer" and how gay people consider that word like the same thing as profanity. I told my psychologist it was just an innocent game little kids play when they don't have enough people for a regular football game and he said it doesn't make any difference. Then we started talking about how I felt about gay people. I told him I didn't really care either way as long as no one tries to get gay with me. I think I only know a few people at school who are gay. They don't tell anyone, but everyone can pretty much tell, especially the girls that are lesbian gays. The male gays are mostly the drama club people and I don't hang out with them anyway. When my psychologist asked me to give him an example of someone I thought fit my definition of queer, all I could think of was Robby. I guess I always thought of queer as being more like a cross between unusual and kind of weird. Then it came out that Robby has never had a girlfriend and my counselor asked if possibly Robby was gay. He said if I ever got to a point when it was important to know, I should just ask Robby because we're already good friends and he should be able to tell me. So I've been sitting here thinking about it and I think maybe Robby really could be a gay guy. Girls scare the crap out of him. Maybe it's because he thinks they're gross. I need to find out if he's gay ASAP! We'll still be friends and everything, but if my best friend is a homo, people might think I'm a homo too. You can't get girls if they all think you're a gay guy.

October 21, 2009

Robby isn't gay and I'm a bona fide genius!!! They should give me a Pulitzer Prize or something!! The chance that all this time Robby has been gay right under my nose was really bugging me today so I finally asked him. I told him to meet me in the chapel next door after dinner because it's basically in my yard and I figured I could sneak over for a few minutes and say I was taking out the garbage or something. But then I decided to just tell my mom that I wanted to go over and just sit and think about stuff for a while and she said that was a good idea. A good idea!!! Genius!!! So I met Robby and no one else was there so I just asked him if he liked girls. He gave me one of those half-assed whiny "I guess," answers that he always does. But I said, "No Robby, seriously. Do you like girls?" Then he got really nervous and wouldn't talk or even look at me. I thought, oh shit he really is gay, and I didn't know what to do so I just told him it was cool if he didn't like girls like I didn't care either way, I just wanted to know. We sat there listening to the old pews creaking for a while and all I was thinking was how complicated stuff was going to get now that I knew my best friend was a homo. Then I guess I started trying to talk Robby back into not being gay by asking him questions like, "So big titties don't do anything for you? You wouldn't want to see Pam Ellerby naked?" That only made him more uncomfortable. Then I asked him what he thought about two men having sex with each other and he looked at me like he had no idea what I was talking about. I asked him to imagine how much that would hurt and he didn't have a clue. Then I told Robby that, when you're a gay guy having sex with another gay guy, you have to do it in the butt and Robby said we couldn't talk about that kind of stuff in church. I reminded him I was on restriction and there wasn't any other place to talk about it. Then I said, "I'm just saying it seems like having regular sex with a girl would be a lot better than having sex with another dude. I'm just asking for your opinion, that's all." Robby stared at the floor real hard for a minute and then he started talking about his doctor stuff. "The female vagina is designed to receive a male penis during intercourse. A male anus isn't. The vagina even produces its own lubricant. Copulation with a male anus would be painful and cause fissures. It wouldn't be very sanitary either." Then I just straight out asked him, "So you wouldn't ever want to stick your dick in another guy's ass?" Robby said, "Not really," and then he wanted to talk about something else. That's good enough for me, except I had to look up what a fissure is when I got home. Now I'm thinking I really need to get that boy laid, but me first.

The tiny old post chapel next to the Bennett home soon became the boys' only parentally approved rendezvous location beyond school and Sunday youth group meetings, which were held at the much larger main chapel adjacent to the fort's hospital. The Bennetts thought their son's troubles with the law had awakened a new spirituality in him and a need to repent for his indiscretions. What better place than a house of God when he needed a peaceful place to meditate and gather his thoughts? For the boys, meeting at the old chapel was simply better than sitting around outside in the cold and wind. There was never anyone there, yet the doors were always unlocked and the heat or air-conditioner was always on.

Robby and Patrick routinely sat in one of the back pews to make sure no one sneaked in behind them unnoticed. Robby clung to his friend's every word no matter how trivial the topic, yet his eyes rarely left the images in the antique stained glass or the many memorial plaques affixed to the old stone walls surrounding them. There was a unique peace there that the boys respected. Every word was whispered, every movement quiet and careful not to disturb. Inevitably sitting in a church every day after school and going to two different Christian youth group meetings on Sunday caused the boys to start thinking more seriously about their faith.

November, 6, 2009

Me and Robby were talking about God today in the chapel. I think he thinks about God and Jesus a whole lot more than I do. I never knew before he thinks most of the Bible is a bunch of BS. It's not like he doesn't believe in it. He just thinks a lot of it is made up stories just to make a point. We were talking about Moses and the Jews fleeing Egypt and he poked a ton of holes in that story I never really thought about. According to Robby, there's a bunch of stuff in the Bible like that that makes no sense. Like Samson turning into the Incredible Hulk just because of his hair growing back. I agreed with that one. It seems too much like Popeye and his spinach to me. I told Robby I thought we humans aren't capable of understanding a lot of the stuff God does, because he's God. If we really knew what was going on, we wouldn't need him. Robby doesn't think that way. I think everything has to make sense to him. We were having a really deep conversation when someone came in so we left. I'm going to ask him what he thinks about heaven tomorrow. I tell you what would be heaven for me. NO MORE RESTRICTION!!!

November 7, 2009

Me and Robby talked about heaven and hell in the chapel today after school. It turns out he doesn't believe in heaven and hell like most people. He says there's no way anyone knows what it's going to be like when we die, but it makes people less afraid of dying if they think they're going to heaven. I asked him what the point was of being a good person if there wasn't a reward from God when you died. He said the reward is being happy now, not after you're dead. So I asked him what would happen to a person if they didn't believe in God, but they still were a good person and went through life and never sinned, what would happen to them when they died. Robby thinks the same thing would happen to them as someone who went to church. Getting into heaven to Robby isn't about believing in God and Jesus. Robby thinks it's all about being good and always trying to do the right thing. I told Robby if that's true then I still don't get the point of religion. Robby said religion is the thing that keeps us humble, that's why we kneel and pray for forgiveness when we screw up. It's about respecting and showing thanks to the thing that created us. I think I agree with him, but I really need to think about it before I go one way or the other. Robby is really smart and everything, but if I get this wrong I might end up in hell with all the atheists and Muslim terrorists.

November 11, 2009

We got the day off for Veterans Day today. Nice job except I'm still on restriction!!! I think my mom is starting to feel sorry for me. I purposely mope and grunt a lot when she's around. My dad isn't budging. Me and Robby met at the chapel after lunch and my dad came over and checked on us. Thank God we were there and heard him come in!!! He sat down with us and wanted to know what we were talking about. I wasn't going to admit I was complaining about my house arrest, so I said we were just looking at the plaques because it was Veterans Day. Sometimes I can't believe how quickly I can come up with a good lie. That's not good though. Anyway, my dad sat with us and started telling us the history behind some of the monuments on the walls. Sometimes I forget my dad is actually a college professor and not just a soldier. He loves military history and knows everything about all the wars we've been in. He even knows a lot about the time when the Army was in charge of killing the Indians that were still loose in the West after we ordered them into reservations. It was really cool listening to him tell us about all the plaques. My dad had to go to Desert Storm when he was a major so he's been in the shit, but I'm not ever going to ask him if he killed any Iraqis. They say you shouldn't ask cops and people in the military if they ever killed anyone because if they did it could trigger some crazy memory and give them PTSDs. We were in there for over two hours talking about Army history and Fort Leavenworth and then the current wars in Iraq and Afghanistan. I don't really care a lot about that fighting terrorists stuff because I think war is stupid. If they come over here and blow up Americans, then we should just drop a giant bomb on them and blow that shit up. And I mean everything from their dogs to their fucking kids. It makes me mad when our soldiers go over there and get killed when we could just kill them all off with a bunch of bombs. So after we talked, my dad asked us if we wanted to go grab a burger or something and we said sure. On the way there we stopped at the post cemetery to see the miniature American flags the Boy Scouts put on the graves. There are thousands of graves there. It's pretty neat how they're all the same white marble stones and in perfect line. There were a lot of people there just walking around so we got out and did the same thing. We didn't really talk or anything. We just walked around reading the gravestones. I've been in a couple of other cemeteries before and they didn't make me feel bad just because they were full of dead people. Everyone dies and we have to put their body somewhere, right? The post cemetery makes me sad though. It's full of people who didn't get to live to be old like most people. Some of the guys in there died before they were even legal to buy a beer. That makes me sad, and it makes me even sadder to know that some of those guys were drafted back in the day and didn't want to be soldiers but we made them do it against their will. That is so crazy!!! After we walked around for a while, my dad took us to the Sonic for hamburgers. I swear Robby took ten minutes to figure out what he wanted. That place has too many options for him I guess. While we were eating we started talking about the cemetery and the military and what Veterans Day was all about. I have to admit I got kind of choked up. I don't know about Robby. You never know what that guy is thinking until he tells you. I read over this just now and wasn't sure why all these extra words were so easy to write tonight. Then I realized it's because I feel a lot more like an adult today than I ever have before.

Patrick's parents decided they would lift his restrictions right after Christmas break, though they continued to leave him in the dark about it. Patrick had additionally managed to talk his parents into letting him return to the gym with Robby after school. He had ninety minutes to get there and back. Patrick was sure to be on time, fearing a tardy return home might result in some additional torture stacked onto his existing sentence. With after school gym visits and meeting Robby at the old church next door to "gather his thoughts in peace" whenever he wanted, the restriction was slowly falling apart anyway.

The boys' parents were also ready for the restrictions to end. Patrick had changed from a lively teenager to one who was often sullen, and both sets of parents were afraid he might slip into a serious depression. None of the adults had any clue that the subtle outward displays of despondency on Patrick's part were a calculated act to get his parents to feel sorry for him. The Bennetts would have also been surprised to learn that managing anger hadn't been spoken of in several weeks at Patrick's psychologist visits. The fifty-minute counseling sessions consisted of little more than Patrick talking about school and sports and how he felt about whatever it was that had happened in his life since the last counseling session. That was usually the shortest part of the conversation because he never did anything. "Doc, I swear, I got nothing to talk about," he pleaded. "I go to school, go to the gym, go to church, and that's it. I couldn't find trouble if I wanted to."

Patrick had been quick to sincerely apologize for what he'd done, and he'd never complained about the fairness of his sentence. Other than the one incident at school, he had no history of violence or bullying. Patrick never displayed emotional problems in front of his psychologist. If you didn't know he'd nearly beaten someone to death in a classroom at school, you'd think he was an all-American teenager with a bright future ahead of him. That was certainly his psychologist's opinion.

Robby's parents felt particularly guilty about Patrick's problems with the law. Sure he'd gone about standing up for their son the wrong way, and it resulted in someone getting seriously hurt. That was inexcusable, but the fact that he did it to shield their son from the abuse of a bully was something they cautiously appreciated. Careful not to intrude on their friends' parenting, the Debruijns stood silently on the sidelines and painfully watched Patrick serve his punishment with apparent dignity.

While Christmas shopping for their wives, Patrick's father revealed to Dr. Debruijn that he and his wife were going to lift their son's restrictions as soon as school resumed after the holiday break. They hoped a final grueling two weeks of house arrest while everyone else was out having a good time would be a perfect crescendo to conclude Patrick's semi-incarceration. Over a lunch break of pizza and a pitcher of beer, the men did nothing but talk about their sons. They were seventeen now, and it was time to seriously channel them toward manhood.

It was too late for conversations about sex with the boys. Robby got his academic lesson at the hospital when he was just ten years old, long before he would feel any desire to actually have sex himself. Patrick received his lesson in two parts—one when he was thirteen and then again right before high school. The first lesson came formally in a junior high school health class. Patrick already had a general idea of how things worked from the other kids running wild in the mean streets of Fort Leavenworth. When Colonel Bennett one day decided to sit down with his son and give him an impromptu lesson about sex and female anatomy, Patrick quickly stopped him and admitted, "I already learned about this stuff in health class, Dad. I got it." Colonel Bennett was relieved.

The second lesson was more about not getting a girlfriend pregnant than actually talking about how getting pregnant happens. Colonel Bennett had a small collection of handguns he occasionally fired at a range at the back of the post, and he decided to have that conversation with his son after a day of target shooting together as the two sat at a table cleaning the guns. Patrick's father laid it out nice and simple. "No one becomes a parent if they keep their pants on and their zippers up." He acknowledged that fighting the urges to experiment with intercourse would be especially difficult because those urges are completely natural, but regardless of nature, Colonel Bennett explained, getting a girl pregnant and becoming a teenage parent would be the worst thing that could happen to all parties involved, no matter how much the two participants thought they loved each other. "Keep your pants on," Colonel Bennett concluded dramatically. "The day you think you can't do it anymore, come and see me." Patrick never mentioned either conversation in his journals.

The two fathers were now concerned that they had less than two years left before their kids graduated and would want to go off somewhere to college, which posed a whole new set of parental concerns. Patrick had been holding out for the chance of a scholarship offer to play football or baseball somewhere. It didn't matter if the offer came from an obscure university he'd never heard of. If the school was going to pay his tuition to be a resident athlete, he didn't care how unknown it was. Robby, on the other hand, needed to worry about surviving high school with grades good enough to even qualify to pursue a college education. It was time, the fathers decided, to step in and play a larger role in their sons' lives.

The boys were lucky their mothers weren't present during that shopping trip. The topic of conversation would have been similar, but the final decisions made over a second pitcher of beer would have been drastically different. I think here in the story is when I learned how similar the boys' parents were, and it further explains why they too had become best friends.

Both couples were extremely close to their spouses. I thought it inappropriate to ask why they each had only one child, but I found the dynamic of their single-son homes fostered a particularly close bond with their boys. Character and being a good person was constantly promoted in both homes. God and fervent patriotism was also always present. I don't know if the mothers came to a point when they consciously decided to step aside and let their husbands become the dominant parent, but they clearly did once the boys reached their middle teens. Disagreements about child rearing were never displayed in front of the boys, although they did happen on occasion. When the boys were little, their mothers held the trump card, and the men usually yielded without a second thought. Teenage boys are different, though, and the fathers decided to reverse the roles of parental dominance in a rather grand gesture.

The fathers decided that it was time the boys had their own car. They went everywhere together, and the constant chauffeuring around town had grown tiresome the year before. The boys had simply outgrown the fishbowl. If getting them their own vehicle would alleviate the need to cart them around all day and also teach them a lesson about responsibility, everyone would win. They assumed their wives would concur.

The dads decided to match the meager savings their sons already had from two summers working at the hospital and use it as a down payment for a used car. They could then finance the remaining balance and have the boys make payments with money earned from their next summer jobs at the hospital. The whole thing would be a big surprise even to their wives and everyone would be very excited. That was the plan, anyway.

The two fathers searched for cars on the Internet throughout the next week and scheduled appointments to meet a few people who were conducting private sales. They found an enlisted soldier on the fort who was selling an old Volvo station wagon for six thousand dollars. The dark blue paint was starting to fade and it needed new tires, but the engine was clean and only had a little over a hundred thousand miles on it. The fathers liked the idea of a slow, uncool, older European model station wagon for their boys. It would reduce some of the temptations that often get teenagers in trouble when they get their first automobiles. As long as it was reliable and got decent gas mileage, that was all that mattered.

The men purchased the car for its full asking price. If the seller had been anyone else, they would have tried to haggle the price down, even though it was a very reasonable starting point. The difference was that the seller was a young sergeant just back from his third tour in Iraq and he needed the money. The two veteran officers understood his sacrifice and thought it cheap and dishonorable to not help another soldier in need. They even gave him an extra hundred and told him to take his wife across the river to Kansas City for a nice dinner on them.

Robby didn't have a driver's license yet so Colonel Bennett handled the insurance. The station wagon was parked down the street from Robby's house, and there it sat inconspicuously for another week until Christmas and then New Year's Day passed. During brunch on

161

the Sunday afternoon just before the boys had to go back to school, Patrick's parents informed him that his restrictions were over. He was now free to be a teenager again. The families then drove to the Debruijns' house to watch an NFL game and for Patrick and Robby to celebrate Patrick's return to freedom.

As they pulled to the curb, Colonel Bennett pretended to notice the *For Sale* sign Dr. Debruijn had secretly returned to the Volvo's windshield. He made a comment about how Volvos were very reliable cars and he wondered out loud what one might cost. After both families piled out of their vehicles, the two fathers walked over to the Volvo and studied it. "Boys, come over here and look at this!" Dr. Debruijn called out before Patrick and Robby made it to the front porch. The game was starting at any minute and they were in a hurry.

"What for?" Patrick yelled back.

"Pat, get over here!" his father insisted.

The boys turned around and jogged over to their fathers and the old imported station wagon. "You know the game probably already started," Patrick said.

The plan was for the two fathers to have a conversation about how great the car was in front of their boys, and then one of them would hand the boys the *For Sale* sign and proclaim the car theirs. Then each dad would hand his son his own ignition key. That was the plan. What happened was the two fathers were so excited to give their sons their first car, they couldn't stop smiling, nor could they stick to the script.

"You guys are loco," Patrick finally said. "This is a clunker. Let's go. It's cold out here."

That was even funnier to the two fathers.

"What's wrong with you guys?" Patrick asked. He looked at Robby. "This is what happens when you have too much champagne and orange juice for lunch."

The two fathers recognized the jig was up, so each reached into his front pants pocket, withdrew a key, and handed it to his son. Robby didn't get it. Patrick immediately understood. "You're kidding," he said with a grin as wide as the Mighty Missouri. "It's ours?"

The fathers nodded warmly that it was.

Patrick grabbed Robby and started jumping up and down. "We got a car, we got a car! Thank you, thank you, thank you!"

Robby was much less enthusiastic, which was expected and completely normal for him. He smiled nervously and offered a stale "thank you" himself before taking his position in the front passenger seat, which would be his spot. The station wagon wasn't a clunker anymore—that was for sure. It was now the coveted vessel that would project them to previously unforeseen territory. No more asking to borrow one of the family cars. No more fear of being told no.

January 3, 2010

We got a car!!! I'm off restriction!!! There is a God!!! Thank you Jesus!!! Thank you Mom and Dad!!! THANK YOU!!! I guess my parents and Robby's parents got sick of driving us around all the time and they've been saving this for when I got off restriction. Finally!!! I'm so excited right now I could blow!!! I guess I'm going to be the driver most of the time. Robby doesn't have a driver's license yet and I don't think he's in any hurry to get one. He will now. It's a Volvo station wagon. It doesn't look very cool, but I don't care. It has lots of room to carry stuff around and the inside is in pretty good condition. The heater works and everything. This is so totally fucking awesome!!!

We get to drive it to school tomorrow morning. I have to make sure I never crash or get any tickets from the cops. I wonder if my probation would get revoked if I got a ticket. I never thought about that before. Now I'm worried. Psych!!! No I'm not. We got a car!!! I'm not going to get any sleep tonight.

Before moving on from this monumental day in the boys' lives, it's worth mentioning how the mothers felt about their sons having their own car for the first time. To say they were unoptimistic would be an understatement. They learned of the vehicle's purchase at the same time the boys did. Watching their proud husbands and the boys share their moment together prevented any feelings of anger or betrayal. The wives agreed it was a man thing, a rite of passage between sons and fathers from which the mothers were excluded simply because of their gender. It would be pointless to dwell on the fact that the decision to purchase the car was made altogether without their knowledge or approval. They did have the right to worry, though, and they did.

The next morning Patrick pulled up in front of the Debruijn house to pick up his wingman. Both Robby and his father came out of the house and descended the porch stairs together. While Robby was loading his backpack into the backseat, Dr. Debruijn crossed to the driver's side of the Volvo and asked Patrick if he could have a quick private word with him. Patrick assumed he was about to get the same reminder about driving safely his parents had given him a few minutes before. It was a very short conversation. Dr. Debruijn simply said, "Thanks for keeping an eye on Robby. You're a good friend," and shook Patrick's hand. Patrick didn't respond. He didn't know what to say.

"What'd my dad want?" Robby asked when Patrick climbed back into the driver's seat.

"Nothin'," Patrick answered. "Your dad's a good guy." The two boys headed off to school in their new used Volvo without another word about it.

Patrick's attitude about his restriction and probation completely changed that day. It was now a badge of honor. He'd persevered, grumbled a little, but mostly withstood his punishment with humility and came out of it with a new anticipation for school and moving on with his life.

January 4, 2010

I think Dr. Debruijn is glad I punched out that kid who was messing with Robby. Today before school he shook my hand and said he appreciated me watching out for his kid. What else could he be talking about? I know Robby's parents are glad I keep an eye on him. I just don't think it's a coincidence that Robby's dad said something about it the day after I got off restriction. I wonder if there's some tiny part of my dad that makes him proud too about what I did. It's not like he can say anything to me about it. You can't tell your kid they did something right when the cops arrest you for the same thing. I bet he is kind of proud of me. Violence is wrong and I get that. I just think sometimes you got to do what you got to do and have the guts to face the consequences when the shit hits the fan. Is that wrong? I got less than a year left of probation and then I'm free and clear. I'm going to knock that out and graduate with decent grades and then my parents will have an excuse to be proud of me again. We've only had our new car for two days and Robby is already complaining about his seat being too hard. We're going to try and fix it this weekend. We also need a better stereo and some of those air freshener things.

Patrick never saw the kid he beat up again. From his perspective it was probably extremely humiliating to have an underclassman kick the living shit out of him in front of a bunch of other students. The kid was also probably smart enough to realize that Patrick had a lot more friends than he did, and many of them were seniors. If there was going to be some form of retaliation, odds were good that he might end up in even worse condition.

Everyone gets a reputation in high school unless they're invisible. The problem with teenage reputations is that they come at the hands of a bunch of other immature teenagers with unbridled hormones who know nothing yet of the real world. Patrick thought of high school as a microsociety of stupid kids doing nothing but judging one another and spreading gossip. If you fell into the right crowd, you were usually on the positive side of those rumors. If you didn't you had to live with being tagged a whore, a fag, a nerd, or whatever other label kids brand each other with until you graduated and escaped into independent adulthood. That was another reason why Patrick was so protective of Robby. There were far too many opportunities for him to become the butt of jokes. What Patrick never anticipated was how solid *his* reputation would grow while he molded and manipulated his friend's esteem. Patrick may have been a popular kid before his big fight, but when word circled campus about what he'd done and why he'd done it, he was instantly elevated to almost legendary status. Say what you want about teenage immaturity, but most do know how to feel compassion for someone who is clearly disadvantaged.

Robby also became more popular. Before the big fight, when Patrick was asked to a party or some other kind of get-together, he usually had to ask if he could bring Robby with him. Now it was always, "Hey, do you and Robby want to...?" Everyone just got it. The boys were an impenetrable force of two, their bond much stronger than that of two siblings forced to coexist because of a shared bloodline. Patrick's recent restriction had only further solidified the boys' relationship. For three months Patrick hadn't been able to socialize with anyone after school and on weekends except for Robby, and Robby had always faithfully been there for him.

Patrick skipped wrestling season and decided not to try out for the track team in the spring. The high school's varsity wrestling team was already full of athletes good enough to compete for state championships in their individual weight classes. Patrick didn't think there was a chance he would make the varsity team, and being a junior varsity wrestler wasn't worth his time. The practices were too brutal and no fun. He felt the same way about the Pioneer track team. Robby was glad to learn his friend wasn't going to disappear into sports again once his restriction was lifted. He was particularly comforted to know that Patrick wouldn't be asking him to help him get in shape for track. Robby enjoyed their workouts in the weight room, but he hated running.

Overall that year's transition to full-time high school went really well for Robby, although he had no interest in extracurricular activities and didn't make any other friends. He could have if he'd tried; he just wasn't a social teenager. There was no such thing as a casual conversation with Robby. He either talked about something specific that he was interested in, or he wasn't responsive at all. He wouldn't even stand still and listen to a one-sided conversation. If you couldn't capture his attention, he'd interrupt and say he had to go, and then he'd simply walk away. Still, he didn't have a rude bone in his body.

The boys gave summer baseball one last season when school was out and got their same jobs back at the hospital. Their paychecks went straight to their fathers to finish paying off the Volvo loan. Patrick had been distracted by a cute redhead named Shelly Tisdale for some time, and they'd started officially dating after months of flirting late in the school year. The delay in asking Shelly out on a regular date had never been about Patrick being too nervous—she was unknowingly being auditioned to see if she could handle the relationship between the boys. Robby was also never aware that he was actually a player in the concerted effort to determine if Shelly was a good fit for them.

May 11, 2010

Me and Shelly went on our first date with just the two of us last night. We went and saw a Harry Potter movie that was kind of dumb. Shelly wanted to see it because she's read all the Harry Potter books. She thought the movie was kind of stupid too. We went to Homer's after that and had chocolate shakes. I told Shelly I wasn't used to not having Robby around because we share the car and we're best friends and basically next door neighbors and everything. Shelly said it was cool that I had such a good friend and she wished she had a friend like that. Then we sat there and talked about Robby until it was time to take her home. I didn't kiss her but I wanted to. I did hold her hand and that felt pretty good. I told Robby about our date today and he didn't care. He just wanted to make sure she didn't mess up his seat in the car.

Shelly was significantly more intellectual and mature than most of the other girls at school and Patrick liked that. His parents were also quite impressed with her. She didn't seem to be the kind of girl who would get their son in trouble—more the type to keep him out of it. Shelly also didn't mind having Robby tag along with them on movie dates. The threesome sat together and went out for a hamburger or just shakes after the show, and then Patrick took Robby home a little after ten. That usually gave Patrick and Shelly another hour or so to have some private time together.

Robby trusted Shelly. She was the first girl he was comfortable talking to, and she was genuinely interested in his passion for the medical field. Shelly had dreams of becoming a marine biologist and was trying to get into a school on the West Coast. She was also a fellow JROTC cadet; her plan was to get a Navy ROTC scholarship to pay for her college. She was the one who first openly suggested that Patrick and Robby should try to get military scholarships and go to college together.

Robby always assumed he was going to college because he wanted to be a doctor. His dream was to study medicine at the armed forces medical school in Bethesda like his father, but Patrick knew that wasn't going to happen. Maryland was thousands of miles away, and the idea of Robby being by himself so far away from home just didn't seem realistic. There was also the problem of Robby not growing out of his shyness and not understanding being an Army doctor meant he also had to be a soldier. How could he make it through a military basic training and medical school if he was still afraid to talk to people, even the ones he already knew? Sure everyone else at school thought he was a genius, but Patrick knew better and so did Robby's teachers. He might make it through a year or two of college, but at some point he was going to be overwhelmed.

Patrick didn't like thinking about his friend not being able to attain his childhood dream. It would be a traumatic day when Robby finally figured it out. It would only be worse if it happened while he was alone in a dorm room in Maryland with some stranger he'd been forced to room with.

Thinking about Robby going to college forced Patrick to think a lot more about his own future. He had been raised to believe a college education was necessary to be successful, but he didn't quite have his options whittled down yet. He still liked the idea of being a physical therapist or a professional sports trainer, which he assumed were basically the same thing. He certainly didn't want to be the kind of doctor who actually had to cut people open and deal with guts and blood and gross stuff; therefore, being an orthopedist was out of the question. He did have visions of being the guy who runs out on the field when an athlete gets hurt and says, "Okay, let's get this knee checked out," and is then in charge of the player's rehab. Let some other guy repair the ACL and MCL tears and the broken bones. He could be the guy who fixed the jocks after their surgeries.

All the therapists at the physical therapy clinic were trained through the military. To a man they confessed they could make a lot more money in the civilian world doing the same thing they were doing at Munson, and they all planned to do just that as soon as their enlistments were up.

Patrick's parents never talked to him about the cost of his college education. It wasn't as if he planned to go to an expensive Ivy League school or anything. Kansas University was right down the highway in Lawrence, and they not only had a big athletic department but they also had their own medical center in Kansas City. Kansas State wasn't that much further away in Manhattan, and they had their own renowned athletic department. Patrick thought he could go to either of those colleges and be a student physical therapy intern. Heck, if he got to do that, why even bother graduating from college?

Last week I asked Robby if he wouldn't mind sitting in the backseat when Shelly is with us since we're officially dating now. He looked at me like I was crazy so I told him it wasn't really a big deal and changed the subject. Shelly felt bad when I told her about it and she thought Robby might be mad at her for wanting to swap seats, so she bought him this really neat leather seat cover that you plug into the cigarette lighter and it gets warm. It also has some extra padding. That was really nice of her. When she gave it to him today I got kind of choked up and I ALMOST told Shelly I loved her. I'm glad I didn't do it. She probably would have freaked out. She really likes me and everything, but we both know it's best we don't get too serious. Probably the worst thing we could do is start telling each other we're in love. I think I may have college figured out. If I go to KU or K State we won't have to pay out of state tuition and it won't matter if I get any scholarships or not. Plus, if I go to KU, I could easily be a trainer on an NCAA championship basketball team and that would surely get me hired by a pro team after I graduate. If I go to K State, I can be a trainer on their football team. They're not going to win any college championship, but they're a lot better than the KU football team. I could still get to go to the Rose Bowl or something. KU's football team won't be in any bowl games. They always suck. So I guess what I have to decide now is whether I want to be a basketball trainer or a football trainer. Jayhawks or Wildcats. I bet the girls at KU are better looking. I heard most of the people who go to K State are farmers' kids. I'll have to check first before I make any final decisions. Shelly wants to go to school in California or Oregon. Maybe she'll change her mind and go to college with me. That would be sweet.

Patrick shared with Robby his idea of going to college at either KU or K State. He suggested that if Robby went with him, they could be roommates, and Robby could take care of all his pre-med classes there before moving on to another medical school to become a doctor if that was what he still wanted to do. They knew they wouldn't be taking the same classes anymore like in high school, but at least they could be roommates and help keep each other focused on their educations. At first it was discussed in very preliminary and random conversations, and then the subject came up in front of their parents during a brunch at the Officers' Club one Sunday. That changed everything.

The boys' parents were visibly skeptical of the idea, which surprised Patrick and Robby. Just about every idea they shared with their parents was shot down with some form of adult logic the boys didn't really understand or agree with. Then something even more surprising happened—Dr. Debruijn went home with the Bennetts.

After Patrick changed out of his church clothes, his father and Dr. Debruijn suggested the three men go for a walk. Just a few yards south of the Bennett home, the tree-lined sidewalk begins to follow a ridge at the top of a steep, grassy hill. Along that ridge stands a battery of antique Napoleon cannons posted there long ago to guard the bluffs overlooking the muddy Missouri River down below. A series of park benches accommodate those who seek the solace of a tranquil view. After a short walk, the men stopped at one of the benches and sat down.

Patrick found himself wedged uncomfortably between the two adults. *What's going on? This just got kind of creepy.* Colonel Bennett was still several inches taller than his son, and the difference in their size was even more apparent when he draped his arm around his son's shoulder. The fatherly gesture made Patrick feel trapped.

They talked about nothing important at first as they sat gazing out toward the brown river churning steadily southbound in the distance. After a moment of absorbing the peace, Dr. Debruijn turned to Patrick and said, "I want to tell you again how much Katy and I appreciate your friendship with Robby."

There it is again. Why do people make such a big deal about being Robby's friend? "He's a good guy," Patrick answered.

"Well, we will always appreciate what you've done," Dr. Debruijn added.

Oh, shit, Patrick thought. *They're moving.*

Dr. Debruijn continued. "Now that you're a young man, I wanted to share with you some things about Robby that I don't think are very clear."

"Like what?" Patrick asked.

"When Robby was a little boy, we began to notice some things about his development that were unusual for a child his age," Dr. Debruijn began. "He was slow to want to stand and talk and things like that. There were some other things that were...well, they were unusual. After a while we took him to some specialists to make sure there weren't any serious problems causing his delayed development, and we eventually learned that Robby does indeed have a disability. He's got a type of autism called Asperger or Asperger's syndrome. Do you know what that is?"

"Not really," Patrick said, confused.

"Well, you've known Robby long enough," Dr. Debruijn continued. "Being uncomfortable around people he doesn't know well, noisy crowds, his difficulties knowing how to act in certain situations—these are the result of his Asperger's. There's something in his brain that's wired differently from ours. We have no idea what caused it and there's no cure. It's just something he's had to manage, and he's going to have to keep dealing with it in one way or another for the rest of his life."

"He's not slow or anything," Patrick said. He almost said "retarded" and was glad he caught himself.

"That depends," Dr. Debruijn said. "Can he do most things on his own? Certainly. Will he be able to someday live in his own place and have a job and maybe even have his own car and travel and see the world? Sure, but he's not going to ever be a doctor. He's barely going to make it through high school."

"I thought he was smart," Patrick said. "He gets good grades, right?"

"He does in some classes," Robby's father answered, "but in others he needs far too much help. I don't think you realize how much time we spend with him at home with his schoolwork."

Patrick hung his head in despair. "I knew this was going to happen. I knew it."

"You knew something was wrong with him?" Colonel Bennett asked.

"Nothing's wrong with him, Dad," Patrick insisted. "Sheesh, what's wrong with everybody? Robby isn't some dope who can't tie his shoes or walk down the street without getting lost."

"We know that, Pat," Dr. Debruijn said. "We're not saying anything is wrong with him, but we are letting you know that Robby has some limitations that will prevent him from attending medical school. He just won't be able to do it emotionally, and he's not even close academically."

"Why doesn't Robby know this?" Patrick asked. "Why are you telling this to me and not explaining it to him?"

"Well, that's our dilemma," Dr. Debruijn explained. "We always assumed that Robby would realize how complicated medicine is to study, and we hoped he would simply grow out of his interest and find something else that he was capable of doing. I never took him to the hospital to coax him into being a doctor. I took him there so he could learn how to interact with people. I wanted him to learn how to think on his feet and take on a responsibility that other people depended on him to handle. He wasn't going to learn those skills being home-schooled. Never in a million years did we think he'd still be talking about wanting to be a doctor at seventeen."

"So what do you want me to do?" Patrick asked. "I'm not going to be the one to tell him."

"No, that's not what we're asking, Pat," Dr. Debruijn said. "What we want is for you to be there for him when this happens. We're not going to tell him he can't go to medical school. He'll hate us for it, and he'll try even harder to get in. What we want to do instead is let him apply to colleges like everyone else and let the process take its course. Let him take some classes, see how difficult the pre-med curriculum is, and then support him when it's time to decide to change his mind. Or if he doesn't change his mind, support him when he ultimately fails."

"I don't like being in on this," Patrick said. "It feels like you're telling me something bad is going to happen to my best friend, but then you don't want me to warn him—just sit back and watch him get hurt."

Colonel Bennett put his hand on his son's knee. "This is hard stuff, Son. It's one of those ugly things in life that adults have to deal with sometimes. You're a young man now. No one is asking you to watch your friend get hurt. What Dr. Debruijn is trying to do is explain to you that Robby is about to face a very difficult time in his life. You're his only real friend and he's going to need you. This isn't kid stuff anymore. If the Debruijns think you're ready to know the truth about Robby's limitations, it's because they respect you. The last thing on their mind would be to ask you to do something that's going to negatively alter the dynamic of your relationship with their son. This is to help you understand what Robby is going through and how critical your friendship will be in his future."

Patrick looked at Dr. Debruijn and warned him, "I'll always be on Robby's side."

"I know you will, Pat," Dr. Debruijn said. "That's why we love you."

Men reflecting on their lives usually describe a day or a moment when their innocence was swept away and they crossed the threshold into manhood—maybe not all the way but far enough to know their childhood was gone forever. This was Patrick's moment. After the revelation that Robby was autistic, Patrick was confused and worried. What did Robby actually know about his disorder? Was there some glass ceiling overhead that would prevent him from ever getting better, ever being like everyone else?

When the men finished their conversation, they returned to the Bennett house and then, after particularly firm handshakes were exchanged, Dr. Debruijn walked across the intersection to his home on Sumner Place. Patrick went straight to his bedroom and sat at his desk with his head in his hands. His mind raced. There was a problem that needed fixing and he had to find that fix before it was too late, but no matter how hard he fought for an answer, there wasn't one. That was what his father and Dr. Debruijn were trying to tell him. Something needed to break first, and when it did, only then could Patrick step in and make things right again.

August 23, 2010

We were talking about going to college at brunch today and our parents were acting kind of weird about it like they weren't sure it was such a great idea. When we got home later, Robby's dad said he wanted to talk about something so we went for a walk with my dad. Dr. Debruijn told me the reason Robby is so shy is because he has some incurable mental problem that he's had his whole life. I guess my dad already knew. I can see why the Debruijns didn't want to talk about it before, but my dad should have said something to me when he found out. I'm kind of pissed about that. Robby could have told me. I guess he's embarrassed about it. I guess I'd be embarrassed too. Dr. Debruijn said he thought I should know because, with college coming up and everything, he doesn't think Robby can pass his pre-med classes so he's pretty sure he's going to eventually flunk out. I suppose he's just preparing me so it'll make sense when it happens and I can help Robby decide something else to do. This is going to be a ton of pressure. I'm worried I won't see Robby the same way I did before. I'm afraid I might treat him differently and he's going to figure out why. They shouldn't have told me. I don't think I was ready to hear any of that stuff. Too late now.

Patrick never mentioned that conversation to Robby. In fact Patrick and Robby never once discussed Robby's diagnosis, although now it was always in the back of Patrick's mind. An Internet search explained every remaining mystery about his friend. The listed symptoms fit him to a T, proof he wasn't just a shy follower whose lack of social skills could simply be outgrown.

CHAPTER 7

The summer of 2010 ended with great anticipation for the boys' final year of high school. Patrick was allowed back on the LHS football team and he flourished in his favorite position—linebacker. The boys began the year with the same arrangements as the year before: they carpooled in their weather-beaten Volvo, their assigned lockers were right next to each other, and they took four of their six classes together. After school Robby did his homework in the library or on the bleachers while Patrick had football practice, and then they drove home together. Robby wasn't playing the part of tagalong though, particularly when it came to their JROTC class. He had been promoted to the rank of second lieutenant. He was now one of the cadet officers in charge.

September 8, 2010

My boy Robby got promoted in ROTC to Second Lieutenant today!!! I got promoted too, but it's not such a big deal to me. It's a huge deal for Robby and his parents. My mom and dad and the Debruijns got to come to class for a short ceremony. They read a promotion letter from ROTC headquarters wherever that is, and then your parents get to pin your new rank on your uniform. We both had our moms pin on our new ranks and they even punched them down like they do when real soldiers get promoted. We weren't the only people to get promoted, but we got the most applause. Robby's probably the most popular kid in our company and he doesn't even know it. I made sure to be the first person to salute Robby. It was pretty cool. I was kind of smiling when I did it because we're friends and everything, but Robby is so serious he saluted me back like I was a real officer. I'm very proud of that guy. It's not really fair that he worked so hard to get promoted and I just kind of went along with the program and we're the same rank. Shelly is a cadet captain and she's the company commander in her ROTC class. She met us in the parking lot after the ceremony to say hi to our parents and congratulate us before 6th period. Since we were all in uniform, me and Robby saluted her which I'll admit is kind of a turn on. Then Shelly congratulated us and gave us both a little unauthorized PDA on the cheek. I thought Robby was going to faint!!! There's no way that kid is gay.

Because he was now a cadet officer, Robby had to command the company during drill practice and help with uniform inspections on Wednesdays. He had no problem telling classmates their uniforms were unsatisfactory in one way or another. It tickled Patrick to watch his friend stand rigid in front of a subordinate cadet and critique his or her attire. It also made him very proud of his blossoming friend.

"Private Jones," Cadet Second Lieutenant Robert Debruijn began, "your collar pin is crooked and you have lint on your lapel. Sergeant Walker, your squad needs some work on their shoes."

Patrick's circle of other friends was even tighter that year, now that they were the big shots on campus. Robby's lack of interaction with Patrick's friends had kept him on the periphery, although he was almost always with the group when Patrick was present. This year would be different. The achievement of being a high school senior wasn't lost on Robby, nor was his position as a promising JROTC officer. For the first time in his life Robby felt important, something that had never happened at the hospital even after all his years working there. By the end of October 2010, the boys had both turned eighteen and Robby felt like there was nothing he couldn't do. He even started to smile for no apparent reason other than being a happy teenager.

Although the boys' October birthdays were separated by three weeks, they'd been celebrating them together on a designated Saturday between their actual birthdates since they were in the eighth grade. Turning eighteen, however, was a monumental milestone they couldn't celebrate with just cake and balloons. They were adults now, regardless of their level of maturity.

Their parents decided to arrange an overnight trip to Kansas City for them as birthday gifts. They bought the boys tickets to see a popular band perform at the Midland Theatre downtown, and they paid for a room at the nearby Westin Hotel so the boys could stay overnight. Each son was also given a hundred dollars to spend on meals, gas, and a T-shirt at the concert. The overnight arrangements weren't made to prevent drunk driving—Robby still couldn't stand even the smell of alcohol, and Patrick wouldn't dare get intoxicated within days of finally ending his probation. The parents simply wanted to make a symbolic gesture to acknowledge their sons' formal entry into adulthood. Patrick described the short weekend on the Sunday night after they got back home.

October 18, 2010

Me and Robby celebrated our 18th birthdays this weekend. Our parents got us some tickets to see a Train concert and then they let us stay overnight at the Westin all by ourselves. It was pretty cool. I can't believe you can watch porno movies right in your room. I thought that was illegal. Maybe that's just in Kansas and not Missouri. We didn't watch any because you have to pay extra to get the porno channels. We even had a miniature refrigerator in our room that was full of tiny whiskey and vodka bottles. We didn't mess with those either. We drove to Kansas City early and ate ribs and mac and cheese at this place called Gates Barbeque. It was really good, but the place was a little too loud for Robby. When you first go in, all the employees are yelling and everyone is in a hurry. They're not mad at anyone. They just want you to hurry up so the line doesn't get jammed. It's kind of scary because all the employees are black and you don't know if they're yelling at you because you're too slow or they don't like you because you're white. We have lots of black friends at LHS and we don't hang out with any racists. At least I don't think we do. Black people sure do make great BBQ. That stuff was the best I've ever had. From now on when we go to KC, we have to go to that place. The concert was okay. The Midland isn't very big and we sat in the balcony. We only know a couple of Train songs so we left after about an hour. It was loud and crowded and Robby wasn't really into it. Then we drove down to the Plaza and just walked around and talked about stuff until everything closed. When we got back to the room we ate our leftover ribs and started watching a really dumb movie about this white trash chick who lives in the Ozarks and her dad who is a drug dealer skips bail so she has to find him and turn him in to the cops before they kick her out of her house. We both fell asleep before it was over. When we got up this morning we had a buffet breakfast at the hotel and then we went over to see the World War

I monument across the street before we drove home. They have a pretty cool museum there we've seen before but we wanted to check it out again. After that we came home and then I went over to Shelly's for a while. She gave me a jacket to put my football letter on even though I didn't get it yet. Sometimes you don't have to get all crazy to have a really good time. Sometimes just being free and hanging out with your best friend doing regular stuff is more fun than anything else. We probably could have had a more exciting birthday, but this weekend was actually kind of perfect.

Patrick was nominated for homecoming king, and if he had to go to the dance, Robby was going to go too. There were plenty of girls in Patrick's crew who didn't have regular boyfriends, so he carefully selected one he thought wouldn't mind attending the dance with Robby so they could double date. Much to his delight, the first girl he asked said she'd be glad to do it, as long as Robby understood they were only going as friends. Patrick promised he could arrange that. The girl, Wendy Miller, and Patrick conspired to have Robby invite her to the dance so he could experience what it was like to ask a girl out.

Patrick knew he had his work cut out for him. There was no way Robby was going to go to a dance and actually try dancing. The idea that he would go anywhere with a girl he would have to talk to was almost unimaginable, but everything Robby did for the first time was once unimaginable. That was how it worked with him; Patrick often had to do some extra coaxing and incorporate some degree of trickery to get him to the finish line. Grabbing Robby by the ear and forcing him to do something rarely, if ever, worked. For this endeavor Patrick decided on the old "Hey, dude, I need a favor," routine.

October 22, 2010

Homecoming is about the stupidest thing anyone ever came up with. I get the whole thing about it being an alumni game and everything, and I get the dance part of it. But why do you have to have a stupid king and queen? Just let the girls be the queen and that's it. Who wants to stand up there in front of everyone like a giant dweeb and have to wear a stupid crown on your head? It's ridiculous!!! I have to go because of football and my parents found out so they're pretty much making me do it. Me and Shelly were going to go to the dance anyway, but we were going to skip out early. Now we're going to get stuck there all night. I'm making Robby go with us. He doesn't know it yet, but he's taking Wendy Miller. Now we have to come up with a way to break it to him. My mom says in some places in Kansas, they used to think dancing was sinful so they made it illegal in school. Sounds like a good idea to me.

Soon thereafter a scheme was solidified and Patrick summoned Robby to meet him inside the old post chapel next door. When Robby arrived he found Patrick sitting in a pew by himself. Patrick heard the iron hinges of the thick double doors squeaking open behind him and waved Robby over to join him on the pew.

"I got a big problem and I need your help," Patrick began. "I got nominated for this homecoming thing so I have to go now. I don't care if I win it or anything, but everyone says being on the homecoming court looks good on a college résumé. If I don't go, they're going to replace me. Plus my parents are making me."

"So go," Robby answered bluntly. *How is that a problem?*

"Well, here's the deal, man," Patrick continued. "You can't go to a dance without a date. Shelly says she won't go unless her friend

Wendy goes, and Wendy doesn't have a boyfriend. You know Wendy Miller. You'd think someone would have asked her by now, but no one has."

"That's sad."

"Hell yeah, that's sad," Patrick agreed. "It's tragic. She's cute, dude. You can't have cute girls sitting at home during homecoming. This is our senior year. This is a once in a lifetime deal, right?"

"I guess," Robby mumbled.

"Dude, I need you to ask Wendy to the dance. You think she's cute, right?"

"I don't know," Robby answered apprehensively.

"Are you crazy? She's hot, man," Patrick insisted. "Look, I'm not asking you to be her boyfriend or anything. Just take her to the dance. You guys can go with me and Shelly."

"Naw, that's okay," Robby answered.

Patrick expected this response and was prepared. "Dude, here's the deal. I need you to ask Wendy to the homecoming dance. If she says no, then I'll tell Shelly and I'm off the hook. If she says yes, we go together, we all have some laughs, and when the night is over you'll get to say you went to your high school homecoming dance. You don't have to go on any more dates with Wendy or anything. Just this one night, man. I need you, brother. You're my wingman."

"Do I have to dance?" Robby asked.

"No way," Patrick answered. "Half the guys there won't dance."

"Can you ask her for me?"

"No can do, buddy. Got to draw the line there. You have to ask her."

"Can I do it on the phone?" Robby hoped out loud.

"Sure," Patrick said. "I'll even help you."

"What do I have to wear?"

"Don't worry about that, dude. We got plenty of time to figure that out. I just need you to lock Wendy in so Shelly will go. What do you say? I'll owe you big time. Free Popsicles and doughnuts for life."

"Okay," Robby said reluctantly.

"You're in?"

"I'll do it," Robby said, "but you have to help me ask her."

"Let's go do it right now," Patrick suggested. "Let's go up to my room and get it over with."

A look of terror crossed Robby's face. "Now?"

"Right fucking now," Patrick insisted with a slap on Robby's knee. "C'mon, let's go."

Patrick gently pried Robby to his feet. He needed to get his friend to a phone and get a number dialed before he had a chance to change his mind. The race was on, but first there was an admonishment from Robby, "You said that word again in church. You can't kee..."

"Jesus Christ, man," Patrick interrupted impatiently. "Okay, look, I'm sorry. Jesus, God, whoever's listening, I'm sorry. Now c'mon, dude. Let's get the fu... let's go."

As the boys left the church and made their way to Patrick's house, Patrick coached Robby on what to say when Wendy answered his call. He assured his terrified friend that the whole conversation wouldn't take more than a minute. The dance later would be a piece of cake. Robby had no time to think—within a few minutes of their conversation in the church, Patrick had dialed a number on his phone and was handing his friend the receiver.

The call went something like this:

"Hi, Wendy, this is Robby Debruijn from school. Would you go to the homecoming dance with me and Pat and Shelly? Okay. Thank you. I have to go now. Bye."

It was the most frightening fifteen seconds of Robby's young life. It was one of the proudest moments for his mentor. As for Wendy Miller, she hung up her phone smiling ear to ear. She was proud too.

Patrick had three weeks to prepare Robby for the dance. He explained that Robby should encourage Wendy to dance with other guys if he wasn't going to dance with her. Robby was fine with that. He was even more relieved to hear he wasn't expected to hold her hand or kiss her. When the big night arrived, Patrick, who much to his relief had lost the homecoming king title, drove the two couples to dinner at the Officers' Club and then to the school for the dance. There they joined the rest of their friends and gossiped the night away between dances. Even when Shelly dragged Patrick out onto the basketball court dance floor and Wendy was dancing with someone else, Robby was never left alone. Early in the evening, Patrick asked all the girls in their group to make at least one attempt during the night to ask Robby to slow dance, thinking he might fight through his fear and give it a try. He refused each and every request, but Robby sure liked being asked judging by the big smile on his face after about the third request. Patrick leaned over and whispered in his ear that it was probably his cologne that was driving the girls wild. Robby believed his friend. What else could it be?

After the dance the boys and their dates went to a party and mingled until it was time to go home. Robby had the time of his life. Patrick enjoyed watching it. When they arrived at Wendy's house to drop her off, she thanked Robby for taking her to the dance and then she gave him a quick kiss on the cheek—Robby's first time being kissed by a date. Nothing could have ended the night better. After church and brunch the next morning, Patrick and Robby sat in the gazebo across the street from Patrick's house and revisited the experience. Patrick was eager to hear what his friend thought.

Robby admitted he'd had a good time, but the music was too loud and he didn't think he'd ever want to try dancing in the future. He thought Wendy was very nice but wasn't interested in pursuing a relationship with her. Patrick asked Robby if he would like help finding another girl to go on dates with. Robby said no. He was too busy with school and working at the hospital to get ready for his career in medicine.

It killed Patrick whenever his friend talked about being a doctor. It was time to try to find him something else to pursue. It was also time for Patrick to get his own act together. The football season was going well, but he wasn't standing out enough to get any scholarship offers. He'd come to the same conclusion about his amateur baseball career.

Although it was protocol for the JROTC instructors to not try talking cadets into joining the armed forces, it was commonplace for staff to occasionally pull aside a cadet who showed superior leadership qualities and interest in the cadet program and suggest he or she look into the college ROTC scholarship program. Of course the endgame of receiving such a scholarship was an officer's commission and obligation to serve at least six years in the military to reimburse the government for its tuition investment. Patrick had a decent GPA. The problem was that little thing on his record that got him temporarily kicked out of school and almost landed him in juvenile hall.

Army and Navy recruiters were frequently seen buzzing around LHS trying to get seniors committed to enlistments after graduation, but Patrick and Robby never paid any attention to them. Patrick had heard the recruiters were all a bunch of liars, promising students anything just to get them to sign up. When Patrick caught one of the Army recruiters talking to Robby one day after school in the parking lot, he sprinted over to make sure he wasn't bullshitting Robby into signing his life away. Robby had already told the recruiter about his plans to be a doctor, and the recruiter told him he should get his start as a medic, and then the Army could help pay for his medical school. Patrick told the recruiter that Robby didn't need any help with his tuition and pulled Robby away to their car while the recruiter was still talking.

Patrick told Robby he shouldn't talk to the armed forces recruiters because they were dishonest and only looking to shanghai him into the military. Robby replied that he thought the recruiter might have a good idea; join the Army first and then let the Army pay for college.

It had never entered Patrick's mind that Robby wanted to be anything other than a general practice doctor, so his statement about a career in the military caught him off guard. Patrick reminded his friend that no matter what job he ended up with in the military, he still had to go through basic training and that would totally suck. Plus he wouldn't have any choice in where he lived, and there happened to be wars going on in Iraq and Afghanistan, which meant he might end up overseas in a tent in the desert fixing soldiers that were blown to pieces. Patrick's intention was to scare some common sense into his friend. Instead Robby was intrigued. Patrick's explanation of military life had just revealed to Robby an exciting new option to his career path. He wanted to hear more.

Patrick didn't have any idea what he was talking about, so he simply started making things up. He told Robby that they never let recruits sleep in basic training and they were yelled at from sunup to sundown. When they weren't peeling potatoes or cleaning toilets, they had to march for ten miles in the rain with a fifty-pound pack full of bricks on their backs, and if it wasn't raining, there would be a drill instructor armed with a fire hose just to make sure everyone got all wet.

"And besides all that bullshit," Patrick pointed out, "you'll have to learn how to shoot automatic weapons and those things are loud as hell, but that's nothing compared to the sound of hand grenades and the other explosives you'll have to learn how to use." The attempt to scare Robby was a complete waste of breath. The more awful a picture of military life Patrick tried to paint, the more Robby was fascinated with it.

Robby innocently discounted the loud explosions and gunfire he'd have to face—he'd just wear earplugs awhile until he trained himself to get used to it. As for hiking wet with a heavy rucksack on his back, he had plenty of time to get in shape for that, and they probably only made you do it once anyway. He'd already learned how to shoot a rifle in JROTC, and that wasn't so bad. As for the sleep deprivation—they did the same thing to medical school interns.

By the time the boys got home from school, Patrick was so worried about Robby joining the Army, he called Robby's father later that night to warn him.

December 8, 2010

I caught Robby talking to an Army recruiter in the parking lot after school today. The guy was already telling Robby he could get his medical training in the military and the government would pay for it. I'm probably going to get in trouble with ROTC because I was pretty rude and yanked Robby away from the guy. I tried to tell Robby on the way home that being in the Army would totally suck. I think he thought I was making it exciting. I got really worried so I called his dad and told him what happened. Dr. Debruijn didn't say much but he said he was glad I called. He probably already put the kibosh on it. Nobody trusts those recruiters when they come to school. They tell you one thing and the next thing you know you signed your life away to be a cook on a submarine or something. I hope I did the right thing and Robby's not mad at me for calling his dad. Whatever. Either way, I'm not going to let any of those recruiter vultures close to Robby again.

Patrick's plans after graduation became the theme of almost every dinner conversation at the Bennett table. With each discussion the sense of urgency grew. Patrick told his parents he didn't think he'd be getting any athletic scholarship offers, and he didn't think he'd qualify for many academic scholarships because his grades were only above average and his assault conviction and suspension from school couldn't be kept a secret. They took his word for it. Colonel Bennett told his son that he shouldn't be concerned with tuition until he figured out what he wanted to do for a career. Once he did that, they could start looking for schools with a degree program that would meet his needs. Patrick was still interested in some form of physical therapy career. He just didn't know where to start.

December 14, 2010

It snowed last night so me and Robby had to put chains on the Volvo's tires before school this morning. It was so cold I could barely move my fingers and my boy Robby started to get a toothache so he wasn't any help. I got chains on the back two tires and then gave up. Then we figured out about halfway to school that our Volvo is a front wheel drive, so it was a total waste of time. What a couple of idiots! I'm starting to think the ROTC scholarship program might not be such a bad idea for me. Shelly got one and now she can go to college anywhere she wants. I don't really want to join the Army, but I guess I could do it for a few years if they're going to pay my tuition. A whole bunch of my ancestors were in the Army. Plus I'd be an officer so that would be cool. I'm going to bring it up to my parents and see what they think. It's supposed to snow some more tonight. Maybe we'll get a snow day tomorrow. I knew I shouldn't have drafted Brett Favre this year for my fantasy football team. It's like my team is cursed. Favre got benched yesterday for the first time in like ten years and I got killed. Tony Romo is my backup and he's out for the rest of the season with a busted clavicle. I shouldn't be writing in this stupid journal right now. I should be finding me a new quarterback for my fantasy team.

After thinking about it a little more and replacing the quarterbacks on his fantasy football team, Patrick revealed to his parents that he wouldn't mind getting into a college ROTC program if it would help with tuition costs. There was no way he was going to make the Army a career, but if they were going to pay his tuition and train him, he could give the military a few years of his young life and get public service checked off his bucket list. Although Colonel Bennett never came out and said it, Patrick knew his father would be proud of him if he gave the military a few years of his life. The Army had been very good to the Bennetts for the last four generations, and Patrick thought it would be the continuation of an honorable family tradition if he volunteered for a short enlistment. It wasn't like a physical therapist would have to worry about getting deployed to a war zone.

The key, in Patrick's mind, was that he needed to get in as an officer or warrant officer of some kind because being an enlisted soldier could result in a career of grunt work. In order to avoid that, Patrick needed to qualify for special training or get a degree under his belt. If the Army picked up the tab for his college education, they would expect a longer enlistment, but he could do that. Heck, Patrick could go to college and knock out an enlistment before he was twenty-eight— at least that was what he thought.

That next Sunday Colonel Bennett and Dr. Debruijn talked at brunch about their sons having some interest in joining the military. Patrick was absolutely astonished that Dr. Debruijn thought it was a good idea for Robby. As far as Patrick was concerned, Robby was much more capable of making it through medical school than surviving life in the military. The idea that Robby could handle anything military beyond the intensity of high school JROTC was total madness.

The fathers mentioned that it might be possible for their boys to join together under a buddy enlistment program, and after basic training they might be able to get into one of the military's support medical fields and get college credits for the training. They could then finish their degrees taking satellite courses from any public university that offered programs to servicemen and women wherever they were stationed.

Neither of the boys wanted to be a nurse, and Patrick was particularly concerned that he might end up being an ambulance driver. Robby didn't understand the underlying text of the conversation and kept trying to consider the various medical fields being discussed as a stepping stone to becoming a doctor. It was difficult for Patrick to listen to. He wished one of the adults would simply step up and tell Robby the truth. Just the opposite was happening, though, and Patrick was disgusted by it. He felt the fathers were openly conspiring to set Robby up. When Robby failed in the military, which he was certain to do, his father could then say, "Becoming a doctor is ten times tougher," and that would be the end of Robby's dream. Patrick angrily folded his arms and leaned back in his chair. He wasn't going to talk about joining the military in front of Robby anymore.

It was clear to Robby during brunch that their fathers were throwing out ideas off the tops of their heads and they didn't really know exactly what they were talking about. Patrick assumed Dr. Debruijn would know more about Army medical jobs, but he was as clueless as Colonel Bennett. Patrick could only imagine one job short of being an actual doctor that Robby would accept, and that was being a nurse in an emergency room where he could give people stitches and shots and bandage their wounds. At the end of the day, that was all Robby wanted to do. He didn't want to spend his life playing hopscotch from one exam room to another, treating runny noses and sore throats and admonishing people about their weight and high blood pressure. Robby wanted to physically fix people. If he couldn't do it as a doctor, he'd have to be a nurse, and Patrick didn't know if his friend would go for that. To find out where he stood, Patrick decided they needed to talk and get on the same page before subjecting themselves to any more of their fathers' nonsense.

Patrick called Robby after they got home from brunch and told his friend to meet him in the chapel. He then walked next door and took a seat in an empty pew. Because it was Sunday, there had been a service earlier, and there would be another in a few hours. Two care-takers were walking around removing used programs from the pews and preparing for the later service. Robby walked in a few minutes after Patrick and sat next to him.

"Dude," Patrick began quietly, careful not to be heard by the two church assistants, "what's up with our dads?"

"They think we should join the Army," Robby replied softly.

"Yeah, do you think?" Patrick answered sarcastically. "Dude, we can't just sign up like two knuckleheads off the street. When they got you, they got you. I don't want to sign up thinking I'm going to get medical training and my college paid for, and all that happens is I spend my whole enlistment being the guy who has to clean shit off people's asses when they can't do it themselves. That's not me, dude. I can't be that guy."

Robby thought about it. He envisioned Patrick towel bathing an elderly patient who had fecal matter smeared on his buttocks. No, that didn't seem like something Patrick would like to do.

"Dude, are you listening to me?" Patrick said, waving his hand in front of his daydreaming friend. "Look, bro, I only see one option if we go the Army route. Okay, now hear me out. What about if they train you to be a nurse—a full-fledged surgical nurse? What about that?"

Nope, that wasn't a good idea, according to Robby, because being an RN required years of training, and that would detract from his regular pre-med studies and medical school. Why not go straight for the big prize?

"Yeah, but, Robby, look," Patrick countered, "some nurses do as much as doctors do in the OR, but they don't have to deal with all that extra bullshit that doctors have to deal with, right?"

Robby wasn't convinced. "That's okay," he answered. "You can be a nurse if *you* want."

I don't want to be a fucking nurse either. "I'm not going to do it if you're not going to do it," Patrick stated firmly. It was the perfect excuse.

That was that. There would be no more talk of nursing school.

None of the Bennetts or Debruijns recall when the decision was made that Patrick and Robby were seriously considering joining the military together, but their fathers were now involved and they weren't letting go. The next Saturday afternoon, Colonel Bennett arranged for an Army recruiter to visit their house after lunch. The Debruijns joined them to listen to the recruiter's pitch. The recruiter had no knowledge of Robby's handicap or background. He talked to the families as if the boys were both able-bodied and ready to sign up to be soldiers right after high school.

Colonel Bennett had asked the recruiter to come prepared to answer questions about the military's various medical fields, so he arrived with a list of jobs the boys might be interested in. He started with examples of the least complicated medical assistant jobs and even some jobs in dentistry. The boys were firmly against the low-level positions, and Patrick was particularly outspoken about not enlisting if there was a chance they might get stuck in one of those career fields.

The recruiter then looked at his list and said, "What would you think about being combat medics?"

During times of war, a recruiter should probably stay away from words like *combat* when sitting in front of a kid's mother trying to talk her son or daughter into joining the military. People get killed in combat and it doesn't make any difference what title comes after that word. It only describes what you're supposed to be doing while someone is trying to kill you. Combat medic, combat radio operator, combat pencil sharpener. There's a reason why that word is in there and moms don't like to hear it. Pauline Bennett and Kathryn Debruijn weren't any different than any other mothers, and it didn't make any difference that their husbands were soldiers.

"Moving on," Mrs. Debruijn said before the recruiter could continue.

"Now, Kate," her husband interrupted. "Let's just hear what he has to say."

Mrs. Debruijn looked at Patrick's mother for support. Pauline gave her friend a subtle wink and then shook her head, signaling to her counterpart not to worry because their sons becoming "combat" anything wasn't going to happen.

The recruiter continued cautiously, explaining that combat medics are basically paramedics for combat troops. Their primary mission is to provide general medical care to troops and stabilize severely wounded soldiers before getting them evacuated to a regular medical facility. There were hundreds of different places the boys could get stationed as combat medics, and between deployments they would probably work in a hospital. There they might work in a clinic or be assigned to various field operations to help with soldiers who'd injured themselves during training. If they were deployed, they'd most likely be assigned to an infantry unit and would be their medical first aid provider with a handful of other combat medics assigned to the unit.

Mrs. Debruijn asked if combat medics carried guns and were on the front lines. The recruiter confirmed they went wherever there was a chance a soldier might need medical assistance and many of those locations would require they be armed.

Patrick's mother asked, "How likely is it that the boys will have to go to Iraq or Afghanistan?"

The recruiter answered that the job of a combat medic is to want to go into harm's way when fellow soldiers are being injured during battle with an enemy. He reminded her that soldiers were going to remain in the Middle East indefinitely, and there would always be enemy insurgents attacking American soldiers regardless of whether the United States was formally at war with anyone. He understood the mothers' concerns, but it was more important for the boys to decide if they thought themselves capable of the bravery and commitment it took to go into battle to save another soldier. If they didn't think they could do it, then they should keep looking for something else.

Did that asshole just challenge us? was Patrick's immediate thought. *Did he just call us out? What did he mean, "if we didn't think we were capable"?* Patrick already thought of recruiters as a bunch of snakes. Now he was livid that one of those snakes had slithered his way into his own home and insulted him and his best friend in front of their parents, and they let him get away with it! *What the fuck, man!*

Both boys had been raised to be extremely dedicated and patriotic toward their country. They understood the words in the Pledge of Allegiance and recited it proudly in school. They understood the significance of the National Anthem and stood reverently with their hands over their hearts whenever it was played. Across the street from the hospital was a national cemetery full of servicemen and -women who had died serving their country. All around them growing up was the history of military service and sacrifice, and rarely was an opportunity missed for the boys to be taught a lesson about how lucky they were to be Americans. That's how the sons and daughters of service members are raised, sons particularly. In Patrick's eyes it was totally inappropriate to have his patriotism questioned.

The recruiter was there for a little while longer. Robby never asked a single question, despite the frequent prodding from his father. Patrick was convinced the recruiter was a prick and told his father he thought the guy had been a little insulting. Colonel Bennett reminded his son that armed forced recruiters were salesman, and sometimes making a subtle challenge was just a maneuver to get potential recruits thinking. It got Patrick thinking, all right.

After the recruiter left, the families returned to the living room and sat down to discuss the presentation. Patrick asked Robby what he thought about possibly becoming combat medics together and Mrs. Debruijn answered for her son, "Not on your life." That was the end of that. The conversation about the other options was almost as short, with those nays coming directly from the two boys.

December 28, 2010

My dad invited a recruiter to come over today to try and talk me and Robby into joining the Army right after high school. He's fucking crazy. They're all fucking crazy!!! The guy was supposed to show us how we could get medical training and get our degrees at the same time during our enlistment, but I smelled a rat the second the guy opened his mouth. We're safe though. The stupid bastard couldn't shut up about the war and being combat medics and I think our moms kind of silently flipped out. He actually implied we might not have the balls to sign up. I'll show him balls. Fuck that guy! I'm so mad right now!!! We got punked right in our own house!!!

Patrick stewed over the recruiter's visit for a few days and eventually realized that even if he did it, being a combat medic would probably be far too intense for Robby. He wasn't worried about going to war. President Obama campaigned on a promise to end American involvement in Iraq and Afghanistan, so there might not even be a war going on by the time the boys graduated from high school and completed their basic military and medical training. Patrick assumed Robby could handle the medical training part with ease, but everything else would be very high pressure for him. Their basic training drill instructors would be yelling at them all the time and constantly trying to wash out the people they didn't think were cut out for the service. Those guys weren't going to be like their JROTC staff instructors. The regular Army instructors would be hard-asses who didn't give a shit about them. Patrick could imagine them zeroing in on Robby and trying to intimidate him into quitting. Patrick knew he wouldn't be able to watch it.

As for joining by himself, Patrick could picture himself learning how to be a medic and doing it for a few years, particularly if it opened a door to being a physical therapist. For Robby, however, it was probably not a good idea. The more he stewed over it, the more he thought it was a really bad one.

January 3, 2011

I've been thinking a lot about this Army medic stuff. Maybe I should just do it. Maybe it's time I need to grow up and stop worrying about Robby so much and just fucking get the hell out of this place by myself and do it. There's no way Robby can. He'd get so stressed out it might make him legitimately mental. ROTC isn't helping. They keep promoting him and it's making him a lot more confident, that's for sure. Half the seniors already know where they're going to college next year. We need to get our shit together, like yesterday! I finished reading the book Shelly gave me for Christmas called The Human Stain. *It was about this black college professor who everyone thought was white. He even got fired from his job because they thought he was a racist white Jew. I was able to follow most of it. Shelly is going to love that I finished it already. It'll give us something to talk about that she's interested in. She reads a lot. They hardly watch any TV at her house. At night they just sit around and read. It's probably a Catholic thing. I could handle that for about ten minutes and then my fucking head would explode. Kaboom!!!! Hey what was that? That was Pat's head exploding because the cable went out and the only thing left to do was read a book. Ha! That's pretty good. Maybe I should just be a comedian. My dad would love that!!!*

The next day, after a lengthy and impressive discussion of Philip Roth's bestseller with Shelly, Patrick went to the Army's online recruiting website and started looking at other medical fields Robby might be interested in. He was amazed that he couldn't find a single medical field the Army wouldn't teach you, including training to be a doctor. From being a dental technician to the guy who takes your x-rays, the Army had a training course for it, and training was taught at either Fort Sam Houston in San Antonio or Walter Reed Hospital in Bethesda.

Patrick's Internet surfing led him to the Medical Education and Training Campus (METC) website at Fort Sam Houston, and there he found links to a handful of training videos he could watch. It didn't take long to figure out that the recruits he was watching in the METC videos weren't Army soldiers. They were Air Force airmen and Navy sailors. That was interesting. Then a new idea struck him. *If the problem with being a combat medic is the "combat" part, why not join another branch of the service other than the Army?*

Patrick immediately rejected the Navy. There was no way anyone was going to get him to live on a ship for months at a time. He didn't like their uniforms either. He could only imagine how goofy he'd look with that floppy white sailor hat on his head and white bell-bottom pants. The Air Force, though, that might just work.

Patrick didn't know much about the Air Force, but he didn't think there was any chance airmen medics would get stationed in a place where they might have to go out and treat the wounded while terrorists were shooting at them. That was a job for the Army and Marines. They might get stationed in a field hospital overseas next to an airport where fresh wounded were being brought in from the field, though. That would be like working in a regular big city emergency room, and that was what Robby wanted. Patrick didn't think Air Force people had to ever sleep in tents or carry backpacks or any of that regular soldier stuff, and he'd heard from other kids in JROTC that Air Force basic training was a whole lot easier than the other branches' boot camps. Patrick felt he was on to something, so he called Robby and told him he was coming over.

He didn't tell Mrs. Debruijn the reason for his visit when Patrick arrived at Robby's house. Instead he pretended it was just a random house call to see what Robby was up to. Because he did it frequently, Mrs. Debruijn wasn't at all suspicious. After making sure Robby's bedroom door was closed behind them, Patrick sat in front of Robby's computer and logged on to the METC website. He then clicked on a video link and the boys began watching a short presentation about the medic program. Patrick eagerly pointed out to Robby that they were watching Air Force airmen and Navy sailors training together. The video showed how almost all the medical training was conducted in a new state-of-the-art facility with mannequins that could actually simulate bleeding and dilated pupils, and they even had one that had had its legs blown off. How cool was that!

The video was about five minutes long and depicted training in almost exactly the kind of procedures Robby wanted to perform. Patrick watched his friend's eyes widen with interest. To keep him thinking, Patrick was quick to point out what he thought he knew about the differences between the Air Force and the other branches of service. They wouldn't be getting yelled at all the time, and they'd probably get stationed at a nice hospital where they could take college classes on the side. What would it hurt if they tried that for a few years? It would be a good test to see if they could handle the real thing, and if they could, then they could apply for a regular college ROTC scholarship and have the government send them to school.

Patrick truly hadn't a clue what he was talking about, but Robby bought it. In ten minutes, with the help of a five-minute recruiting video, Patrick had just talked his friend into joining the Air Force and becoming an airman medic. That didn't mean anything, though, until Robby's parents signed off on it, particularly his mother. Robby wasn't the kind of kid who could tell his parents, "Hey, this is what I want to do and you can't stop me." With that in mind, Patrick suggested that they keep their plans on the down low for a few days until they devised a way to break the news to their parents. In the meantime they could come up with some rebuttals to the concerns their parents would surely have. Robby agreed.

January 4, 2011

I think me and Robby may have figured out what we're going to do after high school. We never thought about the Air Force so I went to their recruiting website to learn about their medical training program. They have everything the Army and Navy has. They even do some of their training together with the Navy. The big difference is that we won't have to worry about being in actual combat. We couldn't even join the Navy and not have to worry about being on the front lines. Those guys are the paramedics for the Marines. There were some Air Force medic training videos online that were pretty clear about what training is going to be like. I showed them to Robby and now he thinks it's a good idea. I never thought he'd make it in the other branches of service, but I think he might be able to pull this Air Force thing off. We're not going to tell our parents until we look into it a little closer. I can't wait to get out of Kansas. It's so gloomy all the time in winter. I don't think the sun has been out since around Thanksgiving. If we join the Air Force, we'll get stationed in San Antonio, Texas. That's almost in Mexico so it's going to be nice and warm. The girls are probably tan all year. If me and Shelly are still going out then I won't cheat on her, but if we break up after graduation, I have a feeling I may really like Texas.

Patrick believed his parents were going to like the idea of the boys becoming Air Force medics so he told them about it during dinner the following night. He began with a rehearsed, "What do you think about...?" which left him an easy escape route if his parents thought it was a bad idea. Colonel Bennett was instantly intrigued. As for Mrs. Bennett, she was apprehensive. Patrick emphasized the idea that there was little chance he'd ever be exposed to actual fighting, but he could get stationed at a field hospital treating wounded soldiers. He also assured his parents that it wouldn't be a permanent career choice but more of a bold test to determine if they, particularly Robby, were truly cut out to work in the medical field. If they liked it, doors would be wide open to go on to whatever else they wanted to do. If they didn't like it, they would have at least served their country for a few years, and then they could enroll in college and have the government help pay for it. The only loser would be Robby if he simply couldn't hack the military. It was one thing being an officer's kid and following your dad around all day in a pediatric clinic. It was going to be a completely different world as an enlisted man with Asperger's Syndrome at the bottom of the armed forces totem pole.

The two mothers, over coffee and blueberry bran muffins, sat down and made the decision to allow an Air Force recruiter to visit the families together and make a pitch for the boys to become airmen medics. The mothers, like their boys, assumed very few Air Force personnel, particularly people in the medical field, ever got close to combat or areas where enemy fighters could reach them. They believed, like their boys, that that was the responsibility of the Army and Marine Corps. After their coffee together, the wives told their husbands to proceed and a recruiter was called. In the interim Patrick went to Robby's house and told him it was time they break the news to their parents together, even though he had secretly let the cat out of the bag a week earlier.

Robby's parents pretended to be surprised at their son's news. When the boys were finished with their brief presentation, Dr. Debruijn told them he was proud of them for taking the time to do some research before making a rash decision about their futures. What Robby heard was, "I'm proud of you for making this decision," and that was all he needed. If his father thought joining the Air Force was a good idea, then that was what he was going to do.

A meeting similar to the one with the Army recruiter was held at the Debruijns' house the following Saturday afternoon. The airman who arrived to make the presentation was a former security policeman and basic training drill instructor who was much more casual in his presentation than the Army recruiter had been. This recruiter, after acknowledging his respect for Dr. Debruijn and Colonel Bennett, said the Air Force was looking for young men and women who were smarter than the average armed forces career candidate who might be better suited for the Army or Marines. He pointed out that advanced computer technology was used by their enlisted ranks throughout the Air Force in almost everything they did, from aircraft support to medical services. Even if the boys didn't have a job that required advanced knowledge of some form of technology, chances were they would be working with equipment that cost millions of dollars to develop, manufacture, and maintain. That was the Air Force of the twenty-first century.

The two fathers understood the recruiter's job was to sell the Air Force, so they didn't mind the subtle jabs taken at the Army. On the contrary both men respected the enlisted recruiter for coming into an Army officer's home and having the chutzpah to imply *The Army's great, but we in the Air Force think we're just a little bit better.*

After a brief overview of the history of the Air Force and its current mission, the recruiter began his presentation about the various medical fields the boys could join if they qualified. He began with the low level jobs that required minimal qualifications and then steadily moved up the ladder. When he finally said, "And then we have our regular medics," the boys leaned forward in their chairs and listened intently.

According to the recruiter, the medic training program would teach the boys how to do almost everything an emergency room triage nurse would do. "Unlike most civilian paramedics," the recruiter said, "our medics have particular expertise with trauma injuries and are trained to treat serious injuries for extended periods of time because they sometimes have to wait for evacuation to a medical facility. And even in a medical facility, Air Force medics often perform duties more likely left to nurses and nurse practitioners in a civilian hospital. Without hesitation, I have no doubt you will save lives if you join us and become airmen medics."

When the last question was answered, the recruiter left the families some pamphlets and his business card and suggested they start preparing the boys for the Armed Forces Vocational Aptitude Battery (ASVAB) testing. They all then shook hands and the recruiter left. As soon as the door was closed behind him, the boys turned to each other and smiled. They were all in.

The discussion after the presentation was brief—actually the part where the two families sat down for a serious discussion about the pros and cons of what they'd just heard was brief. Compared to what the Army had to offer, the Air Force was an overwhelmingly better fit for the boys. If joining the armed forces for short enlistments to learn how to be medics was what they were going to do, then the Air Force was the way to go. The vote was unanimous. With that out of the way, the discussion changed to how to prepare the boys, and that didn't end until later that evening after dinner and martinis. For the first time in a long while, everyone slept very well that night.

January 12, 2011

We met with a guy from the Air Force today and it looks like me and Robby are going to join. I'm nervous and excited about it. I guess the part I'm most nervous about is the basic training part. We can handle the running and push-ups and we both get up really early already. It's the getting yelled at for stupid stuff that worries me. I can probably take it, but I'm not sure about Robby. It's going to be hard watching him get destroyed by a drill instructor and not being able to do anything about it. We have to take the ASVAB test again to make sure we're smart enough for the medic training program. Robby's probably going to ace it. He's practically memorized our ROTC training manuals and he could probably teach half the stuff we're going to learn in medic school. I called Shelly and told her and she said she thought she could deal with us being in the Air Force. She was just kidding around. Her family is diehard Army. Me and Robby went over to Shelly's last month and watched the Army-Navy game at her house, and Col. Tisdale screamed at the TV almost the whole time. I guess the Army hasn't won a game in like ten years. That's got to suck. If you go to West Point, you pretty much have to hate the Navy when it comes to sports. It's the same way I hate the Raiders. I hate the Raiders even more than I hate the Broncos. You can't be a Chiefs fan and not hate the Raiders and the Broncos. It's the same thing if you go to a service academy. The day you get accepted, you automatically have to hate the guys at the other academy. Except I don't think anyone at the Army or Navy academies really cares about the Air Force academy team. I'm not sure they even have football there. I was afraid to ask Col. Tisdale what he thought about his daughter joining the Navy ROTC at San Diego State. I guess if it's going to pay for her college tuition he's willing to deal with it. I'm going to let Shelly tell him I'm joining the Air Force.

Unbeknownst to the boys, their fathers met for lunch during the week and discussed how they could help their sons' transition into military life. They agreed the JROTC program was a godsend for already teaching the boys most of the things they'd learn in basic training. The problem would be how Robby reacted to the manner in which instruction was given in basic training. Being quiet and soft-spoken wasn't going to get him any sympathy anymore. It was going to make him the legitimate target of a drill instructor whose job was to toughen recruits into eager defenders of the country. Dr. Debruijn was the first to specifically mention Robby's Asperger's Syndrome. Robby wouldn't be able to use it as an excuse in the military, and even if he didn't need to, other people finding out he had a mental disability would never work in his favor. Dr. Debruijn decided, and Colonel Bennett agreed by not disagreeing, that Robby needed to conceal his disability as much as he possibly could.

Dr. Debruijn and his wife then discussed how to approach Robby with the idea. It wasn't going to be easy because Robby didn't have a dishonest bone in his body. Dr. Debruijn decided the subject was a good one to address in a father-son chat. The conversation took place one day after Kathryn Debruijn dropped Robby off at the hospital and he and his father walked home after a few hours of pediatric clinic exams.

"Why are we walking?" Robby wanted to know when they stepped into the dark, frosty winter evening.

"I wanted to have a private talk with you," his father answered. "Is that okay?"

"It's cold. Why can't we talk at home?"

"This is better. We need some fresh air."

For extra privacy from the early evening joggers and dog walkers, the Debruijn men cut though a large open field that was once an old cavalry parade ground. Neither man was dressed for a walk home in the snow. Their cheeks stung with each lash of whipping wind, and their toes ached from the frozen ground.

"I want to talk to you about your Asperger's," Dr. Debruijn said as he wiped a drip of snot from his nose. "How are you feeling?"

"Good," Robby answered curtly. It was bad enough they were walking home in a minor blizzard while two perfectly operable automobiles were parked at home. It was completely annoying that his father chose to trudge across a snow-covered field and not use the cleared sidewalk.

"No problems at school? No problems with other kids?"

"No," Robby answered.

"Remember how you used to go to school all day at home? Remember how hard you worked so you could one day go to public school? Remember that?"

"Yes," Robby answered.

"And now you're going to graduate in a few months. Your mother and I are very proud. We can't tell you how proud we are."

Robby was too cold to care. He didn't respond.

"Why do you think we all worked so hard to get you into public school?" Dr. Debruijn asked.

"So I could learn how to be normal," Robby answered.

Dr. Debruijn stopped and turned to his son. "Robby, this has never been about trying to make you normal," his father said. "Look, there is no one standard of normal. I'm not normal; your mother isn't normal. There's something about all of us that makes us different from one another. The thing that makes you different is just more specific, and I'm telling you—listen to me, Robby—you being different is exactly what makes you normal. Understand?"

"I guess," Robby answered unconvincingly.

"You're also a young man now," his father continued as they turned and resumed their walk home. "When you graduate and walk away from high school, a world beyond your imagination is going to open up to you. Some kids your age will look at that world and it's going to scare them, so they'll continue to live with their parents and take simple jobs that don't pay much, and they'll do nothing with their lives except have a few children and perpetuate the same thing over and over again. Other kids will see the opportunity for adventure after they graduate. You know some right now—you know kids your age who can't wait to graduate and move out of Leavenworth, right?"

"Yes," Robby answered. His teeth were starting to hurt.

"That's why your mother and I wanted you to go to high school with other kids. We didn't want you to learn how to be normal. We wanted you to be able to experience the kind of education most other kids your age get. We wanted you to be in a place where you could meet people and have some fun, not spend all your time between your desk at home and the hospital. *That* would not have been normal.

What I'm trying to say is, we thought if you had the opportunity to go to regular school, you would see how some other kids work hard to make something of themselves, and a little of that would rub off on you. It was never about trying to make you like other kids."

"I don't like talking about this, Dad," Robby said.

"Okay, okay," his father yielded. "I'm just trying to say I think it's time we forget about this Asperger's stuff," Dr. Debruijn said. "How about we decide it's over? When you were little and growing up, it caused some problems that you had to overcome, but you've done it. Look at yourself. You're a young man about to graduate from high school."

Robby was thoroughly confused. Was his father trying to say he was finally cured? There was no cure for Asperger's Syndrome, only constant adjustments and new things to learn. What was he talking about?

Dr. Debruijn continued. "I think you've come so far, the only thing holding you back right now is the fact that *you* think you have a disability. I think sometimes you struggle because you expect to struggle. You can't do that anymore because time and time again, you've proven your Asperger's can't stop you unless you let it. If you don't make it into medical school, it won't be because of your Asperger's. It'll be for the same reason everyone else who tries to get in doesn't make it. Medical school is extremely difficult. It's that simple. So I'm suggesting you put medical school out of your head awhile and concentrate on medic training and preparing for a few years of military life. You won't be an officer. You won't have a nice big house, and you won't make very good money. You'll be lucky if you get your own room for awhile, but you will get to treat patients who need help, and that will allow you to decide if you want to continue your medical career later. Is that what you want?"

"I'll be okay," Robby told his father.

"I don't doubt it, Son," Dr. Debruijn answered, "but you can certainly make things easier."

"I'll be ready," Robby answered. "Me and Pat are working out and learning about the Air Force. We'll be ready."

"I don't doubt you will, but there is something I think you can do that will make things much easier. I think, as far as the military is concerned, it's time that your Asperger's becomes something you keep to yourself."

"Okay," Robby answered. That would be easy. He never liked to talk about his disability, even with the doctors and therapists who treated him.

"That sounds simple," Dr. Debruijn said, "but there will be times when it won't be. You are going to have to pass a physical and complete a lot of medical history paperwork, and there will be questions about disabilities. Your Asperger's diagnosis may be a reason to disqualify you."

"Even if I can do everything?" Robby asked.

"I'm afraid that if you tell anyone you have Asperger's, you won't even get a chance to show them you can do it. That's just the way it is," Dr. Debruijn concluded.

"That's not fair," Robby said. "I can do it. I can help people. Even the stuff Pat thinks is gross, I can do it."

"Yes, you can," his father agreed. "So you see we have another obstacle to overcome. We see it coming, we have an idea of what it is, so how do we address it before it becomes something impenetrable or is so overwhelming we can't get around it?"

"We remove it," Robby said.

"Exactly," Dr. Debruijn said. "How can we do that?"

Robby frowned. That answer might take some time to figure out.

"What if we had control over whether the obstacle was there in the first place?" Dr. Debruijn said. "What if we could simply take another path and avoid it altogether? Would that be a wise option?"

"I guess," Robby answered.

"Well, then, if the obstacle is your Asperger's diagnosis, let's get rid of it. Forget it. As far as the Air Force is concerned, it never happened. You've spent almost every day of your eighteen years overcoming that disability and you've done it. How about from now on we consider you cured?"

Robby smiled and said only, "Okay."

Not another word on the matter was spoken. They finished their walk home talking about the colorless winter and what they hoped would be waiting for them on the supper table.

The first order of business was getting qualifying scores on the military's placement test. Without those the idea of joining the Air Force would be moot. The boys wrote out topics and specific questions they remembered from the test they'd taken the year before in JROTC and developed a study guide. The Department of Defense had its own official ASVAB study guide that the boys also used. They'd never even looked at it when they took the test the year before.

The ASVAB was held on a Saturday morning in late March in the JROTC main classroom. Fifty-seven LHS juniors and seniors, not all enrolled in the JROTC program, took the test. The boys answered most of the questions correctly and were just as successful when they had to guess. A few weeks later they received their results. They were more than qualified to enter the Air Force medic training program.

We got our ASVAB scores in the mail today and we both made it. It wasn't even close. I thought Robby would have done a lot better than me, but my score was a little higher than his. I guess there's nothing holding us back now. I'm getting really nervous about graduation, not the graduation part, the part after when you have to go out and try to make something out of your life. Prom is coming up and Shelly wants to go so I'm kind of stressed about that, too. We have to find a date for Robby and then we have to rent tuxedos. The last time I wore a tuxedo I was a ring bearer in a wedding and I was only four or five years old. If we can find a date for Robby, I'm going to ask his dad if we can take their new Camry. We're going to look like a bunch of clowns all dressed up driving around in our piece of shit Volvo.

Shelly took charge of the matchmaking duties and quickly found a prospect for Robby. Few of the seniors wanted to miss their final high school dance. As prom night approached, a mad scramble began for those without dates to find one. Shelly asked a girl named Heather Harris she knew from her advanced studies classes if she would be interested in completing their foursome. Heather was cute and very smart but quiet and not very social. She knew who Patrick and Robby were, although they'd never shared any classes or socialized with one another before. Shelly's proposition was laid out in a simple favor request. Robby needed a date and Heather needed a date, and because Patrick wasn't going if Robby wasn't going, which would ultimately result in Shelly not going, it would be a huge favor if Heather went with Robby just as friends and then everyone could go and they'd all have a good time. Heather didn't need much coaxing. She'd spent most of her high school years at home on weekends. An opportunity to go to the prom with some of the most popular people at school was too good an offer to pass up.

With Heather ready and waiting, Patrick called Robby and told him he had just been talking to Shelly, and she was complaining that one of her friends didn't have a prom date yet. Robby told Patrick that he needed to call him back and hung up the phone. A few minutes later, Robby called Patrick back and said he'd be willing to ask Heather to the prom. Patrick assumed Robby had ended their first conversation to ask his parents if he could go to the dance in the first place before he asked someone to go with him. What Robby had really done was refer to his 2009–2010 LHS yearbook to confirm who Heather Harris was. He did have standards, after all.

The next day after school, the two boys climbed the stairs to Robby's bedroom and, after a short rehearsal, Robby called Heather. She said yes, just as planned, and the date was set. The entire phone call lasted less than a minute. With Heather inked in, Shelly decided to get to know her better and subtly prepare her for Robby's shyness. The girls were soon walking together to their classes and calling each other after school to figure out what they were going to wear to the big event. During their lunch break, they saved a spot at the table for Patrick and Robby. Heather and Robby almost never spoke directly to each other. Their mutual peculiarity was at times comical and other times brutally uncomfortable to watch.

April 23, 2011

Me and Robby got our tuxedos fitted today. We look pretty damn good I must say. We're going all black, none of that colored ties and gut girdles BS. I'm not thrilled about the shiny shoes, but I guess that's mandatory for wearing a tux. Robby's pretty excited about going to prom. I wish he could show it better to his date Heather. She's really nice. Shelly did a good job picking her for Robby. They're both so shy I don't think they could have a conversation if we weren't around. Maybe that's just the way shy people are and that's okay with them. It's really hard to watch though. When just me and Shelly are around, I call Heather "Shelly's Robby." Robby got the okay to use his parent's Camry for prom. He got his license last summer but he won't want to drive so I will. Robby doesn't like to drive with other people in the car. He ignores you if you start talking. He doesn't like the radio on either. I think he's worried he'll get distracted and crash. I was nervous when I first got my license so I don't give him any shit about it. I'd rather drive all the time anyway.

April 30, 2011

We went to our senior prom last night at the Officers' Club. The music was fucking horrible!!! The moron juniors on the prom committee hired a DJ who played nothing but ghetto hip hop and house music. It was like the same bass beat all night. We danced a little but it wasn't any fun. We pretty much spent the whole night out on the patio next to the pool. They had some gas warmers out there so it wasn't too cold. I told the girls some stories about me and Robby when we were little kids and I had them rolling pretty good, especially Heather. I guess she's not that shy after all. A bunch of people saw us out on the patio having a good time and the next thing we knew, people were pulling up tables next to ours and we had our own party outside. I made Robby tell the story about the time me and him and our dads went to a baseball game and I kept farting silent ones in the backseat and our dads thought it was him. No one said anything, but our dads kept rolling their windows down every time I ripped one and then they'd turn around and give Robby the "Hey, give us a break already" look. I was in tears listening to Robby tell that story—"He just kept flatulating and flatulating!" Then we all got in a big debate about whether "flatulating" is an actual word and everybody pulled out their cell phones and started looking it up. Sure enough, they proved "flatulate" isn't in the dictionary, but "fart" is, so Robby then had to tell the story over saying "fart" instead of "flatulating" and that was about the funniest shit I've ever seen. Not that farting is really that funny, but watching your shy as hell best friend who's never said a single cussword or used any slang in his entire life tell a story about me farting my ass off in the back of a car when I was twelve was very funny. And I was proud too. Robby took that story and boldly shared it with a bunch of other people our age and they loved it. They even begged him to tell it again!!! We stopped by an after party off post, but people had already been there for a while and most everyone was getting drunk and smoking pot. We walked around and said hi to a few people and then left. After that we went to Sonic and picked up some burgers and cokes, and then we drove across the street down to Riverfront Park and ate and talked some more while we sat on a piece of concrete watching the river. It would have been nice to ditch Robby and Heather, but we didn't. They had lots of opportunities to go off and be by themselves but they were pretty much attached to us all night. That was fine with me and Shelly. Everyone had a good time. Our curfew was 2 a.m. and we were all kind of fading out anyway so I drove everybody home and that was about it. I'm glad I wrote all this down. Someday my kid is going to get a kick out of it.

May 7, 2011

I'm a gentleman so I won't be specific, but Shelly promised me all week that she'd give me a present for taking her to prom last Saturday and tonight I got it. It was incredible!!! I can't get this shit-eating grin off my face either. I feel drunk without the wobbly/being sick part. You know what they say, "Love is a drug." Well whatever it is, I'm feeling pretty high right now!!! I can't say anything to Robby about it because if you tell him something is a secret, he doesn't want to hear it. He's afraid he might accidentally tell someone I guess. Besides, I shouldn't talk about this kind of private stuff. Shelly is a good girl. It's going to totally suck when we have to split up this summer.

The next two weeks passed in a flurry. The boys crammed for and successfully passed all their final exams. They also received their enlistment paperwork from the Air Force notifying them to report to the Kansas City regional Military Entrance Processing Station (MEPS) on June 12. There they were to have a physical exam and take some blood tests before being sworn in and shuttled to the airport for a flight to Lackland Air Force Base in San Antonio with other basic training recruits from the area.

Dr. Debruijn called the MEPS office and asked that they send him the medical paperwork used during the recruit intake process. After reviewing the paperwork, Robby's father called the civilian doctor in charge of the medical unit within the MEPS and said he was about to conduct a significantly more thorough physical of his son than the center surely was, so if the processing doctor wanted, Dr. Debruijn could simply complete his enlistment paperwork at the same time. He could even perform Patrick's physical exam and complete his paperwork if that would make the MEPS doctor's job easier. The civilian doctor was indifferent to the idea. National Guard recruits often arrived at the processing station with previously completed physical exams. He would review the boys' packages, and as long as the paperwork arrived complete and there was nothing in it indicating the boys weren't qualified physically for careers in the military, the civilian doctor could actually use the help. Dr. Debruijn assured him that both boys were in superior shape and there would be no problems.

May 20, 2011, was an unusually balmy spring evening in Leavenworth, Kansas. Two hundred and ninety-eight LHS seniors marched into the stadium and onto the artificial turf football field behind the high school. Family members and assorted loved ones cheered and called out to their glowing graduates. Near the first group of students to enter, Robert Debruijn and Patrick Bennett stood tall among their peers, each draped in a rented blue robe and matching graduation cap. Both boys' grandparents and one of Robby's aunts and an uncle flew into town to watch the grand pageant with the boys' parents.

The graduates were assembled in alphabetical order, so Patrick and Robby weren't allowed to sit together. Patrick, seated in front, frequently turned to his best friend behind him and smiled as if to say, "Isn't this great?" Robby gave him a thumbs up and then gestured that he should turn around and pay attention to the person at the podium. The principal spoke for a few minutes, followed by the class valedictorian, and then a brief speech was given by a guest alumnus who'd become a state assemblyman. Once the speeches were over, the stage crowded with the event VIPs, who stood in line to dispense the graduates' diplomas and congratulate them.

Patrick was in the first row of students to receive their diplomas. Being popular was never a goal of his, yet he'd become one of the most well-liked kids at school. As he crossed the stage after his name was announced, the seniors still seated before him whistled and cheered, drowning out the modest applause of his parents in the grandstand. When Patrick stepped off the stage, instead of returning to his seat, he nonchalantly moved to the side and allowed the other graduates to walk by him. An underclassman JROTC honor guard member acting as an usher told him he needed to return to his seat, but Patrick wasn't going anywhere.

A few moments later, Robby's row stood up and filed onto the stage. When Robby's name was called, the stadium erupted with applause and cheers. Robby floated across the stage and dryly thanked the principal for his diploma. He then turned to his classmates and threw his hands in the air. The crowd roared at his glorious moment. The seniors on the field could see Patrick waiting for his friend beside the bottom of the stage, and everyone desperately waited for what was about to happen. Another name was called before Robby began descending the stairs, but no one other than that graduate's family was paying attention. The rest of the crowd was glued to the corner of the stage where Patrick and Robby were about to meet.

Robby carefully stepped down the stairs with his diploma clutched in one hand and the corner of his robe in the other. When he reached the ground, Patrick threw his arms around his friend and the crowd roared again; this time the entire senior class stood applauding on the field. In the stands the Debruijns and Bennetts hugged one another and cried. Even those who had no idea who the boys were recognized that they were witnessing something magical.

The principal gracefully gave the boys their moment and then resumed calling names. Patrick and Robby returned to their chairs and watched the rest of the ceremony separately. Theirs was not the only graduation to receive particular acknowledgment that night, but it was by far the most emotional. Immediately after the ceremony, before the boys made any attempt to locate their parents, they were surrounded with well-wishers and congratulations. Shelly joined them and gave Robby a quick peck on the cheek before passionately kissing her boyfriend. Heather even came by and gave Robby a big hug before scurrying off to find her family.

Both families met at the Bennetts' house for a graduation feast and party after the ceremony. Everyone agreed they'd never seen Robby so openly enjoying himself. His short life had been filled with challenges and the milestones of conquering them. This was different; all those past battles and obstacles were fought through for one singular purpose—to get a diploma from a public high school. This wasn't just another minor breakthrough in his development. This was a triumphant achievement, commemorated with an official certificate that was license to venture out into the world and become a man.

May 21, 2011

Yesterday was graduation and we had a blast!!! When Robby got his diploma he turned around and pumped his fist in the air like he'd just scored a touchdown or something and the crowd went berserk!!! Our class gave him a standing ovation and everything!!! We had a graduation party for just our families at our house and it was pretty cool. My dad got his grill going and all the men stood around outside and watched him BBQ while the women got the rest of the stuff ready inside. We were talking about how me and Robby joined the Air Force, and the next thing I knew Robby's granddad handed me a beer and started making a toast. Robby didn't want one but his uncle told him he had to at least take a sip if someone was giving a toast, so he did. After that, Robby just held his until I finished mine and then we swapped cans. He can't stand alcohol. I'm not crazy about it, but it does seem like every time I have a beer it tastes better. My dad told me I could only have two so I saved my second one, which was actually my third, until after we ate. After dinner the adults all started getting drunk on regular booze and were talking about dumb stuff we didn't care about so we decided to sneak off. We walked across the street and climbed up on the old fort wall and watched cars go through the intersection for awhile. It was fun talking about how we used to meet there when we were little kids and we'd play like we were soldiers defending the fort. We talked about how it was going to be weird not living at Fort Leavenworth anymore. We were definitely the kings of our neighborhood. I think the fort is going to be the kind of place you can't wait to leave when you're a kid, but you always want to come back and visit when you're older. When I have kids I'm going to bring them back here some winter and we're going to meet Robby and his kids, and we're going to spend the day sledding together on our old hill. My kids are going to call him Uncle Robert, and his kids are going to call me Uncle Pat, and when one of them starts losing their baby teeth I'm going to tell them about the time their dad got his front teeth knocked out when he dove across the mud over at Gruber Field. The more I think about it, the more I wish that day were tomorrow.

Patrick made a few more casual journal entries before his final entry, which was written a week before heading off to join the Air Force. In his last written thoughts before his great adventure began, he shared his break up with Shelly. His comments about Robby's reaction were most telling.

June 5, 2011

Me and Shelly met yesterday and we went for a walk to try and figure out if we were going to keep trying to go out or not. She's going to college in California and I'm going to Texas and then who knows where, so we both understand trying to stay together isn't going to work out. We both saw this coming from day one. Back then I thought it would be easy to break up when it was time. It wasn't easy at all. It totally sucked. We're still going to be friends and keep in contact with each other. She said she'll send me letters while I'm in basic and tech school. That's going to be nice. No one was crying or anything. It was still pretty sad, though. I called Robby and told him me and Shelly had broken up and he came over to make me feel better. I didn't need it or anything, but I had nothing else going on. We decided to go get something to eat and he actually insisted on driving. I guess he thought I was depressed and didn't want to drive. He drove us out to Homer's and we grabbed a couple burgers and shakes. We usually split the bill but Robby paid for everything. I thought he was just being nice at first. Then I realized him driving me and paying my bill was his way of taking care of me for once. You can't ask for a better best friend than Robby. I'm really worried about this basic training we have to go through. If we fuck this up they're going to kick us out and we'll be branded fuck ups for the rest of our lives. No pressure, right!!! Time to separate the men from the boys!!!

CHAPTER 8

Dr. Debruijn gave the boys their physicals and completed their medical history surveys during their last week as civilians without sharing them with the boys. Patrick was a perfect recruit specimen. Robby was almost as physically fit, but his Asperger's Syndrome diagnosis was an issue. Dr. Debruijn made sure his son's mental health survey made no mention or showed evidence of the diagnosis—he knew full well his intentional omissions were criminal. If Robby ran into a problem related to his disability, and it was discovered that the integrity of his enlistment evaluation had been compromised, Dr. Debruijn could find himself without a job and possibly doing time in the disciplinary barracks. It was a risk he was willing to take.

The boys spent their last night of freedom at Robby's house having dinner with their parents. They asked for rib eye steaks and loaded baked potatoes as their last meal. At dawn the next morning, their fathers drove them to the MEPS in Kansas City and made sure they had their processing paperwork before walking them to the building's front entrance. There they stopped and shook hands as men do—no embraces or parting tears. The boys were excited to begin their adventure and completely overlooked the fact that they were making such a monumental leap into adulthood.

Once inside the processing center, the boys found themselves surrounded by a large group of teenagers and young adults, all nervous and wide-eyed, waiting for their first instructions from the recruit staff. None of the new recruits dared talk or ask questions. Patrick and Robby reported to a clerk and surrendered their recruit packages to the young female Army staff sergeant behind the desk. She withdrew some forms, located the boys' names on a roster, removed airline tickets from a desk drawer, and handed a ticket to each boy.

"Do not lose these," she said. "Now take your things and have a seat. A shuttle will be here in about thirty minutes to take you to the airport. You'll be in San Antonio by eighteen hundred hours. When you get off the plane, you need to go directly to the recruit office near the USO in Terminal B. You check in there and then wait for the bus to Lackland. Do not go wandering around that airport, you understand?"

"Yes, ma'am," the boys answered together.

The boys didn't sit together during their flight to San Antonio. Robby was too busy emotionally preparing for his first night at basic training to notice one of the passengers seated next to him was a very attractive young woman. Patrick spent the entire three-hour flight uncomfortably wedged between two overweight businessmen whose encroaching girth sandwiched him between his armrests. He didn't care what was waiting for him that night. He just wanted off that plane as soon as possible.

The boys met again in the airport terminal and quickly located a sign that directed Air Force recruits to an office near the Terminal B baggage claim. Patrick took a deep breath and looked at his best friend. "This is it, dude. No turning back now."

Robby grinned nervously. "I have to pee."

The boys visited the closest men's room and returned to the terminal. Men and women in fatigues were everywhere, most not nearly as young as the two boys, but none as old as their fathers. The boys remembered their warning not to wander in the airport, so they headed straight for their check-in area. There a group of thirty boys their own age were milling around introducing themselves to one another and sharing what they'd heard basic training was going to be like. Neither Patrick nor Robby was interested in socializing. This was their last opportunity to huddle together and review their strategy. They checked in at the recruit desk and once again had their documents reviewed. After their packets were returned to them, the boys walked to an isolated row of empty chairs and sat down.

"You excited?" Patrick asked his friend.

"Yes," Robby answered without expression.

"You look kind of nervous, dude," Patrick said. "Just remember, the next eight weeks is a big game of psychology between us and them, all right? They're gonna fuck with us until we can't see straight just to separate the weaklings from the herd. We got to stay strong. Keep everything in perspective. Basic is only a test to see if we've got the balls to be airmen. You got enough balls for this?"

"You mean testicles?" Robby asked.

"Yes, I mean testicles! Don't fuck with me, man. This shit is for real now."

"I just wasn't sure if that's what you meant," Robby apologized.

"Look, remember, no volunteering, no bragging about high school ROTC, no showing off, none of that shit, you hear me? This will go down a lot easier if we fade into the crowd—just go with the flow and don't draw attention to ourselves. You got me? We have to keep our mouths shut. The physical stuff is gonna be a piece of cake. Getting up early—we got that covered. All the other stuff, we can do it, but we have to keep our heads on straight and not let the bullshit get to us. Got it?"

"Yeah," Robby answered unconvincingly and looked down at his feet.

"Dude, seriously," Patrick continued, "let's you and me kick this basic training thing in the ass, okay?"

Robby looked up and said, "Yeah, let's do it."

As the afternoon dragged to evening, more young recruits arrived until sixty were assembled together at the recruiting station. Shortly after ten an announcement was made that a bus was ready to drive the recruits to their new home at Lackland. The boys grabbed their bags and recruit packets and followed a staff sergeant to the curb where a charter bus was waiting. Patrick and Robby sat together in silence during the thirty-minute ride to Lackland. There was no talking on the bus, not by order, but because all of its occupants were scared to death of what was waiting for them.

After passing through a base security gate, the bus drove into a cluster of large, ominous, square buildings with exposed steel beams. Each building had a large concrete patio beneath it. As the bus pulled closer to one of the buildings, Robby saw two men standing at ease beneath one of the buildings, both wearing dark-blue campaign hats and camouflage fatigues. As the bus slowed and moved closer, the two men snapped to attention and marched to the curb. The bus driver steered his vehicle to the curb and stopped adjacent to the two US Air Force training instructors. The door of the bus opened and one of the training instructors boarded.

"Welcome to the United States Air Force Basic Military Training Campus!" the technical sergeant announced formally. "This is your new home for the next eight weeks! I am your senior training instructor, Tech Sergeant Aarons! Upon my command you will exit this bus and form into six columns of ten recruits per line! You will then be escorted to the dining hall where you will have fifteen minutes to eat a box meal that will be provided to you as you enter the hall! You will eat this meal whether you are hungry or not! There will be no talking! Do you understand?"

A poorly synchronized "Yes, sir!" erupted from the bus passengers.

"Recruits!" the training instructor began his command, "stand up and gather your belongings and get off this bus in an orderly fashion, now!"

The boys leapt from their seats, crowded into the aisle, and then quickly exited the bus only to be greeted with the chaos of having both Tech Sergeant Aarons and his fellow training instructor yelling more instructions at them. "Hurry up! Six columns! Let's go, let's go, let's go!"

When the formation was assembled—the boys stiffly at attention and frozen with fear—the second training instructor slowly circled the group like a shark deciding who would be his meal. With each step was a sharp click from the steel taps on the instructor's glossy black jump boots. "Don't you dare look at me, son!" the training instructor roared. "You in the middle in the green shirt! Yes, you! Where are you from, recruit?"

"Idaho, sir!" the recruit answered.

"Did they not teach you how to stand in a straight line when you were in elementary school in Idaho? Look to your left, recruit! Your other left! Now look to your right! You got exactly five seconds to figure out what is wrong with that picture! If you can't do it, you better turn around and get right back on that bus, do you understand?"

"Yes, sir!" the recruit answered and slowly crept a few inches forward.

When the instructor's circle was completed, he stopped at the head of the columns and snapped to attention. "My name is Staff Sergeant Andrew Goodings!" he stated dramatically. "I will be your primary training instructor for the next eight weeks! You have three responsibilities while you are here! You *will* do what you are told! You *will* learn what you are taught, and you *will* conduct yourselves with dignity and adherence to the United States Air Force Airman's Creed! If you do these three things, you will have the privilege of joining me in the greatest branch of this country's armed forces! If you do not perform these three things, you will be sent back home to your mothers, and you can go back to your video games and part-time jobs at the mall or the minimart or whatever else you were doing before you decided to grow up and be a man and serve your country!

"From this day forward, you will never go anywhere but the toilet without another recruit with you! You will never speak unless given permission to do so! You will never fight or argue with a fellow recruit! And once again, you will wake each morning eager to take instruction and do these three things! Do what you are told! Listen and learn! Adhere to the United States Air Force Airman's Creed! Do you understand?"

"Yes, sir!" the recruits answered.

"Oh, you think you understand, but you don't," Sergeant Goodings replied, his voice lowered. "Does anyone here even know the Airman's Creed?"

"Sir, yes, sir," a voice from the rear spoke.

"Let's hear it then!" Sergeant Goodings demanded.

Robby cleared his throat and began, "I am an American Airman. I am a warrior. I have answered my nation's call..."

As Robby recited the rest of the creed, Patrick could only bite his lips to contain the fear and anger. No volunteering, they'd agreed. No drawing attention to themselves, they'd agreed. No doing anything that would make them stand out from the rest of the group, they'd agreed, but there was Robby, not five minutes off the bus, completely abandoning the fundamentals of their entire plan to survive basic training. Patrick had arrived nervous and afraid just like everyone else, but he was at least prepared, and that gave him confidence. As Robby continued reciting the creed, Patrick could only imagine how much further his best friend would stray from their plan, and it terrified him.

"What is your name, recruit?" Sergeant Goodings demanded to know.

"Sir, Recruit Debruijn, sir!" Robby answered.

"Where did you learn the creed, recruit?"

"Sir, Recruit Debruijn, sir. At my friend's house in Kansas, sir!"

"And why did you learn the Airman's Creed, recruit?"

"To prepare for basic training, sir!"

"Flight, did you hear that?" Sergeant Goodings asked. "Sixty of you, and only one bothered to learn the Airman's Creed before getting here?"

Robby shot a glance at Patrick. His friend also knew the creed and knew it well. Why wasn't he telling the sergeant he also knew it? Patrick answered the glance with a clenched jaw and subtle swivel of his head. Robby was confused.

"What is your malfunction, recruit?" Sergeant Aarons yelled from the side of the flight into Patrick's ear.

"Sir, Recruit Bennett, sir! No malfunction, sir!" Patrick answered.

"How did you prepare for basic training, recruit?" Sergeant Aarons growled. "Do you know the Airman's Creed?"

"Sir, I have read it, but I have not yet memorized it, sir," Patrick lied.

"But you think it's okay to dance around over here while a fellow recruit, who clearly is taking this much more seriously than you are, shows he's the only person in this entire flight who has one iota of understanding what he is doing?! Congratulations, recruit! You are this flight's new dorm chief!"

Patrick's knees were suddenly weak, sweat now dripping down the side of his face. "Sir, yes, sir."

Sergeant Goodings received a nod from Sergeant Aarons and ordered, "Recruits Debruijn and Bennett front and center!"

Patrick and Robby quickly stepped from the formation and scurried to the front of the columns to face their new training instructor. Sergeant Goodings sized up his two new recruits and said, "Recruit Debruijn, since you seem to be the only person here who knows what the hell is going on, you will be our temporary chow runner. Recruit

Bennett, as dorm chief, you will learn how to do his job with him. Do you understand?"

"Sir, yes, sir!" the boys answered in perfect unison.

Sergeant Goodings paused and looked deeply into the boys' eyes. One already knew the creed, and both clearly knew how to stand at attention and report to a superior. Although their faces were flushed with fear and dripping sweat, there was an air of confidence between them. "You two pay very close attention to what I'm about to show you," Sergeant Goodings continued. "Starting tomorrow morning, getting this flight fed on time is your responsibility. You understand me?"

"Sir, yes, sir!" the boys answered again.

He pointed to a steel door that had the words *Dining Hall* painted in black letters on it. "You two stand over there and watch what I do. One of you hold the door open. After the last recruit enters the chow hall, I want you to find me for your next instructions. Got it?"

"Sir, yes, sir!" the boys answered.

"Then go," the sergeant ordered.

Patrick and Robby jogged to the dining hall entrance and each positioned himself on one side of the door. Patrick hesitated to open the door until he received the order to do so, but then decided the order had basically already been given, so he reluctantly opened the door, expecting there was about a 50 percent chance he was doing the wrong thing.

"All right!" Sergeant Goodings barked at the formation of hungry and tired recruits. "On my command you will enter the dining hall single file, one line after the other starting from your right! As you enter the hallway, you will see a stack of trays next to a stack of meals in brown boxes! You will take a meal and place it on a tray! You will place both hands on the tray and sidestep through the chow line with your tray on the tray rail at all times! When you reach the beverage dispensers, you will take two plastic cups from the rack and you will fill them both with a noncarbonated, noncaffeinated beverage! That means no soda, gentlemen! When you have your beverages, you will lift your tray from the rail and walk directly to a table! You will fill the tables one at a time—no roaming around deciding who you want to sit with, do you understand?"

"Sir, yes, sir!" the flight answered.

"You will not talk! You will not look around the room! You will not sit casually dreaming about the ugly girlfriend you left behind! You will sit and eat, and only when your entire table is finished, you will stand together and walk directly to the garbage receptacle and tray return area! There you will place your garbage in a garbage receptacle and place your tray and cups in the wash bay port! You will then return directly to this assembly area and assume the position of at ease. Fifteen minutes, gentlemen! That's all the time you have, understand?"

"Sir, yes, sir!"

"Flight 587!" Sergeant Goodings sounded off formally. "From the right, single file, forward...march!"

The ten recruits in the far right line stepped cautiously forward and began entering the dining hall. Sergeant Aarons had positioned himself inside the dorm building's cafeteria next to the empty buffet line where the trays and boxed meals were stacked. As he ensured each recruit took a tray and a meal, he also directed them to a cluster of tables where the entire flight would sit together. After the last recruit entered the dining hall, Sergeant Goodings told Patrick and Robby to follow him. He led the boys to two folding tables that had a small podium between them. The tables were placed against a wall at the end of the buffet line where those seated at the tables with the wall behind them could monitor the dining hall as the recruits ate.

"Welcome to the snake pit, gentlemen," Sergeant Goodings said. "Three times a day you will come before this table and one of you will request that your flight be granted entry for a meal. You will stand at attention and wait for an instructor to give you permission to speak. You will then say, 'Sir, Recruit So and So reports as ordered.' When the instructor tells you to continue, you will say, 'Sir, Flight 587 is prepared to enter the dining hall.' When the instructor tells you the flight can enter, you will step back, left face, and go get your flight. When the flight is finished, you will return to the snake pit and advise the instructor that the last trainee has left the dining hall. You got that?"

"Sir, yes, sir," the boys answered, again in perfect unison.

"So it is stop here," the sergeant said, walking them through the procedure. "Right face, like this," he said, pivoting to his right. "Step to the center of the table and stop. Then left face and wait for the instructor to tell you to speak. Then when you're done, you do the same thing backward. Got it?"

"Sir, yes, sir."

"Okay. Go get something to eat. We'll see how you do in the morning. Go!"

"Sir, yes, sir," the boys answered and scurried away to get their box dinner.

No one spoke during the short meal of cold sandwiches, a piece of fruit, and a bag of potato chips. No one dared. The terror and uncertainty was overwhelming—no one made a move without someone else moving first. Their instructions had been simple, yet the entire meal was accompanied by a constant barrage of corrections being hurled at them by both instructors. "Both hands on your tray! I said no carbonated beverages! I told you not to get up until your entire table was ready to leave!"

Robby and Patrick quickly devoured their meals and joined the rest of their flight outside. Once the entire flight was reassembled, their instructors ushered them up a set of nearby stairs to their dorm. It seemed that even the instructors were ready to call it a day. The yelling had finally stopped. The new recruits were assigned beds in alphabetical order, which meant Robby and Patrick were only separated by Recruit Randall Curtis who was from somewhere in Oregon. They considered it their first stroke of luck.

Sergeant Goodings told his recruits to place all their property in the corresponding lockers lining the wall behind their beds and then gave them five minutes to go to the bathroom if they needed to relieve themselves. He then wanted the entire flight seated on the floor in a large dayroom inside their dorm. When they were dismissed, the two bays of single beds filled with the clanging of metal lockers being rummaged through and toilets flushing.

Patrick and Robby bypassed the opportunity to go to the bathroom for fear they might miss something. They were the first two in the dayroom. If Robby had stuck to their plan, the boys would have strategically sat toward the back of the flight, not all the way in the back, but toward the rear where it would be easier to get lost in the crowd. Robby had blown that idea. He'd drawn attention to himself at first opportunity and Patrick was going to pay for simply reacting to it.

As the boys stood deciding where to sit, Patrick whispered angrily, "We're already screwed, dude. We got to sit up front, or at least I do."

"I'll sit with you," Robby said.

"You sure as shit will, you fucking asshole."

Robby was stunned. "What did I do?"

"Dude, are you kidding me?" Patrick snarled. "We're not here five fucking minutes and you're showing off. Don't volunteer, don't draw attention to yourself. Remember that? What the fuck, man?"

"I was just answering a question," Robby said.

"You were fucking showing off, and you pulling that shit got me stuck as the dorm chief. I'm the goddamn dorm chief! Before we even got a chance to piss at this place, I'm already the goddamn recruit in charge!"

"I'm sorry," Robby said and lowered his head in shame.

"Oh no you don't," Patrick said pointing his finger at his friend. "Look at me, dude. Seriously, look at me."

Robby slowly raised his head. His eyes were tearing.

"You got to man up, buddy," Patrick said, "or they're going to eat us alive in here. You apologized—that's it. It's over." Patrick extended his hand.

Robby took his friend's hand and shook it, but when he did, Patrick pulled him close and wrapped his arm around Robby's shoulders. "We got this, buddy. You and me all the way, right?"

"Yeah," Robby answered softly.

Other trainees were walking into the dayroom so the boys ended their conversation and sat.

A few minutes later the trainees heard the approaching sound of steel taps clicking against the floor. Everyone sat up straight with their hands to their sides. When Sergeant Goodings entered the room, he looked angry and tired. "Dorm Chief, front and center," he ordered.

Patrick jumped to his feet and stepped up to Sergeant Goodings.

"Sir, Dorm Chief Trainee Bennett reporting as ordered, sir," Patrick said, his chest puffed, fists clenched against his thighs.

"No," Sergeant Goodings began, "you say, 'Sir, Dorm Chief *Recruit* Bennett reporting as ordered, sir.' And the rest of you, when I call for the dorm chief, you repeat my order loud and clear so Recruit Bennett knows I'm looking for him. Understood?"

"Sir, yes, sir!" the class responded.

"Dorm Chief," Sergeant Goodings asked, "is the entire flight here?"

Patrick knew immediately he'd made a big mistake. He should have walked the dorm and bathroom to make sure everyone was present and ready to go in the dayroom. "I'm not sure, sir."

"You're the dorm chief," Sergeant Goodings growled. "Don't you think it'd be nice for me to know if there's still a recruit in a stall in the latrine? I gave you five minutes to get this flight seated in this room. That was seven minutes ago and you still couldn't do it. Explain how this could have happened."

"Sir, I failed to check the dorm and bathroom to make sure everyone was here as you ordered, sir."

"You failed, all right," the sergeant agreed. "Go figure out who is still missing and get their ass in here."

"Sir, yes, sir!" Patrick answered and scurried out of the room.

Just as he was rounding the hallway corner, another recruit was exiting the bathroom. "Am I in trouble?" the recruit asked his dorm chief.

Patrick whispered, "If the sarge asks what took you so long, say there was a line to the stalls and you only had a few seconds to take a shit. Don't say shit though, okay?"

The other recruit nodded.

"Well, there you are," Sergeant Goodings mocked as the two recruits entered the dayroom. "Please have a seat and join us. Let me guess, there was a line at the crappers and you were the last one in. That sound about right?"

The tardy recruit answered, "Sir, yes, sir."

"What is your name?"

"Sir, Recruit Sanchez, sir."

"Well, Recruit Sanchez," Sergeant Goodings said, "I gave this flight five minutes to do nothing more than drop your things in your lockers, go to the bathroom if needed, and then report to this dayroom. There are six commodes and eight urinals in that latrine. The only reason someone couldn't complete a bowel movement during that five minutes would be because the recruits already on the can were selfish and took their time. Dorm Chief, stand up!"

Patrick climbed to his feet again and locked his arms to his sides. "Sir, yes, sir!"

Sergeant Goodings sat casually on a desk at the front of the room and looked up at Patrick. "When I give this flight instructions, it is your responsibility to make sure those instructions are followed. Do you understand?"

"Sir, yes, sir!"

"The rest of you," Sergeant Goodings continued, "this is your dorm chief. He is an extension of me. When he tells you to do something, you do it. He does not have to say pretty please or ask you politely if you could do this or that. You don't give him any lip or question his authority. Do you understand?"

"Sir, yes, sir!" the flight answered.

"Sit," Sergeant Goodings told Patrick.

For the next twenty minutes the sergeant explained his expectations to his new recruit flight. His demeanor slowly grew more relaxed, allowing the frightened recruits to settle down and pay attention without fear of being yelled at. He explained that the next few days would be spent allocating uniforms, getting haircuts, processing paperwork, learning basic drill fundamentals, and perfecting the art of preparing themselves and their dorm for daily inspections. There would be calisthenics three days a week and drill practice whenever they had the opportunity. In addition to all of this, the trainees would go through a mixed classroom and practical application basic training course that would indoctrinate them into the US Air Force. Each week was a milestone. If for any reason that milestone was not sufficiently achieved, a recruit could be recycled back to another flight for a second chance, or, depending on the reason, the recruit could simply be washed out of the program altogether and sent home.

When Sergeant Goodings completed his orientation speech, he told the flight he would give them the next twenty minutes to take a shower and be in their bunks beneath their blankets ready for lights out. Patrick didn't hesitate to form his plan. As soon as they were dismissed by their sergeant, he was going to jump into action.

"Dorm Chief," Sergeant Goodings said and motioned for Patrick to stand.

Patrick again quickly climbed to his feet. "Sir, yes, sir!"

"On my command you will get this flight bathed and in bed by a quarter after. You will also appoint three trainees to be fire monitors tonight, and I want you and the three you pick to see me in my office ASAP. Do you understand?"

"Sir, yes, sir!" Patrick answered confidently.

"Repeat what I just told you."

"Sir, on your command you want the flight to shower and be in bed by zero fifteen hours, sir! You also request I select three fire monitors and report with them to your office as soon as possible, sir!"

Sergeant Goodings looked closely at his new dorm chief. This kid already knew how to pivot his feet while performing a facing movement. He also knew how to stand at attention and keep his eyes locked straight forward while being addressed. He even understood military time. Goodings was convinced this was a young man who'd either spent a great deal of time preparing himself for basic training or, even better, was an alumnus of a high school JROTC program. "Now you tell them and get it done."

"Sir, yes, sir!" Patrick answered. He stepped back with his right foot and spun around with a perfect about face. "Flight 587, atten...hut!"

The flight jumped to their feet and stood erect, waiting for their orders from Recruit Bennett.

"On my command you will return to your bunks and gather the toiletries necessary to take a shower! You will then take a shower and prepare for lights out! This task will be completed by zero fifteen hours! The first three trainees to complete their shower will return to this dayroom and we will report to Staff Sergeant Goodings for further instructions! Flight 587, dismissed!"

The members of the new basic training flight ran from the day-room like firemen responding to an alarm. While Patrick waited for the last trainee to leave, Robby asked him, "Do you want me to be one of the fire monitors?"

"No way, dude," Patrick answered. "You need to get some sleep. That chow runner deal you got yourself into is going to be hard enough. Hurry up and go get your shower. I'll see you right before lights out."

The boys parted and Patrick went straight to the bathroom and positioned himself at the doorway. "Let's go, boys," he pressed like a high school football coach. "Quickly, quickly—no time to goof off. In and out. Let's go, let's go." As the first three recruits prepared to leave the shower, Patrick reminded them to meet him in the day-room as soon as they dried off and put on some clothes. There was no grumbling.

A few minutes later, when Patrick was satisfied that the bulk of the flight had showered, he retrieved his toilet kit and returned to take his own shower. Much to his disappointment, there were still members of the flight standing in towels waiting to bathe.

"Hey, come on, guys," Patrick said firmly. "Get in and get out. If we fuck this up, Sergeant Goodings is going to go through the roof. Hurry your asses up." Patrick's pushing increased the speed of the assembly line moving through the shower room. Even when he was able to take an open spot beneath one of the spigots, he continued to push the others to move quickly. "C'mon, guys. Let's get out of here and in bed. Ten more minutes."

After Patrick rinsed and dried off, he returned to his bunk to check on Robby and put on some dry clothes before reporting back to his training instructor. He was relieved to see Robby had showered and was sitting on his bunk ready to go to sleep.

Patrick lowered his head so no one else could hear him. "Did you brush your teeth?"

Robby looked up at his friend with red, tired eyes and answered. "Yes."

Patrick gave him a gentle tap on the shoulder. Once he was dressed he met his three new fire monitors in the dayroom and then the four went together to their training instructor's office, which was between the two bays of single beds. Patrick knocked on the door and stood at attention.

"Enter," Sergeant Goodings said from inside.

Patrick opened the door and took one step forward. "Sir, Recruit Bennett reporting as ordered with three fire marshal volunteers, sir." *Did I just say fire marshal?*

"Fire marshals?" Sergeant Goodings repeated with a chuckle from behind his desk. "Let's go with fire monitors."

"Sir, yes, sir."

The sergeant ordered the fresh recruits to enter his office and close the door behind them. He told them to stand at ease and listen very closely to his instructions because they would have to relay those instructions to the next group of recruits who became fire monitors. Sergeant Goodings explained that a single recruit from the flight would be designated as the fire monitor at all times, twenty-four hours a day, even when the flight wasn't present in the dorm. In addition to reporting smoke or fire in the dorm, the fire monitor would also ensure that the dorm entrance was always secure and anyone requesting entry into the dorm had the authority to do so. Fire monitor shifts would last four hours during the day and two hours during lights out. He told one of the other recruits standing with Patrick that he was the head fire monitor and in charge of creating a schedule of monitor volunteers. Sergeant Goodings then dismissed Patrick and his entourage so they could privately decide who would take the first night's shifts.

Everyone was exhausted, but Patrick knew he'd score some respect points with the flight if he volunteered to take one of those first shifts. "I'll go first," he said to no objections. After the other boys selected their shifts, Patrick returned to the front of the first bay of beds and announced, "Five minutes, guys! Everyone needs to be in bed in five minutes!" He walked to the second bay and made the same announcement.

A flurry of slamming locker doors and squeaking bed springs followed as the recruits rushed to prepare for bed. Patrick wasn't going anywhere for the next two hours except a chair next to the front door, so he decided to check on Robby one last time before absolute silence was ordered.

"How we doin', buddy?" Patrick asked his friend, who was lying stiffly at attention between his sheets.

"Good," Robby answered and yawned.

"I'm gonna be the first fire monitor tonight, so if you need anything, I'll either be sitting by the door or walking around making a security check. You got your nose stuff?"

"Yes," Robby answered and withdrew a small bottle of nasal spray from beneath his pillow.

"Okay, well...get some sleep," Patrick said with a comforting smile. "Big day tomorrow."

"Good night," Robby said and rolled over onto his side.

"Good night, dude," Patrick responded and took his post at the front door.

A few moments later Sergeant Goodings exited his office and found every member of his new flight tucked in bed and completely silent. "Your wake up in the morning is at zero eight hundred hours!" Sergeant Goodings announced as he walked through the two bays. "Enjoy it, gentlemen, because it's the last time you will sleep through dawn while you are at Lackland! When I turn off these lights, the only time you will leave your bunk before zero eight hundred is if you have to use the latrine or you have fire monitor duty! There will be no talking! Do you understand?"

"Sir, yes, sir!"

"Dorm Chief!" Sergeant Goodings yelled.

"Dorm Chief!" the flight echoed from their beds.

Patrick hurried to his training instructor. "Sir, Dorm Chief Recruit Bennett reports as ordered, sir."

"I don't want to hear a peep out of this flight tonight, do you understand?"

"Sir, yes, sir!"

"I'm going to be in my office," Goodings continued. "If there's a problem, you let me know. Now I'm going to order you to prepare the flight for lights out. You are then going to stand before each bay and advise the flight that it is lights out. Then I want you to walk through both bays and make sure everyone is in bed. When you're done report back to me that every member of the flight is accounted for and prepared for lights out. Got it?"

"Sir, yes, sir!" Patrick answered confidently.

"Dorm Chief, prepare this flight for lights out!" Goodings ordered.

"Sir, Recruit Bennett preparing the flight for lights out, sir!" Patrick then performed a flawless about face and stepped to the head of the first bay of bunks. "Flight 587, lights out!" He marched to the head of the second bay and repeated the command and then marched down the center aisle of both bays to ensure everyone was present and in bed. When his check was completed Patrick returned to Sergeant Goodings, who remained outside his office door. "Sir, Recruit Bennett reports as ordered, sir!"

"What is it, recruit?"

"Sir, Flight 587 is present and accounted for and prepared for lights out, sir!"

"I'll take your word for it," Goodings answered. "Turn off all the lights except the one that has a red switch and then return to your post."

"Sir, yes, sir!"

Goodings turned away from Patrick and stepped back into his office. Patrick found a row of light switches next to the front door and started turning the lights off, careful not to turn off the switch that was colored red with a marker. Within moments the dorm was dark except for the glow coming from the exit signs at the back of each bay and a small light between the bays next to the latrine. There Patrick sat in the near darkness for the next two hours and fought to stay awake.

The first thirty minutes of his watch passed quickly. There were too many thoughts racing through his head to lower his guard, so he decided to stand and make a security check. Many of the recruits were snoring, some shuffled half asleep from one side to the other, but only one seemed wide awake—Robby.

When Patrick came upon him, lying on his back staring at the ceiling, he kneeled next to his friend and quietly whispered, "Dude, you got to close your eyes and go to sleep."

"I'm nervous," Robby replied, his eyes locked onto nothing above him.

"About what?" Patrick asked. "There isn't anyone here more prepared for this than you and me. Just relax, man. Close your eyes and think about how cool it's going to be when we get out of this place. Think about how ugly we're going to look tomorrow after they shave our heads. Who knows, I may be even uglier than you."

Robby didn't move his eyes from the ceiling. "I'm nervous about breakfast. I don't remember what I was supposed to say."

"Dude, don't sweat it. I don't remember either and I got to do it with you. If we fuck it up we fuck it up, and guess what? I guarantee you we're going to get it wrong somehow. What are they gonna do, yell at us?"

Robby didn't respond to his friend's attempt at lighthearted sarcasm.

"Dude, you got to take a big deep breath and relax," Patrick whispered. "We haven't even been here a whole day."

Robby continued to stare silently into the open space above him.

"Robby, I need my wingman to have his head on straight, right?" Patrick said. "You're my wingman. I'm *your* wingman. No matter what, we're in this together, right? Don't get freaked out over some shit we have no control over. Let these other guys freak out over that shit. We're the A-Team, buddy. We're above all this."

Robby looked at Patrick and whispered, "Thanks for coming here with me."

Patrick gently grasped his friend's hand. He didn't know what to say.

He returned to his post and spent the next ninety minutes wondering. Did Robby actually think he'd only joined the Air Force because of him? If that was the case, did Robby think Patrick could somehow protect him through basic training or act as some kind of mentor? The seriousness with which the two friends had prepared for their life in the military had given Patrick some degree of confidence that Robby could survive his entry-level training if he could only keep his mouth shut and not draw unnecessary attention to himself. In that he'd already failed miserably at his first opportunity. As the night crept by, Patrick realized he was no more prepared for the events about to unfold than the other fifty-nine recruits who slept under his watch.

He made three more security checks throughout his shift, and each time he found Robby lying with his eyes wide open, staring off into space. He wouldn't look at Patrick as he passed his bunk. Patrick didn't stop to offer any more encouraging words. He had nothing else to say.

At two Patrick gently nudged awake his replacement and soon after climbed into his own bed for the first time. He could look over the recruit sleeping in the bunk between them and see Robby still lying on his back with his eyes open. Patrick was too tired to be frustrated and decided the lesson Robby was about to learn might be one of those he couldn't really teach anyway. With that Patrick closed his eyes and slowly drifted off to sleep.

The boys' story becomes understandably cloudy here. The next day they were given a small postcard to mail home to confirm to whomever they sent the card that they had safely arrived at Lackland and were busy with their training. There was no room on the card to provide any details to their loved ones about what was going on. They were permitted to make their first call home after their first week, and those calls home are how the families learned about that first night.

The boys wrote their first letters home in their second week of training. Both short letters portrayed two young men growing comfortable in their new environment, although they were clear that the training was difficult and they were doing more things wrong than right, particularly Robby when he tried to get the flight in and out of the chow hall. Before every meal the training instructors monitoring the chow hall would pepper him with questions before they gave him permission to bring the flight into the large cafeteria. "When was the Air Force founded? How many flights are needed to make a squadron?" Robby knew the answers to most of the questions; he just couldn't spit them out fast enough. Then, in the early evening of the first day of July, the Bennetts received a frantic call from Patrick. Robby had found his way into trouble, and he was being recycled.

The circumstances are vague, and those with knowledge of the specific details weren't excited about sharing them. It appears that Robby was relieved of his chow runner assignment and found himself in a group of recruits in charge of keeping their dormitory bathroom clean. There was a squadron inspection coming up, and the group had made significant effort to prepare the latrine and shower area. Unfortunately whoever was doing the inspection decided to postpone it for a day, and that meant the bathroom would have to be cleaned all over again. Someone on the cleaning detail came up with the brilliant idea that if everyone in the flight only used the sinks to towel bathe for one night instead of showering, that would cut their cleanup duties in half before the next day's inspection. When the bathroom crew ran it by their dorm chief, Patrick said he didn't care as long as the entire flight agreed. The flight then had a vote and the plan was approved.

That night the flight went without showers, but each recruit was supposed to towel bathe with soap and water in a sink. Apparently that wasn't enough for one prospective airman, and when he showed up in formation the next morning smelling like a homeless transient, their training instructor was furious. Patrick explained to Sergeant Goodings what had happened and that the flight had voted as a team and never intended to break any rules. If anyone should get in trouble, it was him for not putting the kibosh on the idea when he had the chance. Throwing himself on his sword wasn't enough, though.

The recruits on the bathroom cleaning detail were summoned to Sergeant Aarons's office. When the meeting was over, all the boys but one, who had only been on the detail for a day, were recycled. They were to immediately clear their lockers and report to another flight that was one week behind theirs. Robby and Patrick would have to finish the rest of basic training and their medic training on their own. When Patrick learned Robby and the other two members of his flight were being recycled to another recruit flight, he asked for an appointment with Sergeant Aarons and again insisted that he was ultimately responsible for what had happened and he too should be recycled. Aarons denied the request.

Being separated from Patrick early in their basic training was like being thrown into pounding ocean surf to learn how to swim for Robby. He was never comfortable talking about the specifics of how he was handling basic training on his own. When he called home, it was only to reassure his parents that he was still there and doing well. There is a gap in the written correspondence here of about six weeks, when the boys mostly communicated by phone with their parents and friends. I think it is safe to say it was an extremely stressful period for everyone.

I don't think being recycled was humiliating or embarrassing to Robby. He'd have to think he did something wrong first, and I don't think he did. What we do know for certain is that the boys remained in the same squadron, so their dorms were in the same building. This provided the opportunity for the boys to occasionally see each other in the outside break area and visit while other recruits were calling home from a bank of old payphones. I only found one letter that mentions Robby's recycle and how Patrick felt about it.

July 9, 2011

Hey Mom and Dad,

How's it going? I'm still alive and doing well. Training is going fine. I'm really getting the hang of this stuff. I'd probably be doing even better if I wasn't so worried about Robby all the time. I got to talk to him yesterday for about ten minutes. He's doing good and that made me feel a lot better. He doesn't seem freaked out about getting recycled at all. I think being sent back a week actually gave him a chance to reboot and start over fresh. I'm hoping now that he's doing better this will go by faster. We get our first liberty in a few weeks. I really need a hamburger. You can only eat so much chicken à la king. Say hi to the Debruijns the next time you see them.

Love,

Pat

I'm sure there are some interesting details within the subplot of the boys being separated in basic training. All we know for sure is that both boys took Robby's recycle as a wake-up call. The failure that was an option for their parents certainly wasn't an option for them. With renewed fervor to succeed, both boys became exceptional recruits and leaders.

Any hopes that the boys would be reunited during the medical portion of their training were dashed the day of Patrick's basic training graduation. Each member of the flight by then knew where he'd be going to continue his specific job field education. Most of the new airmen would be flying off to another Air Force base somewhere. Only Patrick and a handful of new airmen training to become security policemen would be remaining in San Antonio. What Patrick learned just before his graduation ceremony was that his medic class would be starting the next week, two days before Robby had his basic training graduation. Now their paths were clearly headed in different directions—not opposite, but off track enough to force the boys to accept that they were on their own, and their futures were in their own hands.

Whereas the primary eight-week basic training course is designed to break recruits down and then bombard them with constant tests of their physical and emotional stamina, the medic training program is an eighteen-week, forty hours per week course consisting of primarily classroom instruction and practical application testing in an academic environment. Arriving by bus at Fort Sam Houston just a brief drive across the city from Lackland, both boys were relieved to see that the Medical Education Training Campus looked like a brand new junior college campus. Young airmen dressed in green camouflage and young sailors dressed in blue camouflage wandered casually from building to building. There were no intimidating training instructors to dodge. Patrick was even more impressed with his new living quarters—a single dorm room he'd only have to share with one other airman.

Hi Mom and Dad,

This is going to be quick but I'm really busy so don't be mad. My first week here at METC was pretty easy. A lot of the stuff they're teaching us is basic lifesaving I already learned in ROTC. Me and my roommate are getting along fine. We rented a TV together for our room. Robby is probably somewhere on another floor in my dorm, but I haven't seen him yet. Mom, don't bother sending me a phone. There are so many rules about where and when you can use those things around here, it's probably better I don't even have to mess with it. We're going to start really getting into it next week. I probably won't be calling or writing home that much for a while because I'll have to study a lot. We have a study room here with computers so I can drop you an e-mail when I get a chance. That's about it. Talk with you later,
Pat

Before the letter was received at the Bennetts' home, Pat sent an e-mail saying he and Robby had found each other and were going to spend the following Sunday exploring Fort Sam Houston together.

E-mail August 10, 2011

Hi Mom and Dad,

I spent the day with Robby today. We went to the chapel by our campus for a service and didn't really like it that much. It was packed with other people from our training group and we kind of wanted a day to get away from those guys. After the service we started walking around to see what we could find. Sam Houston has been here forever so there are lots of really old buildings everywhere like Fort Leavenworth has. It's not a very pretty place. It's flat and not nearly as green as back home. They do have palm trees on some of the streets, which is pretty cool. We found a place to buy a couple subs and then we walked around a little more and stumbled onto an old church they still use. It's a lot bigger than the memorial chapel next to our house on the fort. We decided we're going to try it out next Sunday. Robby looks good and is excited to get into his medic course. Since I'm a class ahead of him, I can fill him in on what's coming up in his training so he's prepared. I don't think he's going to need it. So far everything I'm learning is going to be a piece of cake for him. Got to go. Talk with you later,

Pat

E-mail August 17, 2011

Hi Mom and Dad,

I hope everything is going well up there in Kansas. We're doing good down here in San Antonio. Me and Robby tried out that old church this morning that I told you about last week. The chapel part is a round room with a balcony where the choir and organist sit. Instead of a steeple, they have a big dome like a government building or a museum might have. The place creaks and smells just like the inside of our chapel at home. It made me and Robby a little homesick. We were the only trainees there. Everyone else was regular people from the fort. After the service we walked across the street and got a couple subs and something to drink and took it to a place called the Quadrangle. It's a tiny fort within the fort that looks just like someplace they would have built back in the day when the colonists were fighting the Indians, except the walls are stone instead of wood. A lady at the church told us there was a park inside where they kept Geronimo when he surrendered, so that's what we were

looking for. It was pretty cool. They have wild birds like peacocks and swans just randomly walking around. They even have some deer in there that will walk right up to you. It's one of the few places where the grass is nice and green and there's plenty of shade, so we hung out in there for a while and just relaxed and talked. Everything else is still going good. Another three months and it'll all be over. I can't wait. Later,
Pat

A nearly identical e-mail was sent to the Bennetts each Sunday evening over the course of the next three months. The boys met on Sunday mornings and walked across Fort Sam Houston to attend a service at the old post chapel, and then they bought sandwiches and ate them on a park bench in the shade among the wildlife freely roaming the Quadrangle. Both boys were confident in their medic school progress and barely ever mentioned any specifics of their training to their parents. When they did talk about campus life, it was usually complaining about duty assignments outside of their medic studies. After a few months of repetitive content in his correspondence, Patrick sent the following e-mail. It was clearly written by a young man who had experienced a moment of reflection in his life.

E-mail December 4, 2011

Hi Mom and Dad,

How's it going up there. We're still good down here in ol' San Antone. Me and Robby had our usual Sunday get-together today. Graduation is less than two weeks away. I can't believe it's already here. I'll find out where I'm going to be stationed sometime next week. As long as it's not Elmendorf (Alaska) or Minot (North Dakota), I'll be fine. I was

thinking today how much we've had to grow up since we've been here. It's crazy how much Robby has changed. He's still a quiet one, but when he does talk, he's not the mumbly little geeky kid he used to be. I don't think he's afraid of anything anymore. Seriously, he's flying through this medic training like it's a refresher course and he's actually helping me a lot more with homework than I'm helping him. I used to be really scared about what's going to happen when we get stationed to different places. I guess there's still a chance we could go to the same place, but I doubt it's going to happen. It doesn't matter anymore though, and that's the thing. I don't think Robby needs me. I think coming down here made him a man. It's made me one, that's for sure. You should see Robby with all of his gear on. You'd never recognize him. He's bigger than half the other guys in his flight. With a weapon in his hand he looks like a regular combat soldier. I know he's not afraid to kill someone. We talked about what would happen if he had to shoot somebody and he said he wouldn't have a problem killing anyone who was the enemy. I don't think we're ever going to have to worry about that, but I had to ask. He's the real deal. If they want us Air Force guys to be warriors now, well, they sure made one out of Robby. You guys are still coming to graduation, right? Talk with you later,
Pat

A few days later Patrick learned he would be stationed at Kirtland Air Force Base in Albuquerque, New Mexico. He didn't know anything about Kirtland, but being in New Mexico was a lot better than Alaska or North Dakota. On December 15, 2011, Airman First Class Patrick Bennett graduated from the joint Air Force–Navy Basic Medic Training Course. His glowing parents were there to see it. After a brief ceremony, the Bennetts piled into a rented car and fulfilled their son's only graduation wish by driving straight to a Sonic restaurant for hamburgers and fries. The family spent the rest of the afternoon and early evening together in San Antonio visiting the Alamo and then having an early supper down on the River Walk. Patrick was then returned to his dorm for his last night at Fort Sam Houston. Saying good-bye to his parents again was easy. There was nothing left for him back at Fort Leavenworth, and he looked forward to finally having some of his freedom restored once he got to Kirtland. He'd never been to Albuquerque before. Exploring a new big city would be exciting, but before his new journey could begin, he needed to say good-bye to Robby, and that *wasn't* going to be easy.

The boys met in the lobby of their dorm and walked outside together after almost everyone else on campus had called it a night. They sat on a bench and talked briefly about Patrick's graduation day. Patrick then talked for a few minutes about what he thought was in store for him at Kirtland. There was discussion of Robby's chances of also getting stationed there, but both knew better than to get their hopes up. It was oddly not that important anymore.

When the forced small talk was concluded and with curfew drawing near, Patrick reached over to his best friend and offered his hand. Robby took it, expecting a handshake, but was suddenly yanked into Patrick's chest. The two young men locked in an embrace, Patrick fighting to keep the tears welling in his eyes from spilling onto his face. "This has been quite a ride," he said and cleared his throat.

"Yes, it has," Robby answered. "When we get our first leave, let's meet back home."

"The chapel or behind the wall?" Patrick asked playfully.

"Wherever you want," Robby answered. "You just tell me where, and I'll be there."

The two young airmen broke apart and stood. Patrick wiped his face with his sleeve and they shook hands. "We did it, buddy," Patrick told his friend. "We really fucking did it."

"Yeah, we did."

"I love you, man," Patrick said before his voice cracked and he was no longer able to speak.

"I love you too," Robby said.

The childhood friends then embraced again and returned to their dorm. Two years passed before they saw each other again.

The week after Patrick left for Kirtland, Robby learned he was going to Davis–Monthan Air Force Base in Tucson, Arizona. Robby didn't really care where his first duty assignment was as long as there was a hospital he could work in. His parents and grandparents attended his medic school graduation. After the ceremony Robby showed them the old church where he and Patrick went on Sundays to get away from their dorm, and then he took them to the Quadrangle to see where they sat and had lunch and watched the birds and deer. Robby was almost unrecognizable to his mother. He'd grown two inches and put on at least fifteen pounds since his high school graduation. As Robby conducted their tour, he pointed out things he thought were interesting or worth mentioning with a casual confidence she'd never seen before. Dr. Debruijn was just as impressed, but he'd expected the changes, having experienced basic training himself over twenty years earlier. The day ended with a large Mexican dinner at a River Walk restaurant in San Antonio.

With the young men now completely separated, the story of Patrick and Robby growing up together comes to a close. Patrick was no longer keeping journals or writing letters home. When he wanted to correspond with someone, he was now free to call or send e-mail or text messages, almost none of which were saved. Robby was never one to correspond with his parents under his own volition. If they wanted to talk they could call him, and they did so regularly.

Training continued at their new assignments, and as new airmen they were often required to put in longer hours than the more senior airmen medics in their new squadrons. Establishing themselves at their new bases took up so much of their time that the initial e-mail exchanges between the two soon slowed to monthly, and then to even less frequent short blurbs about their fledgling careers as members of the armed forces. None of those messages were saved, either.

I received a copy of a short thread of e-mail between Patrick and his parents that describes what the parents knew about their son's first deployments overseas. This seemingly innocuous correspondence revealed an unexpected change in Robby's career path that, once clarified and understood, left his mother almost paralyzed with fear.

March 27, 2013

Patrick- *Hi Mom and Dad, everything still good here. Hey, did the Debruijns tell you about Robby being at some training up at Fort Dix? You guys know they have an infantry school there, right? What is Robby doing at an Army post? He said it's for more medic training, but Air Force people don't train at Fort Dix. Did you hear anything about that?*

Pauline Bennett- *Kathryn says it's a course to prepare medics for deployment in Iraq and Afghanistan. I suppose you may have to go too.*

Patrick- *No one from here is going and no one even knows about it. Our last day here is April 12. The people who have already been to Kandahar say it's not that bad. They say the hospital is really busy so the time flies. That's good news. It's not a big deal or anything, but can you see if Robby's dad knows what Robby is doing at Fort Dix? Thanks.*

Pauline Bennett- *O.K.;)*

March 28, 2013

Patrick- *Hey mom and dad, you guys aren't going to believe this, but Robby is up at Fort Dix taking an Army combat course. I found out today they are taking Air Force medics and running them through a short infantry school and then attaching them to Army units in Iraq and Afghanistan. Do the Debruijns know that?*

Colonel Bennett- *Son this is your dad. I called Dr. Debruijn and he was under the impression the training at Fort Dix is just an orientation for Air Force people before they go to Afghanistan. Are you saying that's not true?*

Patrick- *Dad, it's frickin' combat school. Robby is up there qualifying to be a combat medic.*

Colonel Bennett- *Interesting. Let me get back to you.*

March 29, 2013

Colonel Bennett- *Son, it appears you're right. Robby volunteered for a combat medic course and was selected. The Debruijns didn't realize what he was getting into. I imagine he either purposely wasn't forthcoming with them or he was just being Robert and wasn't clear about his intentions. Either way, you were right. Can you reach him?*

Patrick- *His phone has been disconnected and he's not returning my e-mail. If he's in the field, he wouldn't have access to a computer anyway. I'll let you know if I hear from him.*

He never did.

CHAPTER 9

July 27, 2013, Bagram Air Base, Afghanistan—Operation Enduring Freedom

"Scramble! Scramble!" the PJ control operator yells over his shoulder to the small group of Air Force Pararescuemen, otherwise known as *Parajumpers* or *PJs*, crowded behind him. "Everyone, go, go!"

A crackling speaker above a row of command post computer monitors fills the room with the sounds of young men yelling chaotic commands into their portable radios. "Control, this is Hotel One," a voice breaks through clearly. "We got a lot of our people hit out here, and we're still taking small arms fire from the west side of town. Both birds are down, I repeat, the first two PJ birds are down. We definitely have some KIA. At least five serious who need immediate evac. Scramble every medic you can get out here. We also have some ANP (Afghan National Police) and Nasro friendlies down."

"Roger, Hotel One," the PJ control operator answers. "We got the world rolling your way, buddy."

The operator spins around in his chair and yells, "Airman Jones!"

A young African-American woman in camouflage fatigues runs into the room. "Yes, sergeant."

"I need you to run over to the bee huts and make sure every available combat medic we got is headed out to Nasro. Tell them to hook up with one of the reaper teams for a ride."

"Yes, sergeant," she answers and darts back into the hallway.

The control operator spins back to his console and picks up a radio receiver. "This is PJ control. I'm hoping to get some extra medics to you guys. I have no idea how many we can round up, but whoever we find is probably going to need a ride out. Can you guys secure a couple extra MRAPs or make some room in what you got? Great."

The plywood PJ command post door flies open and Airman Jones rushes out toward the medical services housing area. As she crosses the dusty airbase, a loudspeaker blares, "All available combat medics report to base security headquarters, ASAP! All available combat medics report to base security headquarters, ASAP!"

An airman medic stops to listen to the PA announcement. "Hey, what's going on?" he yells to Airman Jones who is jogging across the desert-powder and loose gravel street.

"A team was out doing vaccinations in Nasro, and some of our people and Afghan police got hit with sniper fire and RPGs. A PJ team flew out and both birds got hit."

"Did they make it back?" the medic asks.

"No, they're down," Airman Jones answers. "From what I heard on the radio, it sounds real bad. They're calling for some extra medics to go out and help triage in their perimeter. Can you go?"

"Sure," the medic says. "Where do you want me?"

"You're already here. Go with us."

The medic thinks for a moment. He doesn't have any supplies and his gear is in his locker. If he wastes time retrieving it, he might miss his ride. "Can I go like this?" he asks.

"Run inside," Airman Jones says and points to the PJ command post. "Tell Sergeant Teague you're a medic and you need a gear bag. He'll take care of you. Hurry, the guys are already on their way out to the flight line."

The medic runs to the PJ command post and asks to see Sergeant Teague, who he finds sitting in front of the row of video monitors. "Sergeant, I'm a medic with the 163rd. If you let me borrow some gear, I can go with you guys."

"Take mine," Sergeant Teague answers and points to a row of lockers across the room. "Number seven. My bag is loaded with bandages and first aid stuff. Just take the whole thing. The bird has everything else you'll need."

The medic locates the locker and drags a large camouflage bag out of it. He quickly opens it and sees it's crammed full of medical supplies. He reaches up and pulls a combat vest and helmet from the locker. Without testing their fit, the medic grabs the bag and borrowed gear and runs out the door toward the flight line and waiting MH-60 helicopters.

As the medic rushes onto the tarmac, he sees four heavily armed pararescuemen climbing into the side of one of the helicopters. He sprints up to the helicopter as the last man is climbing aboard and yells above the propellers' roar, "I heard you guys need some extra medics! Can I get a ride?"

All four PJs frantically wave him in and one points toward an area where he can sit. The medic hurries to his seat and straps himself into a safety belt draped behind his shoulder. The lead pilot leans over and looks into the rear of his helicopter. One of the PJs gives him a thumbs up and a few seconds later the rescue team is jostled as the helicopter lifts off, nose dipping, and begins its race to the small Afghani village of Palah-ye Nasro, three miles southeast of Bagram's airfield.

During the short flight one of the PJs motions for their medic passenger to show him what supplies he has in his bag. As they conduct a quick inventory, the PJ, noticing the bag is incomplete, removes some IV bags and vials of morphine and syringes from a supply compartment and hands them to the medic. The noise in the back of the helicopter is deafening.

As they approach the small desert village, two small plumes of smoke rise from an open dirt lot on the north side of town. As they get closer, it becomes clear that the dark smoke is coming from a crashed and toppled Air Force PJ helicopter. Close by is a second helicopter that appears to have landed safely but is nearly engulfed in flames. About twenty yards south of the wreckage, where the dirt walls of the village begin, a crowd of American and Afghani military personnel have encircled a large group of wounded servicemen and civilians.

"That's Reaper Five!" one of the PJs yells over the noise of the helicopter turbines. He points to a line of US Air Force armored trucks with .50-caliber machine guns mounted on their turrets, all firing into a field west of the village. "They think the village is clear, but that doesn't mean shit! Nasro is crawling with al-Qaeda! Keep your head down, okay?"

"Okay!" the medic answers.

"We're going to take the two most serious and get them out of here! We need you to go around and stabilize the bleeders! Can you do that?"

"Got it!"

The nose of the helicopter slowly pitches upward and then begins a slow descent.

Four PJs with the medic close behind jump to the ground and jog over to a young Army officer covered in dirt and sweat. The officer yells, "Glad you guys are here! We got five airmen KIA, not counting the locals, but we're going to have a few more if we don't get them out of here! We already cleared your downed birds! Sorry, boys, three of the KIA are yours! It looks like two IEDs went off while some reconstruction team medics were doing vaccinations for the locals! It's bad, fellas, real bad! There was some small arms fire after the explosion and they fired off a couple RPGs! Looks like the cavalry is here now! Let me know if you need some extra hands!"

One of the PJs steps back and gives his command post an update via his radio. When he finishes he steps back to the other men and reports, "They have ambulances rolling from Bagram. We'll have four birds up. Let's just grab whoever's in the worst shape and the next team can take over!"

The men jog into the perimeter where nine casualties are lying on the ground and another seven are sitting up nursing their wounds. The medic goes directly to those who appear the most gravely injured. He sees two other medics he recognizes from the base and yells to them, "What about these guys! Have they been triaged yet?"

"No!" both airmen respond in unison.

The medic drops to his knees next to an airman lying on her back, her head propped up slightly by a wadded fatigue shirt. She is staring into the sky and holding the side of her neck and jaw. Blood is seeping through her fingers, caked over her hand and shirt, pooling beside her.

"Let's take a look," the medic says as he effortlessly slides rubber gloves on and removes a large bandage wrap from his borrowed medic bag. The airman slowly removes her hand from her wound, exposing a large open gash on her jaw where much of her cheek has been blown away. The medic carefully examines the wound to determine the main source of the bleeding. He discovers a gap in the airman's jaw where several teeth are missing. The medic stuffs a wad of cotton into the injured airman's mouth and then places a large bandage over her wound. "Are you strong enough to hold this?" he asks.

She nods and gently places her trembling hand over the bandage.

"Okay, you're going to be fine," the medic says. "You have a cut that's going to need stitches. Most of the blood is coming from inside your mouth, so I need you to keep that gauze in there, okay? It hurts, I know. Lots of nerves in there." As the medic talks, he prepares a pre-packaged morphine syringe. "So this is morphine. It's going to make you feel better."

The injured airman turns her head and winces in anticipation of the shot. She knows what's coming. A sharp sting pierces her right thigh and her head begins to fog. The pain and fear then slowly escape from her body, and she thinks about how much she misses her beloved dog waiting for her back home in Georgia.

"Little help!" another serviceman yells across the makeshift triage area. The medic scrambles to his feet and looks in the direction of the call. He sees an Army Military Policeman kneeling over a lifeless body on the ground. The medic grabs his bag and sprints over to render aide. At first sight the burned and bloody body is almost unrecognizable as human. Rifle fire suddenly erupts. Army MPs and Air Force security are firing wildly into the hills. An explosion shakes the ground, and then another before a cloud of debris rolls through the triage area.

"Vitals?" the medic yells over the cacophony of battle.

"I don't know how, but this guy is still alive!" the MP shouts and coughs. "He's going in and out!"

The medic scans what's left of the badly burned and mangled body. This soldier is going to die. All that's left is to fill him with morphine and let him pass in peace. The medic grabs another morphine pack from his bag and opens it. There is no thigh left for a point of injection. He rips off the remains of the soldier's combat vest armor, searching for a piece of muscle large enough to fill with the drug that will end this warrior's suffering. He tears the soldier's uniform open and pushes his T-shirt up to his neck. The soldier's skin is bloody and pale, but his chest is strong and round. The medic tries to pinch together some skin near his abdomen, but his stomach is too tight. A cloud of sulfur and dust wafts over them again and the medic's eyes burn in the chemical poison. He rubs the stinging tears away and refocuses on the dying casualty. He grabs a handful of pectoral muscle and delivers the dose of relief with a steady hand.

The soldier's eyes slowly flutter and then open. They are like two brilliant white lights on a dark moonless night. The medic freezes. The battle goes silent. The world stops spinning. The soldier isn't a soldier after all; he's another airman medic—his best friend.

"Pat?"

The dying airman fights to respond, "Ro...?"

Panic suddenly returns to the desert village and the sounds of chaos reappear. There is frantic shouting and more explosions. Two AH-64 Apache gunships roar past overhead and unleash a stream of missiles toward the hillside. The medic lifts what's left of his friend and hoists him onto his back. He races to an evacuation area shouting hysterically over and over, "Wounded warrior! Wounded warrior!" When he reaches the evacuation area, he slowly lowers his friend onto a large plastic tarp and kneels to comfort him. He holds him and gently strokes his hair, whispering it will all be okay even though he knows he is watching his friend pass before him.

"Hhh...hol...hold my hand," the dying airman pleads softly.

The medic grasps his friend's hand and draws it to his cheek. "It's okay, Pat. I'm going to get you home. It's going to be okay."

The two men watch their childhoods pass in each other's eyes. A stillness envelops them, a mysterious calm amid the savagery. Then, slowly, the dying airman's grasp weakens, his stare grows distant, and his last breath is set free.

EPILOGUE

It took four hours for the young airman I met in the Bangor airport to tell me this story. It took me a few more weeks to make some follow-up phone calls before I started writing it. As the story was shared with me I had many questions, but I learned early on in our encounter that my initial interruptions were a distraction to the young man, so I mostly sat quietly and listened. He didn't like talking about himself and almost never did. Everything was about his friend, what he'd done for him and how they'd become brothers.

Before I sat down and developed an outline for this book, I took a few days to review my notes and the recording I'd made at the airport. I wanted to make sure I had enough facts to give a completely accurate account of what I knew of the boys. It was very important to the airman who shared his story with me, so I felt he deserved to have it told in his words—inevitably his friend's words—and not mine.

I later tracked down the parents and interviewed them—the Bennetts at their retirement home in Rhode Island and the Debruijns in New York, where Robby's father had opened his own private practice. They all shed a great deal of light on the relationship between Robby and Patrick, and this is when the story began to gain some

271

color. Both sets of parents were also pleased that someone was writing about their boys.

I didn't attend Patrick's funeral. He was buried only a few days after I met Robby, and at the time I had yet to realize how involved I would become in their story. I have gone to Pat's grave recently. He has a beautiful location among a cluster of dogwood trees in a family plot in a historic garden cemetery just north of Providence. His parents didn't want to bury him in a military cemetery. In their eyes Patrick was never a warrior. He was just a regular kid from Fort Leavenworth, Kansas, who one day when he was eleven years old decided he was going to befriend another kid who was oddly peculiar and weaker than everyone else. I don't think I'll ever understand what it's like to dedicate oneself to someone like Patrick did, but I wanted to know, and that's the reason why this story often reads as if he were the storyteller. It allowed me to walk in his shoes.

Robby went back to war and is now in Afghanistan somewhere, attached to a company of Army Rangers. He sends me an occasional e-mail, usually no more than a paragraph or two, and he never writes of the war. I asked him one day if he was going to quit when his enlistment was up. This was his entire e-mail response:

Hi Avery. How are you? It's hot again today, how about there? I'm not going to quit until the war is over. They still need me. I miss Pat.

I sent this reply to Robby. *Then be safe, my friend, and just so you know, although I never met him, I miss Patrick too.*

Made in the USA
San Bernardino, CA
03 January 2016